I0645830

SPIRITS OF THE FLAME

THE RED PATH

OTHER WORKS BY THE AUTHOR

When Spirits Touch the Red Path
Book 1 in The Red Path Messenger Series
ISBN: 0-9786664-0-2
First printing, November 1993

The Message
Book 2 in The Red Path Messenger Series
ISBN: 0-9786664-1-0
First printing, December 1994

The Season of the Long Shadow
Book 3 in The Red Path Messenger Series
ISBN: 0-9786664-2-9
First printing, February 2003

Watchers From the Shadows and the Light
Book 1 in The Red Path Spirit Adventure Series
ISBN: 0-9786664-4-5

The Brotherhood
Book 2 in The Red Path Spirit Adventure Series

Lumen
Book 3 in The Red Path Spirit Adventure Series
More information on Speaking Wind may be found at:

www.dolphinmedia.com

Spirits of the Flame

▼

A Red Path Novel

Patrick Quirk "Speaking Wind"

Spirits of the Flame
A Red Path Novel

All Rights Reserved. Copyright © 2006 Dolphin Media, L.L.C.

No part of this book may be reproduced or transmitted in any form or by any means, graphic, electronic, or mechanical, including photocopying, recording, taping or by any information storage or retrieval system, without the permission in writing from the publisher.

Published by Dolphin Media, LLC

For information, please contact:

Dolphin Media, LLC
6275 University Drive, Suite 37
Huntsville, AL 35806

www.dolphinmedia.com

Cover layout and design by Cliff Collier and Jim King.
Back cover photo by Bryan Rohbock.

ISBN: 0-9786664-3-7

Printed in the United States of America

This book is dedicated to all of the spirits who came to Speaking Wind's Huntsville seminars. The memory of our experiences at Kinlock will be with us always.

Thank you Patrick.

Table of Contents

INTRODUCTION

As we enter this domain that is the Earth Mother's, we will find ourselves in a place that our people have come to call "Standing With The Spirits Of The Flame." This is a time when we will find ourselves standing in our world with no idea why things are falling away from us. This place where we will stand will be a time of great crying and calling for help from anyone who will be willing to listen to us. This place is where we will come to feel as if our entire world is on fire. And, as all things that are ours seem to go up in the flames, we are frightened into thinking that we will burn up as well.

However, from the teachings of our people…those teachings that can be found echoing from the great stone walls of our lands…those messages that are continually carried to the ones who can hear them, they will remind us that this is not a time for us to wear the face of the frightened one…that this is not the time. Those things that have been either taken away from us or those things that have seemed to leave on their own, they were not ours to begin with. And to keep them would only keep us back from doing those things we have a need to do.

This is a time when we will experience a great growth on this life path we travel with the Earth Mother. This is the time when we will find many of those things that have left us…that they did not have real value to us for those things we are searching for. This is the time when we will be passing through the fires of the Ancient Ones…those same fires that our ancestors have held in a sacred place among our council fires of sharing. This time…this time when we will feel the burning away of those many things we once held onto…this is the time when we will find our face of truth. This is the time when we will come to know who and what we are and how to continue forward on the path of the spirit. All that will remain with us, once we have passed through each of these flames of the spirit…all that will be allowed to continue with us, they will only be those things that hold the face of truth with them…this face of truth that will allow us to one day see this path we seek to travel…this path we have chosen to follow…this path where we will find the greatest blessing of all ourselves.

Calling Thunder,
The Land Of The Pueblos

How we will come to treat ourselves, this will be how others will treat us. How well we will come to know ourselves, this will be how much others will know of us. How well we can see ourselves for who and what we are, this will be the mark of how well we can share ourselves with another. If you will wish to have a friend, first become a friend to yourself. If you will wish to have another give to you their love, you must first be willing to love yourself so that they can see this in you.

Grandfather, Spirit Caller
From The Land Of The Pueblos

Part 1

The Coming of
The Spirits of The Flame

Spirits of the Flame

Chapter 1

▼

THE CALLING

It had been many seasons since I was living on the lands of the mesa with Grandfather, Two Bears, and Cheeway. I had taken many faces to myself...faces that I did not always know were to be my own. However, in those seasons since we had all been together...in those seasons that we had come to call ourselves the Council of Four...I had been away from the lands of my beginnings...these lands where so much of my teachings had taken place...those teachings that were preparing me for the path I had willingly chosen to travel in this domain of the Earth Mother's.

But for the passing of those many seasons from these lands of the mesa...and from the loss of Grandfather, Two Bears, and my best friend, Cheeway...there were many events that had come to me...events that had seemed to be standing in my way...standing between myself and the path I was willing to travel. It had seemed to me as if there was a great obstacle that had been placed in the front of me. And the closer I would get to it the further away all that I had come to know would go from me. It was almost as if I had been given a choice...a choice that was telling me that if I wanted to continue on this path that I had been prepared for...this path that had been shared with me by Grandfather, Two Bears, and Cheeway...that I would have to give up all of these things that I had come to have. That there was not going to be a way for me to continue to hold onto those things that I had worked for and still continue to travel on this path of the spirit.

Just before I had left the lands of the mesa, Grandfather and Two Bears began their great spirit journey to the waiting place...this spirit journey that was soon to be followed by my best friend, Cheeway. During those many growing seasons that we had been together, Cheeway and I had been presented with all of the teachings of the Silent Brotherhood...those teachings that shared with both of us many great faces of truth...faces of truth that would allow us to see through those many events that had come to us…to see them as having a important lesson to offer us. And, if we would allow ourselves to see them not as the problems they could be but to see them as this arrival or offering of a lesson to teach us…a lesson that would allow us to gain a higher level of understanding for ourselves and all that was around us…then we would be allowed to continue to travel this path of the spirit…this path that would eventually share with us what it was that we had entered this domain of the Earth Mother's to do.

So it was that for those many seasons that would pass us by, I would attempt to look for those lessons that would be offered to me. To look through those events that would enter my life path with the hopes of seeing something to learn from them. But, for the most part, I did still see many of them for problems…problems and obstacles that were preventing me from doing those things that I held the believing in me that I should be doing. And there was nothing that I could find come to me from my within place that would offer me assistance for this. Nothing seemed to allow me to hold the clarity of vision to what it was that was taking place in this life path. I could only see myself getting further and further away from the place I wanted to go…to the lands that were home to me.

However, as the seasons continued to grow with Cheeway and myself… they did not see us continue with the rapid rate of growth that we had seen while we were still sharing a life path with Grandfather and Two Bears. As a matter of fact, the seasons that would be born to both of us would show me that we were spending less and less time together. Less and less time was spent between my best friend, Cheeway, and myself. For whatever reasons the Ancient Ones held in the front of their thinking minds, Cheeway would be taken to the tip of the Yucatan…this place where he would begin almost twenty-two years of his work in archeology. And I would spend the next twenty-two years working in almost every country in the northern hemisphere…working at those things that did bring to me a share of happiness.

But nonetheless, they did manage to keep me away from these lands of my beginnings…away from the lands that I had come to know and love. It would seem to me that each time I would try to return to these lands that were my home…that I would end up in a place that was further away… further away from them than I had begun from…further away from all of those things and places that I had come to know and grow up with…further away and in lands that I did not know the language of nor did I know anything about the people who lived in them. The only times that I would be allowed to return to these lands of my beginnings would be when I had enough vacation time and money to make a visit...to make a visit to the lands that I had come to call my home.

This did not seem correct to me. I could feel that there was something that was standing in the front of my path. But I just could not make out what it was. I felt as if I were trapped on a slow moving ship...one that would allow me to come close to the place I wanted to go. But when it would come close, then it would immediately turn around and head in another direction...another direction that would always be further away from what I thought was to be my destination. It was as if I were being tormented with this thought of returning to the lands of my beginnings...tormented with this thought while being forced to live and work in many strange and unfamiliar lands and the customs of the ones who lived there.

Each time I would be allowed to return...though it would only be for a short time. However, each time that I would return, I would always manage to find Cheeway...the one I had grown up with on the lands of the mesa...the one who had been prepared in the same way for this great quest we had taken up for the Earth Mother. However, as each of these times would come to us...and we would find ourselves back on the lands of our beginnings...we would both share that we felt the same way for what was happening to each of us. Cheeway would tell me that each time he would try to return to these lands on a permanent basis, that would be when something great would be discovered in one of the digs he was involved with. And because of this great discovery, he would always have to put the idea of returning home behind him. I would share with him that for each and every time that I would try to put in for a job that would allow me to return home, that would be when all of the offers would just seem to grow away from me and the only one I would be offered would be one that would take me further away.

Always it would seem that each time either of us would try to return to these lands...return to them for something other than a visit...that there would be something come up that would keep us from returning. Some kind of invisible hand would seem to keep us away from the lands we had come to know as our home. Each of our visits would bring this subject into the forefront of our discussions. And each time we both would share with the other our levels of frustration for it being so. Neither of us knew what was taking place.

Neither of us was happy with this turn of events...especially since it seemed to keep both of us from doing those things we had discussed with Grandfather and Two Bears...those things that we were supposed to be doing for the Earth Mother...those things that we had come to the place of believing that we would be doing together. We each felt as if we were being kept from performing those things we had entered this domain to perform...those things that would allow us to share our teachings with the many...the many who did not have the knowing or the understanding for the teachings that were to be found on the path of the spirit...those teachings that had been presented to both of us by Grandfather and Two Bears. All we had managed to come to the place of knowing was that because we were both being kept away from these lands of our beginnings...because we were not being allowed to return, that we could not begin to do those things that we said we would do. In the front of both of our thinking minds, we did not have the believing that we could have performed this great task until we had been allowed to return to our lands, to our homes and together.

As we both continued to travel more and more seasons of our life paths with the Earth Mother, this is the thinking mind that was in front of both of us. These were the thoughts that were keeping us in their company, as we would see season after season pass us by. Because of our not being able to return to our lands of the mesa and because we were not being allowed to spend a great deal of time together, both Cheeway and I had reached the same conclusion. And that conclusion was that if the Old Ones wanted us to begin our great quest for the Earth Mother, then they would see to it that we would no longer be kept from our home lands. Then they would ensure that both of our paths would return us to the lands of our beginnings together. And if they were not ready for us to begin this journey on the path of the spirit, then perhaps it was just not time. Perhaps the times that were told to both of us that would be over the face of the Earth Mother were simply not ready yet. That we were only going by our clocks and not the time of the Ancient Ones.

However, as we both held this thought in the front of our thinking minds, it did not seem to be the correct one. All of those endeavors that we would attempt to perform…all of the people that we would begin to have a great liking for, those things would only be allowed to spend a short time with each of us. Each time either of us would become successful in attaining enough money to return to our lands, something would happen that would require us to spend it in a different way. There was either something that would take place in our own life path that would require this money to be spent in a repair…or there would be something happen in another's life path that would require us to spend this money in an effort of assisting them to overcome something. But in either case, we were not being allowed to keep sufficient money that would allow us to return to our lands together…return for anything more than a short visit.

As we continued to feel this invisible hand keep us away from our lands…as this hand continued to keep us away from being together, there were more things that it would bring to us with its presence. Each time we would begin to make friends…each time that we would begin to become comfortable in the lands that we had been sent to…all of this would be taken away from us once again. All of those people that we had come to call our friends would either be offered a better opportunity in a different land…and, if they would take it, it would not be long before both Cheeway and I would lose all contact with them…or if they would not take this opportunity that had been offered to them, then it would be Cheeway or myself who would be taken to yet another place…another land and other people. In the times when I would become comfortable in the lands I had been delivered to and I could find a place where I would make a power place for myself…a place where I could feel the oneness with myself, that would be the time also when I would be taken from this land and delivered to another.

When Cheeway would make these same attempts, he would not be taken from those lands. Rather, the place where he was making his attempt of blessing with the assistance of his own spirit…this place where he too would be able to travel without worry into the spirit of silence…this place we had both been taught to return to for those answers we were seeking… when he would have almost made all of the preparations for this place on the land he was on, then something else would take place for him…something else that was much different than it was taking place for me. The land where he was making this attempt of creating this safe place for his body to rest while he would travel into the spirit of silence, this land would also be taken away from him as well. However, he was not being allowed to leave the place he had been delivered to.

Instead of his being removed, there would be something either built over the piece of land he had come to know or the ones who were in charge of this land would open it up to the public and create many tours over this land…tours that were filled with many people traveling over this same piece of land that he was trying to prepare for himself. And as so many would cross over this small piece of land that Cheeway was trying to prepare in the ways of our ancestors…as they would cross over it, they would leave those things of themselves on it…those things that all will leave behind them as they will continue to travel in this life path with the Earth Mother…those things that we have come to call the trace of their presence on a land. So it was that as these people would leave their own traces over this small piece of land that Cheeway was trying to prepare for himself, their presence was literally destroying his attempts of making this piece of land into what he was trying to make it into.

When you will make a power place for yourself, you must take something of spiritual significance from yourself and place it in a shallow part of this land. After placing it in a shallow place of this land, you will next mark it from the four corners…the four corners that are in reminding to the spirits of the land. Once this is done, you must be willing to spend many hours sitting and waiting…in silence as you will ask these spirits of the land for their permission of blessing…their blessing that will allow you to continue to mark this small piece of land for a safe place to yourself. And once the spirits of the land will grant this assistance to you, then this piece of land…this small place that is on the face of the Earth Mother…this place will become one of power to you. It will be from this place that has been shared with you by the spirits of the land that you will find many open doorways… doorways that will allow you to continue traveling between the domain of the Earth Mother's and the domain of the Ancient Ones…those same ones that will offer to you many blessings that will shed their light on all things that have been placed before you…a light that will then be carried with you even as you will travel this domain that we have come to know as our temporary home with the Earth Mother.

From this light that will travel with us…this light that will be seen by many who travel in this domain of the Earth Mother's…they will perceive this light as something that is good coming from the one who is carrying it. They will feel a great peace that will be coming from the carrier to them. However, this light that will be carried with us from beyond the great doorway of the Ancient Ones…this light will give to the carrier the ability of seeing all things that are being presented to them with the vision of clarity. There will not be anything that will be hidden from them. There will be nothing that will not be answered for them…nothing that they will have a need to come to the place of knowing and understanding.

However, for those places that Cheeway was attempting to prepare for himself…those same places where others would cross over or others would build another structure on, these events would completely destroy all of the efforts that he had been willing to make…all of those efforts that he was attempting to do, just as I was, so that we could come to a place of seeing…a place of seeing why it was that we were not being allowed to return to the lands of our beginnings. But for all of those efforts that Cheeway had been making, those articles that he had placed in their shallow places in the earth…when the others would cross over them, their levels of spiritual significance would be dropped. And if one will allow their spirit articles to drop in their energies, then soon, they will no longer have the value they once held. Soon, they will become an article that will be of no spiritual significance. This happens when others will either touch them and by doing so they will have a part of themselves enter it or, as was the case of all of Cheeway's efforts, the presence of the ones where they were, who were crossing all of the places where he was attempting to create, was enough to lessen the desired effects of what it was he was doing…all of the places he was attempting to create…this power place where he would be allowed to enter the great doorway of the Ancient Ones and bring back with him their light…their light so that he would be able to see what it was that was taking place for both of us.

Well, from all of the ones who would venture across this land…their presence would be left on it as well. And, in a very short time, all of the spirit energy that Cheeway once placed over it would be so infused with the others…so complicated by their presence that it would no longer be of any use to him. When a power place is created for one, then this is the one that should use it…only him. When others will cross over it, then the effect of only one or two would not be so bad. But when there are many, well, this will take all of the power from this place and confuse it…confuse it so much that there will no longer be your identity over it. And without this then there can be no efforts of crossing over the great doorway at all.

Each time that Cheeway and I would return to the lands of our beginnings and would share with each other, we would always arrive at the same conclusion. Each of us was not being allowed to return to the lands of the mesa and neither of us was being given permission to enter the great doorway that would take us to the place of the Ancient Ones…this place where we would be allowed to see why things were taking place in our life paths as they were doing…this place that would share with us the face of truth for all that was taking place for us. For both of us, it would always be the same result…the result of allowing us to know all of the steps that were needed to make the journey into the silence…this silence where we would be able to see the location of the great door way that would lead us to the Ancient Ones.

But just as we were about to complete the preparing for ourselves…this preparing of the place on the land we were on so that we could travel…we would have it suddenly taken away from us. Both of us were of the knowing that there was to be nothing for either of us while these conditions were being held over us…that neither of us would be allowed any measure of success in trying to perform those things that were necessary…those things that were necessary for us to find our way back or to come to the place of knowing why we were not being allowed to return. So it was, that when we would leave each other's company on the lands of our beginnings, that we would make our plans for our next return home and we would continue to try to understand what it was that had come to close us off from those things that we were both trying to do — from returning to the lands of our home.

All of those seasons that were to pass both of us by remained the same. That is, until I received a letter from Cheeway…a letter that shared with me that he had been taken ill and was being returned to the lands of the mesa…the lands of our beginnings. When I received this letter, the first

thought that crossed my thinking mind was that this hold over us was finished…that Cheeway was being allowed to return to our home lands and
that soon, I too would follow…and that when we were both together, then
the first thing we would do would be to travel into the silence and enter the
great doorway of the Ancient Ones…this doorway that would allow Cheeway to be healed. Once he had been healed, he would then be allowed to
begin this great quest we had both been given…this great quest that was
in service to the Earth Mother in her great time of need.

However, when I returned to the lands of the mesa and saw Cheeway, I
could see that this illness that had come over him was one that would not
easily go away. During the times of our sharings, I was told that he would
not have one more complete season with the Earth Mother and that the
level of this illness was such that it could not be reversed. This much I
had heard from one of our spirit callers called Calling Thunder…one who
had been a great friend to Grandfather and Two Bears for the times they
shared in this domain that is the Earth Mother's. From the speaking words
of Calling Thunder, I was assured that all that could have been done for
my best friend, Cheeway, had been done and that the calling voices of the
Ancient Ones were already all over these lands of our beginnings…their
calling voices to him…their calling voices that were in need of his return
to them.

Hearing these speaking words from this one called Calling Thunder
gave to me a feeling of complete abandon…a feeling of being all alone in a
life path where I was being choked off from even doing those things I had
been prepared with…those things that had come to me from the teachings
of Grandfather and Two Bears. "Calling Thunder!" I cried to him as we
were both standing on one of the spirit ledges of the mesa.

"Yes, Speaking Wind. What is it that is giving to you this great weight of
concern? Is this face you now wear before me the result of feeling as if you
are one of the ones that has been left behind?" came his response to me.

"Yes, Calling Thunder. I have this feeling within me…and it is a feeling
that has been growing within me for all of these seasons that Cheeway and
I have been kept from returning to these lands of our beginnings…these
lands of our home. I have the knowing that we were both prepared in the
ways of our people for performing a great quest for the Earth Mother and,
since we received this preparation, neither of us has been allowed to return

here. Neither of us has been allowed to be together. And neither of us has been given any opportunity of traveling into the silence and asking this question of why to the Ancient Ones.

"These events now that are coming over this face that I wear are only added to this knowing that I have been given. This knowing that now Cheeway is being taken away from this domain…and still, I am not allowed to ask the Old Ones why. Still, I am being held away from them as the lands of my beginnings.

"Calling Thunder," I said, trying to keep the sound of an emotional cry out of the tone of my speaking words. "I feel as if my entire world has been set on fire and there is nothing that I can do to alter it. This is what has come over the face I now wear that you see. I do not have any knowing why all that I have ever held close to me has been taken away…why I have been held against even myself and all of the efforts that I have taken in returning to these lands of the mesa.

"I just feel so alone, Calling Thunder. I feel so alone and without any assistance from anyone," I shared with him.

"Speaking Wind," Calling Thunder said to me as he placed his right hand over my left shoulder. "All that will take place in any of our life paths is for a reason. There is no thing that will ever be presented to any of us that does not have its reason…and the times that this reason cannot be seen or understood. Well, these are the times when we are not looking for the answers that are being presented to us. This will be the time when we will only want those answers that we want and not the ones that are."

"So then what can I do, Calling Thunder? All of the efforts that I have been trying to do have been stopped. I have not been allowed to create a power place for myself that would allow me to come to the Ancient Ones with this question."

"Speaking Wind," Calling Thunder said with a knowing look that had come over his face. "Perhaps the reason that you were being stopped was that you both were trying to travel a path that you were not ready for yet. Has this occurred to you? Did you remember that there were other ways in which one may call upon the assistance of the Ancient Ones?"

"I am not sure that I completely follow your speaking words, Calling Thunder. What precisely do you mean those other ways?" was my return.

"Learn to call on them, little one. This is a good day to do such a thing,"

Calling Thunder returned to me. Finishing his speaking words to me, Calling Thunder rose from the sitting position we were both in and began to walk away...to walk in the direction of the village...the village where my best friend, Cheeway, was resting. I did not have a complete knowing of what it was that Calling Thunder was sharing with me. However, from those many seasons that I had been allowed to spend in learning the ways of our people from both Grandfather and Two Bears, I held the knowing that I should do what had been shared with me to do. Even if there was not a clear level of understanding for those speaking words that had been shared with me, I had learned that when one of the wise ones, one of the ones like Calling Thunder, was among our people...when he would share something with anyone, that it too held its own life of reason within it. And it was from this knowing that I decided to follow the path he had suggested for me...this path of asking.

Chapter 2

▼

THE VISION

Watching as this one called Calling Thunder returned to the village, I could not help but think on those many things that had been shared with me. Those many things that had come to me on the back of the speaking words from Grandfather and Two Bears. And as I listened for them, there was a direction that had come to me on this day. It was a direction of calling…a calling to the ones who had been so willing to share with me all that would be needed…all of those things that I would need in order to perform those great quests for the Earth Mother.

"When you will have a need for an event that has come to you, little one," came the beginning of the speaking words from Grandfather from my within place, "…when you will be presented with events that do not allow you to see their face of truth…this face of truth that will allow you to see them for what they are, then you will be in the place of having only one course open for you to follow.

"It is a course that is still to be found on this path of the spirit…this path where all that we have shared with you has prepared both you and Cheeway equally…prepared both of you to find the meaning in my speaking words.

"When you will feel as if you are trapped inside of a large canyon…one that is too high above you to allow you the freedom of leaving…when you will have this feeling little one, then you will also come to a place of believing that your world has been set on fire…that your world has begun to burn up and these flames will also take you up with them.

"When this time will come to you…and I assure you that it will…for it comes to all who are traveling in this domain…then you must take the time to look deep into the face of the sky and ask for assistance to come to you…assistance that will share with you those things that you will need.

"When you will do this, little one…when the spirits of the land will see you asking for assistance in this way, then they will come to know that there is not anything more that you can hold within you. Anything else would be to put you in a place where you would no longer be of any service to any.

"It will be at this time when you will call into the face of the spirits that reside within the sky that they will come to you. They will come to you if they see that part of yourself that you are presenting to them bears the face of truth.

"They will allow your speaking words and the face they carry with them to be born on the spirit wind. And the spirit wind will make itself known to you at this time…this time when you will feel your totem carry off those things that you are holding a need for.

"Do this when you can see no other way of assistance come to you, little one. Follow these steps that I have been willing to offer to you. For when you will do this, then you will receive those things that you will need… those things that you will need so that you will be capable of staying strong on this path you have been willing to travel…this path of the spirit that we have prepared you for."

Hearing those speaking words of Grandfather's come to life once again from my within place…this gave to me the piece of direction that I needed…this piece of direction that shared with me what it was that Calling Thunder had suggested I do.

The sun was still low in the morning sky on this day. As it would fill our lands with all of the blessings that would come to us, I could see the morning shadows were beginning to fall away…to fall away and hide themselves into the one who had been creating them. Looking at this process, I could feel the calming of these lands of the mesa…this calming that would come to those who could feel it…the same ones who had learned to have a love for this land of the mesa…this land that I had once been allowed to know as home.

Remembering those speaking words that had first come to me from the one called Calling Thunder…those speaking words that were just supported by the speaking words of Grandfather from my within place, I held the knowing that they had all come to me for a reason…a reason that I would not have the understanding for until I would follow their advice…their advice that shared with me that this was the path I should follow…this path that would show me that now was the time to ask for assistance in the way I had been shown. That this was the time to call on the spirits of the land to assist me with those things they were willing to assist me on.

I had received from those speaking words of Calling Thunder that it was now time for me to do such a thing. And, because those speaking words of Grandfather's had returned to life once again from my within place, I had come to have the knowing that when this would happen, then it would be for a specific reason. And that reason, even thought it might not be obvious to me at the time, would be shared with me when it was time. Those speaking words from Grandfather…those speaking words that had come to remind me that there were other methods that could be used in calling to the spirits of the land…other methods than the ones both Cheeway and I had been using…these methods would serve me well now. They would serve me well because now it was time.

Returning my eyes to the sky that was above me, I could feel a drawing on me. It was a kind of drawing that I had received before. One that shared with me that this would soon have me in the between place. The place where I had tried to travel to so many times before…but before now, I had been stopped. It was at this time when I was presented with a thinking picture from my within place…a picture that shared with me all of those events that had come to me for the past twenty-two years. And this one last event that had come across my life path, this event that had been given to me of the passing of Cheeway…this one who has always been my best friend…the one who had been prepared in the same way as I had…but now, he was the one who was being allowed to leave, to leave and begin his great spirit journey to the waiting place…this place where Grandfather and Two Bears are waiting for us. I was seeing this last of these many events of the twenty-two years cross my thinking mind. And as each of them would cross me, I could feel the weight that each of them was bringing with it…this weight that had been given to them by my not having the understanding for them…this understanding that would have allowed me to see what it was they were offering to me.

Instead of seeing them with the face of fear and hostility for what they were being seen by myself…as this weight of the passing events continued to fall on me, I could also feel this fire that seemed to consume all that would come near to my life path…this fire that would run those away before we could begin to know one another. This fire that would burn away those things that would come to me and this same fire that would grow even greater each time that I would attempt to return to these lands of my home. For each time I would make this attempt and have them stopped.

Looking deep into the dark blue sky that was over me, I could feel that there was more in them than just the wind spirit. I could feel others. Others whose presence I had felt in many of the events that Grandfather and Two Bears would point out to us. Because of this knowing of them in this place and on this land, I had no understanding of why I did then what I did. All that I can see for my actions was that it was something that just came out. I was standing on the spirit ledge of the mesa when I found myself listening to my own speaking words come out of my mouth. Listening to them and following them as they would not only go up and into the sky that was above me but also as they would bounce off the great stone walls that were around me and then travel into the sky above. "Grandfather! Two Bears!" came the first of these unattended speaking words from me. "It is I, Speaking Wind, who calls to you on this day.

"I know well that your time is to now sit around the great council fires of our people. But I have a great need…a need that only you will be capable of assisting me with.

"Look into me. Look into me and see the trapped one who resides within. See the one who is confused and cannot see the spirit quest that was once offered to me.

"Assist me in calling to the Ancient Ones. Those Ancient Ones of our ancestors who have not been listening to my speaking words of calling. Those Ancient Ones who have for so long provided our people with the guidance and wisdom that we have always sought.

"Assist my calling of this spirit face that I present to you, Grandfather and Two Bears. See the stains of the tears that have run down my face… these tears that have been falling from my within place. These tears that show to you and all who will see them the great hurt that I now carry with me. A hurt that I cannot see my way. A hurt that is cutting through my heart.

"Add to my calling voice the calling voices of your own. Add to them so that together they will find their way to the ones we have come to know as the Ancient Ones.

"Grandfather, my world is on fire. My whole world is on fire and I do not know what it is that I am to do.

"Hear me calling to you. I am showing to you my face of truth. This face of truth that is me for this day that I am now in.

"I need your assistance, Grandfather. I need your assistance, Two Bears. I am lost in this darkness of unknowing where I am going. I am lost in the night of passing and cannot see my way.

"Take the time from tending our council fires to take my message to the Old Ones. To the Ancient Ones and stand in front of them for me. Stand in the front of them and hold to them where they can see this face of truth…this face of truth that I have been willing to share with you. This same face of truth that carries with it a great hurt. A great hurt from one who is wondering and lost.

"Listen to my speaking words of the spirit, Grandfather. Listen to my speaking words of truth, Two Bears. For it is I, Speaking Wind, who is calling to you. Speaking Wind who remembers you well in his heart. In this heart of our people. In this heart that you have assisted in forming for me.

"I ask for your assistance so that I might gain my clarity of sight for all of these events that have been presented to me. These events that have been offered to me. Offered to me with a lesson to learn from them. A lesson that I have yet to know.

"I have not forgotten you. I have not forgotten this path I have been willing to travel. This path of the spirit. But I need your assistance for this cloud that has come over me. This cloud that carries a fire to my life path. A fire that I cannot understand. A fire that will not go away."

Looking up to the sky that was over me, I could still feel this pulling… this pulling that was attempting to draw my spirit up to a place that was beyond where I could see. Beyond this place where I was standing on the spirit ledge of the mesa. Suddenly, there was a noise that was beginning to grow. A noise that was beginning to grow in a place that was just beyond where I could see. A place that was close but not within my sight. I could hear this sound as it was gaining its momentum. It was like the sound of a great stampeding herd of the children of the hoof. A herd that I knew was nowhere close to these lands of ours. Suddenly, as the noise was continuing to grow in its life near me, I saw that the once dark blue sky was no longer clear. It had been filled up with a great cloud. One that would usually mean the water spirit was near to bless our lands. However, I did not smell any promise of his blessings. I did not even see the approach of this one coming to our lands. It was as if this great cloud had been hiding from my sight. Hiding until this moment. This moment when it would make itself known to me. In the process of this great cloud blocking the reflection of the Great Spirit in the sky, the noise was becoming louder.

And, with the increase of its sound, I felt a very familiar hand come over me…over me and in a way that I could not mistake. For the noise I was hearing was from my spirit totem. It was the calling of the spirit wind, and he was sharing with all of the children of the Earth Mother that had come to call this land their home that there was soon to be a great blessing here. A great blessing that would not include them but one that would include one of those who traveled on the two legs. Having this knowing that those spirit words that I had asked assistance with had been answered, I knew that there would be a new face for my understanding. And this new face that I would be shown would soon be presented to me. Presented to me as I had finally been answered. Answered for all of the events that had been taking place with my life path. For all of those things that had come to me. Those things that I had been allowed to come close to them to have them be taken away. Even those events that had been keeping my best friend, Cheeway, and me separated and away from these lands of the mesa. These lands that we had come to know as our home.

Not wanting to stand any further, I took a place that was on this face of the Earth Mother and sat down. As I did this, I could feel the arrival of the spirit wind over this land. I was surprised at his suddenness of arrival. But most importantly of all I was feeling very honored. Honored to have one of the spirits of the lands such as this one do me this honor. This honor of being the deliverer of those things I had asked assistance for. Assistance from Grandfather and Two Bears. Assistance from the Ancient Ones of our people. The ones who had always been willing to provide us with the needed direction and guidance that we held a great need for.

And now, now I was sitting down on this spirit ledge of the mesa. This spirit ledge where so many of the lessons of wisdom had been shared with me by Grandfather and Two Bears. This land both Cheeway and I had come to call home. In my sitting position, I could still feel the pulling of my within place to the in-between. The in-between place that is between the sky and the face of the Earth Mother. The place where many of our unanswered questions will be shared with us by the Ancient Ones of our people. As I was feeling this pull of my within place for my spirit, I could feel the strength of the spirit wind begin to increase. Trying to keep my eyes open, I could hardly see the village that was just below me. It had been blocked out by all of the small pieces of earth that were being moved to other places. Other places where the spirit wind held the knowing that they could find more lessons for themselves. More lessons that would allow them to continue to grow on this life path they had come to the Earth Mother for.

I was beginning to see that there is not ever any one action that is taken up by any of the spirits of the land that would only involve one. That for all of those efforts that were shared in this domain, there would always be many who would benefit. Many who would benefit if they would have the eyes and ears of the spirit to see and hear with. Feeling the sureness of my spirit totem fill the lands that were ours to travel on, I could feel a peace of knowing filling me. A peace of knowing that this path the spirit wind was traveling was no different from any other he had been willing to travel.

However, the one thing that was holding the great difference for me now was that I was no longer being held behind the blind of uncertainty. For the first time in many seasons with the Earth Mother, I could feel that this time for me was right. That all things were now taking place on my life path as they should be. That all was in a balance as they were meant to be. Even this growing scattering of the small ones of the earth that were flying across my face. Within a few minutes, I found that the back of my neck and back were beginning to sting. Beginning to sting from the flying pieces of earth that were being moved. And for a while, I felt as if I were the one who was in their way. Just as soon as this thought crossed my thinking mind, the stinging of the small pieces of earth stopped. It was as if they were sharing with me that I was not standing in their path. That this was a path that could very well be shared by all. And this knowing gave to me a good feeling. A good feeling that was filling me from the within place. This within place where my spirit resides. And this within place that was now feeling even more the pulling from the spirits of the land to the in-between place. This place where I was being taken to. This place where I would see those things that I held a great need to know.

However, the force of the spirit wind did not diminish on this day. It was gaining in its strength as it would cross our lands. These lands that I and my best friend, Cheeway, had come to know as our home. I could feel the force of the spirit wind pushing across my back. And the continued pulling of my within place to the between place. This place where so much assistance was to be found for our people. Our people who have been before as well as the ones who were here now.

Just as I was feeling this pulling and pushing that was with me, I was very surprised to see a vision of myself. It was one that I was a part of but separate from at the same time. In this place where I had gone to…gone into without any warning, I could feel all things that were around me. All things seemed to be a part of myself and I felt as if I were a part of all that I could see. From this place of seeing, I would only have to look at the place where the great stone face of the mountain was. And as I would continue to look at it, it was becoming very easy for me to become a part of it. A part of it in a way that I knew all things that it was feeling. That I could become a part of all things that it was thinking. And in a way that allowed me to share with it all of the knowing and understanding that it had been allowed to achieve for itself.

As I would look at the trees that were on this land, I could feel the same things for them as well. I could not only feel their being but I could share in the path they travel in this domain of the Earth Mother's. This path that has allowed them to be known among our people as the great communicators and unselfish sharers of their life force. All of this was very new to me. And I did not have a knowing of this place that I had been taken to. This place where I knew many of my unanswered questions were to be revealed to me. Those things that were behind all of the events that had been taking place for Cheeway and myself for these many seasons.

As I could feel myself blending into all things that were before me… blending into them but still maintaining my own identity among them, I could hear the sounding of the beating of drums. This I had come to know was the calling card of many of the spirits of the land. And it was they who would be sharing this sound with those who would enter close to them…those who they had accepted into their domain. And it was this beating of the drums that was a signal to me that it was not only the spirits of these lands that I had come to call home but it was also the spirits of many of these other lands that I had come to know. Those many other lands that I had been directed to over these last twenty-two years that had come to my life path.

Listening to this sounding that was coming to me, I could hear those speaking words that had been shared with me many seasons ago…those many seasons ago and on these same lands that I had shared with Grandfather and Two Bears.

"Listen to the sounds of the beating of the drums when they will come to you, Speaking Wind. Listen to them and open your heart to those things that will be presented to you.

"For it will be at this time when you are being signaled by the spirits of the land. This will be the sign they will give to you that all those things you have come to them with have been heard. That they have not only heard those speaking words you have formed for them to hear but they have also felt the inside of your heart…this heart that wears the face of our people and our path of the spirit.

"The sounding of this beating drum you will hear. The sound of only one drum will be the calling sign of the spirits of the land on which you will stand. This will be their welcome to you…their welcome for you to enter the between place. This place that is located between the Earth Mother and the face of the sky.

"This will be the calling to you for you to enter…to enter their domain with their blessing. However, little one, there will come a time for you when there will be more than one drum beating that you will hear. A time when there will be a great need by you. A need that has not only been seen by the spirits of the land but a need that has been seen by the Ancient Ones themselves. A need that they will have seen you prepare yourself for. A need that will come to you with such clarity that you will feel the need to close your eyes to this face of truth. To this face of truth that will be presented to you.

"But you will soon find that there will be no need to close your eyes at all, Speaking Wind. For when you will see this great face of truth that is being presented to you, there will be an immediate knowing that none of those laws that have applied to you in this domain that is the Earth Mother's will apply to you in this place. In this entry way that is through the spirits of the land.

"For when you will be in this place, little one...when you will have been accepted by them, you will no longer be with the constraints of the body part of yourself. And you will not have these constraints over you because you will be traveling with your spirit. This spirit that is you.

"Now, when you will hear the beating of more than one drum playing for you at this time...when you will hear many of them coming to you... coming to you and all with their own sense of tempo, then you must keep in the front of your thinking mind this.

"That for each of these tempos that you will hear...these tempos that are from the same rhythm of the Earth Mother's heart...that for each of these variations that you will hear, they will represent yet another set of the spirits of the land. The ones who have been given dominion over another part of what we have come to know as the face of the Earth Mother.

"Do not worry if you will think this will bring about a confusion over you. For in truth it will not. Their presence around you is giving to you an honor. It is an honor that they are willing to share with you. And it is an honor that they have already shared with the Earth Mother and the Ancient Ones long before they have made their presence known to you.

"You see, little one. This time that I am sharing with you is much like the times that our hunting parties would come back to the village. Come back to our homes with their baskets filled with all of those things that our people needed...all of those things that would allow us to continue with our life path with the Earth Mother. And when our people would see them coming into the village, then they would all gather next to the path these successful hunters would return by. They would gather on both sides of their path and give to them their signs of approval and admiration. This would be their measure of thanking them for doing what they said they would perform for all of us and perform it so well.

"When you will have come to the place of hearing more than one set of drums come to you...come to you from the between place of the spirits of the land…this same place that is our spirits path…to receiving a knowing from the ones we have come to know as the Ancient Ones.

"And it will be when you will have this great need of knowing…this great need of knowing that you have allowed yourself to become prepared for. It will be then that you will hear the many different tempos of the beating drums. Those beating drums that will be sounding for you to hear…to hear the welcome of the spirits of the land.

"From the many tempos that will come to you on this time, Speaking Wind. They will be the numbers of the spirits of the land that are standing on either side of this path they have allowed you to enter…this path that they have accepted you on…this path where you will find the wise council of the Ancient Ones. The ones who will present you with the knowing for those questions that you have brought with you."

Hearing these speaking words of Grandfather's come back to life from within me…this brought to me a great peace. And it was a peace of knowing. A peace of knowing that for those many years of seeing all that would come to me…all of those things that would come close to me being taken away. That now the time was right for me to receive a kind of an answer. However, as I have learned from the many teachings that had come to me from Grandfather and Two Bears…that when the knowing will come to you from the Ancient Ones, that there will also be a price to pay for this. And this price that one will have to pay will be in the amount of effort they are willing to place in understanding all that has been offered to them.

"When the Ancient Ones will present you with answers to the questions you have been allowed to place before them, Speaking Wind," began the reliving of the speaking words from Two Bears. "When they will present you with a spirit vision…a spirit vision that will share with you all that you have been asking…well, it will not come to you with the answers that are carried on its back in the same way that we have become used to seeing and hearing.

"When the Old Ones will present you with those things that you will have a need for…those things that will be quite necessary to remain on this path of the spirit, they will present them to you at a much higher level of understanding than they hold over you now.

"The reason this comes to you in the way it does is really very simple. It all has to do with the kind of knowing that you are seeking. This knowing that has resulted from those questions that you have held out to them. Held out to them with both of your hands turned in the upward position.

"When they will see that you have prepared yourself sufficiently to have a need to those answers you have asked of them, they will be more than willing to offer them to you. However, they will offer them to you at the same level of understanding that you will need in order to see their answers clearly.

"What this means, little one, is this. That when you have come to them with these questions, you do not have the understanding for those events that have been presented to you. The understanding that would have allowed you to look at them and see the lesson they have been offering to you so that you could learn from them. And it is this lack of understanding at this higher level that has created the problems you are having at this time.

"At the time of your asking, the Ancient Ones will see where you are. Where you are in these many different levels of understanding that we have entered this domain of the Earth Mother's to learn from. And they will see that you are standing in a level that is really too low for what it is that you are asking of them. A level where you would not have the knowing to come to the place of understanding what it is that they are willing to offer you anyway.

"So what they will do is this. They will see the level you are currently standing on now. And they will also see the higher level of understanding that you will need to be on. To be on so that you will be capable of coming to the place of understanding what it is they are presenting to you.

"Once this determination is made, then it will be from this higher level of understanding that they will allow their offer of assistance to reside on. This higher level that is necessary for you to travel to anyway.

"And this will be the reason that for many of the spirit visions that you will receive from them will not seem to make a great deal of sense to you in the beginning.

"However, as Grandfather and I have shared with you, this will only take place for you in the beginning times. Those beginning times when you will still be new to this path that will allow you to go to them. This path that resides in the between place.

"After you have come to know this path well, that will mark the time that you will begin to see these answers that will be presented to you more clearly…these answers that will be left for you to see at the higher levels of understanding. These higher levels of understanding that you are attempting to reach anyway.

"What they are doing for you is great. This blessing that they are willing to share with you does not lie so much in the answers or the spirit vision for that matter. The true mark of the blessings the Ancient Ones will be willing to offer to you is assistance…assistance in attaining this higher level of understanding that you have come here to learn…this higher level of understanding not only for yourself but for all things that are as well.

"And, little one, keep this in the front of your thinking mind. That the higher levels of understanding we will be able to attain in this domain of the Earth Mother's, the more successful we will have become on this life path we have been given…this life path that has so graciously been given to us by the Earth Mother.

"Remember, Speaking Wind, it is not the knowledge or the understanding that will mark the success or failure of a life path. But it is the wisdom…this wisdom that will allow you to use this knowledge and understanding that you have discovered. Without the wisdom to use these things that will be presented to you, then you will become like the great book that no one will ever come to read. This book that no one will ever read because none can come to understand it.

"In order to come to have this wisdom, little one, you must be willing to travel into these higher and higher levels of understanding. These places where you will begin to see more clearly all events that will come to you. When you will come to achieve another level of understanding that is higher than the one you were on before, then all things that had come to you…all of those things that you once held the believing in that you knew, they will all change. They will all change because you will not have seen one of them fall away and another take its place. Rather, you will now have gained the ability of seeing more clearly that face. That face of the things you only thought you knew more clearly.

"And with this ability of seeing more of this face of truth to all things that are around you, you will first come to believe that all things are made new. But this is not the truth of what has happened. As you will continue to travel in this path of the spirit, you will see that they have not changed but that you have. And this will give way to seeing more completely those things that you have entered this domain of the Earth Mother's to work with. You will begin to see things that are around you as they are or at least more of what they are.

"So it will be that in the time you will be willing to travel on this path of the spirit…this one and only path where the Ancient Ones will be allowed to offer to you their assistance, you will be assisted in attaining higher and higher levels of understanding for all events that will be presented to you.

"And the higher levels of understanding that you will attain, then the more of the faces of truth you will be able to see…these faces of truth that will reside in all events that will come to you. It is from this attaining of the next higher level of understanding that we will learn the wisdom that will allow us to use the understanding and knowing for all that had been presented to us from the one just below. From that level of understanding that we have just passed.

"So it is that when the Ancient Ones will offer to you their assistance for those things they have seen you are ready to receive, they will leave them on the next higher level of understanding for you…this next higher level of understanding that you must be willing to attain. And when you will reach this next higher level of understanding, little one, that will be the time when you will be able to look over to the last level you had been traveling on…this last level of understanding where you had so many questions about and see the answers for yourself. Those answers that you have had a great need to see more clearly.

"This then is what will bring to you the greatest blessing of all. This is what our people have come to call the Light of Direction that the Ancient Ones have always been willing to share with us. This ability of seeing for ourselves all those answers we have been seeking. But to see them from the next higher level of understanding that they will have shown to us. This next higher level of understanding that they have shown to us and how to arrive at it. This then is the face of truth to the spirit visions that are shared with us, Speaking Wind. It is the greatest blessing of all when one of us can attain the next higher level of understanding and come to the place of wisdom to where we have just passed. To attain the wisdom that will allow us to use wisely all that we had come to know and understand from our last level of understanding.

"You would do well to keep these speaking words in the front of your thinking mind, Speaking Wind. Do this and they will always bring to you a knowing of what is being presented to you…those things that will come to you in the path of the spirit vision. This path that has been created for us by the Ancient Ones. The Ancient Ones of our people."

Feeling myself in this domain where I was a part of all things and all things were a part of me, I could not help but know that all of those speaking words of Grandfather's and Two Bears were also being shared with the one. With this one that I had been so welcomed into. And it was this knowing that shared with me that they too were allowing me to share in their acquired wisdoms. These wisdoms that will come to all life that is within all domains that have been created by the Great Spirit. I was receiving a very good feeling from my within place. It was a feeling that I was not only taking in all that was being shown to me in this new place. But I too was sharing. That I too was giving. And this had always been shown to me that this is the way it should be. That this would allow one to come to the place of understanding the meaning of the balance of the life path. The balance of the life path whether it was being traveled in the spirit form or in the body form.

Resting with this understanding that had come to me, I closed my eyes and began to feel the oneness that was coming over me. This oneness that allowed me to be a part of all that is but still maintain my own separate identity. As soon as I had closed my eyes, this closing of my eyes to feel more of the oneness that had been presented to me, I felt a sudden surge in the pulling. This pulling that I had experienced earlier while I was sitting on the spirit ledge of the mesa. I knew that the spirit vision that I was seeking was about to begin. This spirit vision that was being presented to me by the Ancient Ones of our ancestors. This spirit vision that would allow me to see the direction to the next higher level of understanding. This next higher level of understanding for myself and all things that are of life. The next higher level of understanding that would allow my spirit to advance one step closer to all of our desired goals. This goal of being prepared to rejoin with the Great Spirit. To rejoin with the Great Spirit and become one once again with all that is.

Chapter 3

▼

SPIRIT VISION OF THE ANCIENT ONES

The next thing I had come to know was that it did not matter if my eyes were open or closed. I could tell that these things that I was now seeing were coming to me from another place, another direction. In this place as well I did not have any knowing of. This too was a new place where I had been taken. This place where I held the knowing that was where I was to be given this spirit vision…this spirit vision of the Ancient Ones. In less time that it would take me to complete one half of a breath, I began to see the face of this offering to me. This offering that was coming to me from the Ancient Ones of our people. Once again, I had been taken to another place. Another place where all that was before me was new but somehow familiar.

I found myself sitting on the top of a large mesa ledge. A large ledge that had been built into the side of one of the faces that looked down and over a great valley below me. Just behind me was the wall of this face and above me was only a clear blue sky. A clear blue sky that was sparsely dotted with the attendance of little white and fluffy clouds. In this new place that I had been brought to, I did not receive the same feeling of being a part of one with all that was here. However, I did hold the knowing that this oneness was here. And while it was available to all who shared in this land, it was not available to me.

I could feel the firmness of the earth that was under me on this place. This place I had been brought to. And, I could feel the presence of the spirit wind on these lands as well. This presence of my totem that was serving only as a gentle reminder to me that I was not alone on this land. Looking over the edge of this ledge I had been placed on, I could see below me and into a great valley. A great valley that seemed to go on forever in any direction I could see. In the middle of this valley were what looked like two separate paths. But their destination could not be seen by me because they both seemed to follow the length of this valley. This valley that I could not see either the beginning to or the ending of.

However, as I was sitting on the top of this ledge portion of a mesa, I could see there were many groups of animals and people. Groups who seemed to be moving as if they had a place in the front of their thinking minds. I was receiving a feeling from those groups. And this feeling that was being presented to me shared that there was some kind of a migration taking place with them. A migration that they knew of but a migration that was not entirely clear to me. Realizing that there was nothing more for me to see from them, I continued to sit and observe...observe their actions that were taking place on these two paths. There seemed to be equal numbers of these groups of animals and people who were traveling on both of these paths. Equal numbers of them who would stop from time to time and seem to share a direction with the others who were with them.

Knowing that there was nothing more that I could come to understand from what was being shown to me, I sat back in my sitting position and allowed myself to find a place of enjoying these things that they were doing. I was surprised to see that there were many who had taken leave of one of these paths and would jump across to the other one. This other one that was not too far from each other. I did not have a place of understanding for this. But as this continued to take place, I could see that the ones who would perform this seemed to have their own reasons for doing so. Reasons that I had come to the place of believing were beyond where I was looking from. Looking over to the ones who seemed to be jumping from one path to the other, I could see a look of knowing what it was they were doing. This was becoming very obvious to me from the looks they held over their faces. These looks that would come to them as they would make their jump.

There was one thing that did come to the front of my thinking mind though. One thing that seemed to fill up all of my thoughts as I was looking at these two paths that had been set into the bottom of the valley below me. I was remembering the description of the two paths that are available to all who will enter this domain of the Earth Mother's. The two paths that are described for our people and are within the teachings of the silent brotherhood. As I was looking at these that were now being shown to me...these two paths where there seemed to be a great migration taking place on them, I was reminded of the path that leads to the right and the path that leads to the left.

I was reviewing…the path that leads to the right is the one that is traveled by the others. These others who have not yet found the way to their own spirit. These who travel the path of the others are always giving themselves away to accommodate the many. The many who are always telling them how they should be and what they should do. And by giving to these others this level of controlling their own life path, they are made to believe that they will always be taken care of. That they will not ever be alone because the group they travel with will tell them that they will always be there for them. But, from those others I have seen traveling this path that leads to the right, I have yet to see a time when they will stop to assist one who is in need. Instead of assisting them, they will literally turn on them so they will not have to be reminded that this time of need could come to them as well. And, in the front of their thinking minds, they believe that if they will not have to look at one who is having a great need then they will not have this kind of a time come to them.

So it is that while the ones who will travel on the path that is leading them to the right, they will spend all of the seasons that have been given to them in chasing shadows in the night. Those shadows that promise you if you can catch them, then they will give to you their great secrets. Secrets that will make you strong on this path you are on. However, as the ones who travel on this path that will lead them to the right…when they will come to the end of those many trails they will be shown, they will find that there is only one place any of the trails on this path will lead. They will find that all of these trails that are on the path that leads to the right end up in the great darkness. This place of the great darkness where only sadness can exist. And, when they will discover this, for the most part, they will believe that it is just too late for them to change. Too late for them to change from the path they are currently on to the path that will lead them to the left. However, as I have seen, this is not so. I have seen many change paths and from all places where they have been traveling.

Now the other path that I was looking at in this valley below me…this other path seemed to remind me of the path that leads to the left. This path that has been found by our people. This path that was taught to both Cheeway and myself when we were of our short seasons on the lands of the mesa. Those short seasons when we were being prepared by the speaking words of Grandfather and Two Bears. This other path did remind me of the path that leads to the left. This was the path that will eventually lead one to the path of the spirit. It is the path where you are always asked to learn from yourself. To learn from all events that will come to you. And this learning from those events…this is what will bring to you your next higher level of understanding. This next higher level of understanding that will advance your own spirit while you are still in this domain of the Earth Mother's.

As these thoughts were crossing my thinking mind and how similar these two paths that I was looking at were to the ones that had been talked about…those paths that had been shared with me from the silent brotherhood, I was suddenly taken from my sitting place on this ledge of the mesa and was taken to another one. I was taken to a place that was just between the two paths that I had seen from my high place of observing. I was standing directly in the middle of them. From this place, I could more easily see the faces of the ones who were jumping back and fourth between these two paths. The looks that were being worn over their faces were almost as I had left them from the place I was at before.

However, as I was looking over them from this close place…this close place where they were traveling on their respective paths, I noticed that there were none of them who noticed my presence among them. It was as if I did not really exist. However, I was so close to them that I could have reached out and touched any of them I would have wanted to. I did not have the knowing of why I had been brought to this place. But as it is with all things that will come to us, there will be nothing that will take place by accident. There will always be a lesson to be learned or a direction to be followed from them.

So it was that I had decided to remain in this place…this place I had been brought to by the Ancient Ones…these who were bringing to me this spirit vision. Waiting on this piece of ground I was placed on…this piece of land that was residing between these two paths, I was able to observe the ones who seemed to be in this migratory movement even better. And, it had crossed my thinking mind that this might be one of the lessons that was being offered to me. One of these lessons that could be seen so much better by me now that I was standing this close to the event.

Looking over these people and animals who were traveling on both of these paths, I could see that every now and then they would stop. That this stopping of their direction on either of these paths would allow them to share events among themselves. And that just before their groups that they were traveling on would stop, there would be a particular face each of them would place over themselves. It was a look of either a great confusion or one that was filled with frustration. But in either case, this look was one that did not allow them to continue on the path they were traveling. Not continue at least in the same way they had become used to doing.

Turning my head from the left to the right, I could see there were many more of these groups who would travel on the path that was to my left. But on the path that was to the right of me there were more individuals traveling. And, this allowed me to reinforce my own thinking mind with the differences there had been in the two paths that had been shared with me…these two paths that had been shared with me by the teachings of Grandfather and Two Bears…the two paths that had been shared with them by the teachings of the silent brotherhood.

However, from the place of seeing…this place where I had been placed that was between both of these paths, I could tell that there were events that were coming to all who would travel on them…to all of the people and animals that were traveling on both of these paths that I was now being shown. But, there was no place for me to see what it was that was taking place for them. I could not see nor did I hold the knowing of what it was that was coming to them. Those events that were seemingly coming to all of them in such a rapid succession. Such a rapid rate that would make them continually change their minds and jump from one path to the other.

Even though I could not see what these things that were taking place with all of them were, I could tell that whatever events were coming to them…that they were great. That they had been presented to them in pretty much the same way. I held this knowing because of the looks that would come over all of their faces just before they would jump from the path they had been on onto the other one. I could feel that these events…whatever they were…that they held something very significant for me to learn from. I held this knowing because of the immense importance they held over all who would travel on either of these paths.

So I continued to look from the standing position I had been given. This place I had been brought to that was directly between both of these paths. Without any warning or sound, there appeared before me a great white object. At first I could not tell what it was because it would only appear as a great white blur to me. However, there was such a brilliant light that was coming from within it. A white light that was illuminating all that was around me that I was sure I had been the one to try to instinctively block this light from my eyes. I believe that this was my first reaction to it. But within a few short heartbeats, I found that even when I would look directly at this white light…this light that was coming to me from the object that had appeared in the front of me…that there was really no need to turn away from it. It was brighter than any other light I had ever been shown. But its brightness was in the greatness of wisdom and not in the directness of its shining. So, standing in my position, I continued to look at what had come to me from out of nowhere. And, I would look at it with my eyes fully opened and standing square to it.

As I was focusing my eyes onto this new appearance that had just placed itself before me, I was noticing that there were none of those who were traveling on either of these paths that had taken notice at either my presence or that of the large and glowing white light that had appeared before me. However, as I continued to look at them…look at the ones who were traveling on both of these paths, they did not allow this appearance of either myself or this large white light to interfere with their direction. They were still performing those same things that I had observed in them earlier. The looks of having an event come to them. An event that was very strong. Strong enough to have them make a choice. A choice of crossing paths.

Realizing that I would not be able to see what these events were…these events that I held a believing were very important to my situation…this situation that had created so many questions for me to ask…I realized that if I would allow these events to take place and in their own time…that I would be shown all that I had a need to see. Allowing this to come to the front of my thinking mind, I was then able to focus my attention to the event that had just come to me…this event that had appeared before me as a great white light. Looking over to the place where this appearance had formed itself, I was surprised to see that it was a buffalo. It was a buffalo and then it was a bear. I could not follow the number of times that it would change itself. But within one blink of an eye, it would change from being a white buffalo into being a white bear.

As it would change itself into these two forms, I could feel a deep and growing peace that was coming into me…a deep and warming peace that was growing. Growing each time this white light would change itself from one face to the other. Even though there were no speaking words being shared with me from this one…this one who was sharing itself with me as being two, I could feel that there were many messages that were being given to me. Messages that I could not understand at this time but messages that were being stored within me. And, when I would come to the place of a higher level of understanding, I knew that they would come to the surface for me…surface to me from the within place…this place where all things are stored with my spirit.

The changing faces of this one who had come to me did not vary. There were no other noticeable changes that were coming. And, we both or all three simply stood in the between place of these two paths looking at each other. Sharing with each other. Sharing from a place where no speaking words could reach. A kind of sharing that is only known and understood at the same time. This was the kind of sharing that I had been prepared for by all of the teachings that Grandfather and Two Bears had been willing to show me. This was the path the Ancient Ones would often take for us. This path that would allow us to have this knowing and understanding at the same time. These things that would not require so much time for us to come to the place of understanding that was within our own reach. This place of understanding that was with us already but we had not yet seen it for what it was.

I could feel the great amount of wisdom that was coming to me from both of these spirits of the Ancient Ones. From the white buffalo, I could feel the bounty of many blessings that had been given to this one by the Earth Mother. Many of those blessings that this one had earned…those blessings that this one had been given to share among those who would also earn them while they were traveling in this domain. From the white bear, I could feel the wisdom that comes when one will go to the within place in search of wisdom. Wisdom that will come to them from the understanding they have received by working their way through all of the events that have come to them. This wisdom that was being shared with me from this white bear was the kind that I had only heard of from many of the song legends of our people. And, the bounty that I could feel pouring from this one, it was more than enough to fill me from every side. As I stood in my position looking at this changing that was taking place before me, I could feel a swelling within me. A swelling within me that left little room for my heart to live.

And, as we two or three were looking over the others' place, I received the feeling that I was looking into the spirit of ones who had known me for many seasons. For many more seasons than there were stars in the night sky. As this feeling of knowing came into me, there was another sudden change that took place. Another change that became the next step in this spirit vision of the Ancient Ones. My attention was taken from looking at this changing of the white buffalo and white bear that was before me to one above. I found myself looking up at the sky that was over me. And as I looked up, there was yet another great event that was being presented to me.

It was an event that had begun from the between place of two small clouds that were sitting very still in the sky above me. Looking to the place that was between them, I could see there was beginning to form another small but very bright light. And, from this light that was beginning to grow in a life place of its own, there was another path coming to me from it. A path that was much different from the two that I had been looking at. There were no others on this path. None like the ones who had been traveling between these two that I had been shown before. However, as I observed this path beginning to grow to me…grow to the same place where I was standing…when it reached the place where my feet were, the white buffalo and bear were on it as well.

But, they were no longer the ones that I had seen before. They were not sharing the same body and changing between themselves. Now the white buffalo was standing on one side of the pathway from the sky, and the white bear was standing on the other. Both of them were looking at me with the face of wisdom and understanding…this face of wisdom and understanding that I had only heard about in those most ancient of our song legends. This face that shared with me that they were about to offer me a great event…a great event that I would learn from. Silently, they both came closer to the position I was standing…this place that was directly in front of the new path that had come to me…this path that led up into the sky itself.

As they reached me, both of them took one of my arms and began to lead me up this path…this path of the sky. Taking me by each arm, we began to climb up this path that was before me. And, as we began to climb, I could feel the swelling of my heart become larger than I was. This swelling that was coming to me from the feeling of greatness that was around me. This feeling of greatness that was coming to me from both the white buffalo and white bear. It had been from the many song legends of our people that I had the knowing of who these two were. They were one of the many forms of the Ancient Ones. Their forms that will come to those who have a great need to understand many events that will come into their life path.

And it is from the form the Ancient Ones will take up for you that you will eventually have the knowing of why they chose as they did. Why they chose to show themselves to you in the form they had taken. However, as the teachings of Grandfather and Two Bears had filled so many of my younger seasons came back to me, I had been reminded that these forms the Ancient Ones will share with you…that this will be the face of wisdom…this face of wisdom that you will need to travel to so that you will be capable of finding your way. So that you will be capable of finding your way through the darkness that has come over you. These were the thoughts that were filling me as these two Ancient Ones were leading me up this path way to the sky. These were the thoughts that were assisting me in finding the understanding that I needed at this time.…this understanding that was needed by me so that I could continue on this path of the Ancient Ones' spirit journey…being led by the two Ancient Ones' forms. Those two forms that had come to me as the white buffalo and the white bear.

We continued to go higher and higher on this path way that was leading into the sky. Climbing higher on this path…this path that I was being assisted on by the two Ancient Ones, I still had not taken my eyes off from the two paths that were below me. Even though we were heading into the higher place that was above me, I was still observing the two paths that we had just left. And, even though we were rising much higher than the ledge was on the mesa…this ledge that I had begun from…still, I could not see the ending or beginning of either of these two paths I had seen before. These two paths that were going through this great valley below me.

Soon, my attention was drawn to the two Ancient Ones…the two who were assisting me in traveling on this path that was leading into the sky. I could feel them more than hear them as they were making a point clear to me. It was an understanding that was coming to me from them, but it was coming to me with all of the understanding that was needed. This understanding that would normally have to be worked through in order to attain it. I could feel them sharing with me that it was now time for me to learn a great lesson…a lesson that would assist me in coming to the place of seeing. A place where I could be more capable of seeing all of those answers to the questions I had been holding with me. And, just as they had finished with this sharing with me, they dropped me.

They dropped me and I immediately began to fall into the valley below…this valley where the two paths were crossing through. Feeling the air rushing past me, I held the believing that this was much more than a dream. To me, it was holding the face of reality. This face that I had come to know would bring results to all things that were done to it. This face that shared with me that for every action there would be a reaction. And this was filling the front of my thinking mind. I knew that if I would hit the bottom of this valley…this valley that was below me, then I would surely have grave consequences to my body part. And, I would not be wearing a good face over myself when this would happen.

However, I did not react to this event in the way I had anticipated. I did not scream nor did I try to reach for my balance. I only remained in a stretched out position and looked at the valley below me…this valley that I was traveling to very quickly. Looking at this end to the journey and holding nothing more in the front of my thinking mind, I heard a voice come to me. It was a voice that held an echo within itself…an echo as if it were coming to me from every place. "Do you know yet?" came the voice as I continued to cut through the air and toward the valley below me.

"I think I do!" was my response.

"You do not know yet," came the voice once again. And, once again there was a silence over me. And, with this silence, I continued to fall, seeing how much closer I was getting to this valley. This valley that I knew would stop my direction of falling. Again, the same echoing voice returned to me. "Do you know yet?"

Looking at the downward direction I was falling to, I could not move my attention to the ground that was coming up to me very fast and say, "I think I do!"

And again the same voice repeated to me, "You do not know yet." And I continued to fall into the direction of the valley below. Once again the voice came to me, "Do you know yet?"

And once again, I responded to it in the same way: "I think I do!"

"You do not know yet!" came the return. Hearing this same dialog was giving to me a concern. It was a concern of how intent I had been looking at the place I was falling to…this valley that was below me. And, as this thought was crossing the front of my thinking mind, I decided that to continue to look in this direction was bringing to me no great advantage. All it was doing was keeping me from looking at anything else.

Not wanting to concentrate on the place where I was falling to…not wanting to look at it any longer because this was all that was filling my thoughts, I turned over. I flipped over in the air and was now looking at the sky that was above me. My first reaction to this was so that I would be able to take my mind off from what was coming to me…this event over which I did not have any control. And to look at something else. I was thinking that if I would not become so intent on looking at this ultimate ending to my falling, then I might be able to see what it was that was being shown to me…this lesson that was being offered so that I could learn from it. Even if this learning would only come to me instants before I would end this fall…if I would be allowed to see this lesson, I was thinking…then I would have some time with it. And to have at least some time with this knowing…this would be better than not having been with it at all.

However, as I turned over to look at another place…one that was different from the one I was falling into, I was filled with a great surprise. It was a surprise that I was not ready for. But it was one that was holding this lesson I had been told about…this lesson that was being echoed by the calling voice that had been coming to me. This voice that kept asking me if I knew now. Looking up to the sky that was above me…this place where I could only have the thinking that I had begun my falling from, I could see that there was an identical scene that was above me as was the one below.

However, from the one that was above me, there was much more detail that was being shared. Much more detail even though I was falling away from it at a very fast rate. Looking to this scene that had been shown to me...this scene that was now in the sky, I could see that there were the same two paths that I had seen in the valley. However, these two paths were much more clear to me. And all of those events that had been hidden from me before...they were all being shown to me now. From the two paths that I could see in the sky, I could still see the same migrations that were taking place. And, I could also see the same groups of people and animals that were traveling on them in their small groups.

However, from what was now being shown to me, I could see that the path that was on the left...it was leading to the left. And the one that was on the right...it was breaking in the opposite direction. It was leading to the right. This much was much clearer for me now. I could see that those things that had filled my thinking mind were becoming much clearer to me now. I could see that those things that I was holding to me...those things that were being shared with me from those teachings of seasons past, that there is the path of the others. This path that leads to the left. This path that not only leads to the left but to the place of the great sadness that is filled with the darkness of not understanding. And, the other path that I was being shown...this path that would lead to the right...this path that has been sung of in so many of our spirit songs, this was the path where so many of the events were taking place on. This path that reminded me of the one that would lead to the path of the spirit.

Looking closely at this path that was leading to the left as well as the one that was leading to the right, it came to me that what I was seeing was the portrayal of all those teachings that I had been prepared with. The teachings of the silent brotherhood. The same ones that Grandfather and Two Bears had taken so many seasons to prepare both Cheeway and me with. Now I was looking at those things that had been shared with me. I was looking at the face of truth to those teachings and this was giving to me a great feeling of belonging. A great feeling of freedom. One that was greater than this fear of falling into the valley below me.

As I would look at these paths, I could see there were the same numbers who would continually jump from one path to the other. However, I could also see that there were many who would not change their path. And while their numbers seemed to be small, I could not help but think on how well they each seemed to travel on the path they had chosen for themselves. Even the ones who were traveling on the path to the left. Even they, who seemed to be traveling on a path that would lead them to no place...no place where there could be any spiritual growth. They would still carry with them an air of dignity. This dignity that came to them from staying the path they had chosen to follow. This path they had seen a need for themselves on.

Looking over to the path that was leading to the right, I could see that there were a number of the travelers who would also stay there. A number of them who, like the ones I had seen remain on the path that was to the left, they too held themselves proudly and with the wisdom that had been worked for by them. This path that was on the right. It was the one that held the Great Mystery to it.

And as I would continue to fall into the valley below me, I could not take my eyes away from these paths in the sky that I had been shown. Especially the one that was leading to the right. On this path that was leading to the right, there seemed to be many flames that were coming out from it. They were not all coming out in one place. Rather, they would seem to stagger themselves all this place. This place where the path to the right would pass.

I looked at those who were traveling on the path to the left. And, as I could see the faces they would wear over themselves, I could see that for each one who was traveling through the flames...those flames that were on the path that was leading to the right, they would have a look of awe and admiration over them. I could feel that this look that had come over them...over the ones who were watching those on the path to the right pass the flames...that this look that was coming over their faces was the result of seeing those others possess this ability...this ability of passing these flames.

However, not all of those who were on this path to the right were successful. Many of them, just as they were about to enter these flames on their path, would stop in the place where they were. They would stop and I could see that they were filled with a great fear. They would be filled with this fear of now having the understanding of what was taking place to them. This fear that will come to all who will not understand that all things that will happen to them will bring with them a great offering…an offering of a lesson…a lesson that they need in order to attain this next higher level of understanding.

However, because they did not possess this understanding…when they would come to the place of the flame…this place where they could either pass or turn away and jump over to the path that was leading to the left, many of them would choose to leave this path of the flame. This path that would eventually take them to the path of the spirit. And, when they would cross over, it was done in a great jump. This same jump that I had seen when I was observing these same two paths on the floor of the valley below me. This same valley that I was now falling into.

For the ones who remained on the path that was leading to the right… this same path that was filled with many flames…those same flames that would appear then disappear…when they would be about to enter the portion of the flame, I could see the look that was over them was one that seemed to be very heavy. They always seemed to be stooped over as if something was resting on their back and they were having to carry it for a long distance. The look that was over their face was a tired one. It was a tired one until they would reach the face of this flame…the face of this flame that was staring at them.

And as they would enter this flame, it was always done with a look of fright over them. But it was not the same kind of fright that we would often find when we were being chased by a large animal…one who we had made very angry at our actions to it. This look of fright was more of a knowing one. A knowing look but a frightening one. And it would fall completely over them. So much that they would forget this great weight that they seemed to have been carrying. As they would enter this flame, there were sudden jerks that would be shown all over their body. And there were a kind of muffled screams that they would let go as they would first enter. However, all of this would pass away very quickly. And when they would exit from the flame…which did not seem to take very long, they would be standing very straight and have a look of peace come over their face.

This was bringing me to a place of remembering…a place of recalling those things that I had been taught those many seasons before. "When you will see one who is traveling very heavy…traveling as if they are carrying a great weight over them. And this look that will come over their face will be one that will show to you a heavy heart. Then you will have seen one who will be carrying many events and lessons with them. Events and lessons that they have not yet reached the place of learning to understand from," came the beginning of the speaking words from Grandfather back to life for me once again. "You will see these others who will not have taken the time and effort of working their way through all of the events that have been offered to them. You will see them as very frightened individuals. And this look of fright will come to them from wondering just how much more weight they will be able to carry with them. This weight that has come to them from all of their lessons they have not been willing to work their way through.

"When an event will come to you, little one, it does so as a very innocent child. A child that will carry over it only one face. And this face is one that is the face of truth to this offering they are willing to share with you. This offering of the lesson that you and the Earth Mother have designed for you to learn from. However, when you will not be willing to look at this little one's face of truth...this same face of truth that you have called to yourself to learn from, then this child of the offering becomes very sad and will begin to think that he has been presenting himself to you in a way that would not be recognized by you.

"These small children of the offerings will have only one purpose in the front of their thinking minds. And this purpose will be to share with you all of those things that you have entered this domain to learn from. And, when you will not accept them as they are when they come to you, then they will learn to put on another face for themselves. They will place over themselves another face for you to see. Hoping that this face will become more acceptable to you and you will not continue to ignore them.

"But as these little children of offering will place this other face over them, it will have to be in addition to the one they have originally carried to you. And for each additional face they will have to wear for you to see them, then the more weight they will carry on them. This weight that will be carried on them will be seen on the one who is not looking at their offering. This offering that is being presented to them.

"It will be when you will not be willing to make this effort of working your way through this lesson that is being presented to you...this effort that would have allowed you to come to the place of understanding what it was that was being presented to you to learn from…this will be the time that another face and another weight will be added to the original offering.

"The number of faces that will have to be placed over them will give to this offering additional weight…additional weight that will have to be carried by you…additional weight that will over time hide the original meaning of what was being offered to you.

"It is because of all of these additional faces that have been worn over the original lesson…it is because of them that this additional weight will soon be apparent to the ones who will come to see you. And to them, you will appear to be one who is carrying a great weight on their back…a great weight that is causing you to walk in a bent over position. But it will be a weight that no other can see. They will not be able to see it because it can only be felt. And it is only felt by the one who is carrying it.

"There will be only one way that this weight will be allowed to leave you, little one. And this one way will only be when you will be willing to look into the face of the original offering that had come to you…this original lesson that had first appeared to you with this lesson that was created for you to learn from.

"However, before you will be able to see this original offering once again…you will have to be willing to work your way through all of these other faces that have been placed over it. These other faces that must be worked with one by one until they have all fallen away.

"Only then will you no longer have this weight to travel with. Only then will you be able to see the original lesson that had been presented to you. And, little one, only then will you be able to go on to the next one.

"However, for the times that will come to many…the ones who have entered this domain to perform many great tasks for the Earth Mother. They will not have the time to perform all of those things on their own. They will require assistance in their learning. This learning that will bring to them to the place of being prepared. Prepared to begin all of those things they told the Earth Mother they would do. Prepared so that they will be capable of seeing what path they will travel in this domain. The path that will bring them to know the face of not only themselves but the face of the Ancient Ones as well.

"These faces that will bring to them the opened eyes and ears of the spirit. Those same eyes and ears that will share with them the pieces of the faces of the great truths that have been set into motion in this domain for us to learn from. These same pieces of truth that have been placed so that we could all find them. And, when we will place them all together, then we will be in a place where we will begin to see the face of the Great Spirit…this face of the Great Spirit that will allow us to see the one…this one that we are all attempting to return to.

"But, as I have been willing to share with you, when one will see what it is that they must do, this required work that will have them work their way through all of these additional faces of the lessons that have come to them…those same lessons that they had not been willing to work their way…they will find that they are confronted with a great number of seasons in order to do this.

"When they will receive this knowing. They will ask for assistance. Assistance from the Ancient Ones, the spirits of the land, the Earth Mother, as well as the Great Spirit. Assistance that will allow them to work their way these things quickly.

"This kind of assistance is not freely given, little one. And you would do well to keep this in the front of your thinking mind. This kind of assistance is not freely given because for the most part all of this work was meant to be done by you. And the reason for this is to give you the learning and understanding that is needed by you. This learning and understanding that will share with you what not to repeat when other lessons are being presented to you.

"And, little one, you must keep in the front of your thinking mind that there will not ever come a time when another will be able to do this work for you. That there will not ever be another who will be able to gain this learning and understanding for you.

"They will only be capable of sharing with you those things they have come to the place of learning and understanding for. But from this sharing of their experiences, you will have to perform the rest of the work for yourself.

"It would be in the same way to ask another if you could travel on their path. To ask such a silly question would mean that you are willing to give up all that is of value to you. To give up the advancement of your own spirit so that you could tag along behind them. To tag along behind them and learn nothing of your own.

"So it is with the assistance that will be asked for…this assistance that will be asked for by those who are carrying this great weight of the unlearned lessons on their back.

"Remember, little one, that there is no request that is not heard. That all voices that are raised for assistance, well, they are all heard equally. Equally from the most quiet to the loudest. However, they are all heard but you must remember that the ones who are listening are also looking into you as well.

"They are looking into you which gives to them the knowing of what you need as well as those things that you only want. And, this is the place where the assistance is either given or held back from you.

"There are many who do not have a place of understanding for this, little one. But these are the ones we have come to know as the selfish ones in this domain. They will ask for assistance. And, when they will not see it come to them, then they will have only one place of understanding. And this understanding will tell them that they are not being heard.

"You see, little one, these are the ones who are only thinking of themselves. They are not thinking of others and why they will have to do this work on their own. They do not see this lack of assistance they have asked for as an answer to them. They will not see that for all those things they are not receiving this assistance for, that they are in truth being given assistance. But this assistance that is being given to them is one that they cannot see. They cannot see it because they are being shown that they have some work to do of their own now. That it is they who will have to perform this work for themselves because there are a great many lessons for them to learn from. Lessons that will only come to them from feeling alone while they are doing this work.

"For these who will be required to do this work…this work that will not come from any but themselves, well, this is what they are in great need of. This great need is to share with them that they must first come to the place of believing in their own spirit. This spirit who is residing within them. This spirit who is them.

"Once they will learn to grow this strength that is within them…once they will come to the place of believing in themselves and being able to stand strong on their own, then they will have prepared themselves to receive higher lessons…higher lessons that will allow them, when they will work them, to be in a place where they will be able to perform great tasks for the Earth Mother.

"And it is the ones who have reached this place that will see the face of assistance. This face of assistance they have requested from the Old Ones.

"So it is that there will not be any who will not be heard, little one. There will not be any who will not have this request for assistance who will not be seen. But at the level they are this will determine how this assistance to them will come. Whether it will come to them on the path they travel from their own efforts or if it will come to them from the Old Ones. The ones who are seeing them and the needs their spirit holds.

"When the Old Ones will see that you have reached the place of the preparing…this place where you are now ready to perform great quests for the Earth Mother, then they will have this knowing that I have already shared with you. They will have this knowing that the times you are in now do not carry with them the same opportunities that have been with our generations of the past.

"They will have the knowing that in order for you to see those things that you can perform in service to the Earth Mother and all who are within this domain…that this process of working each of these faces of the original lesson…that there is just not the time available to you to do this.

"And, little one, this will be when you will be given this assistance you have requested. This assistance that will allow you to look through all of the faces that have been worn by the original offering…to look through all of them so that you will be able to come face to face with what it was that had been originally offered to you…this face of the child of the offering.

"When you will come to the place where there will be nothing that will come to you as a path…a path that will share the direction for those things you have come to know…those things that you have a knowing of that you alone must perform for the Earth Mother…when this path will not come to you and you can feel the need growing within you…then you will ask for the assistance of the Old Ones…this assistance of the Ancient Ones of our people.

"And when they will hear this request of yours and see you for who and what you are, they will see that you have been prepared and are in great need of their assistance…this assistance that will allow those many faces that have been gathering over you to fall away. It will be at this time that you will be given an answer. It will be an answer that will be carried to you on the back of your spirit totem. And this answer will share with you that this assistance you have requested is coming. That it will arrive to you very soon.

"Then the Ancient Ones will begin their journey to the place where you are spiritually. Their journey has been marked by many of the song legends of our people…these song legends that have been held within the teachings of the silent brotherhood. These same teachings that you have entered this domain to share with the many who will have a great need to re-remember them once again. The ones who have forgotten to remember their own face of truth.

"And when the Ancient Ones will arrive to you with this assistance that has been requested… this assistance that has been requested by your own speaking words, they will come to you in a way that cannot be ignored or looked away from. Their presence over you will be such that there will not be any mistaking them for who and what they are. There will not be any mistaking all of their efforts for anything but what they have come to you as.

"When the Ancient Ones will come to you in this way, little one…we have given to them a name. It is a name that will share with the many who will come to them for their assistance how they will come to them. We call this path they travel for us to learn from "The Spirits Of The Flame." This is the name we have given to them for this time of their assistance. And, this is the name that will fit over them the best. It will fit over them the best because this is what they will bring with them. They will bring with them this spirit of the flame so that it will cause those things that are over you…those things that do not hold the life of truth to them…those things that do not have anything to do with the original offerings of lessons…to fall away from you.

"And, little one, it will be by your passing through these flames that they will fall away. They will fall away from the heat that is within these flames. This heat that is increased only higher for all that does not hold the face of truth to it. This heat that will not exist for those things that are of the face of truth.

"They will present themselves to you in this way so that you will be able to continue on with those things that are ahead of you, little one. It is not anything that you would have had the time to do on your own. And the number of lessons and quests that are still ahead of you for the Earth Mother, they are great. And this time that is over all of us now is very short.

"When you will come to the place of being offered this assistance, little one…this place where the Ancient Ones will come to you wearing this face of the spirits of the flame, you will be in a place of the great knowing…this place of the great knowing that will share with you that you are about to begin your work…this work that you had originally come into this domain to perform.

"However, the face that will come to you…this face you will find over yourself as you will first encounter this place of the spirits of the flame, you will come to the believing that all of your world is on fire. And, there is no thing that you can do to put out the flames.

"Remember, Speaking Wind, remember well that when you will arrive at this place, that the best thing for you to do will be to walk into them. Walk into those flames that have come to you. For, as you will exit from them, there will only be the face of truth to all those things that had once been attached to you and this path you are trying to travel. There will only be those things left that will benefit your spirit. And, from those things that will be left, only learning will come from them. And as you will continue with this learning you will become lighter and lighter. Which will give you a good face to wear.

"But remember these speaking words little one. The time of the spirits of the flame does not come only once to you…there will be many times. Many times when once again you will be in need of assistance from them…assistance that will allow you to gain in the strength and believing in your spirit that will keep you strong on this path of the spirit…this path of the spirit that will lead you home once again."

Hearing those speaking words of Grandfather's come to life within me once again, they gave to me the understanding I had been looking for... this understanding of why so many who were traveling on both of these paths would see a great event come to them...an event that would cause some to cross over to the other path these events that had caused others of them to observe...to observe those things that they too needed. And this caused them to also cross over to the other path. With this knowing and looking up to the sky above...this place where I had been shown the two paths more completely, this allowed me to place the falling behind me. This falling that was taking me into the valley below. As I felt the wind passing the back of my head and body, I no longer was concerned with the sudden stop that was waiting for me at its end. This no longer held any interest to me. For what I had come to understand in this place...this lesson that I had been shown of the spirits of the flame, this was all that mattered. This was what was filling me now. And with a great cry, I shouted, "I understand now!"

As the last of the last sound of these speaking words passed my lips, I found that I was no longer falling. I had been returned to the face of the lands and in a very gentle manner. One that left me with the feeling of being a feather in flight...a flight that had just come to its own end. Standing on this face of the earth that I had been set on, I remained in the silence...this silence that had come to me by my own choosing. I wanted to take this time to look back on all that had been offered to me...all that I had come to the place of understanding for in this spirit vision...this spirit vision of the Ancient Ones.

When, from all places that were around me, I heard a very strong but peace filled voice come to me, "These are my children, Speaking Wind. Show them the path of returning to me." As the last of these speaking words came to me, I found myself back where I had begun. I was no longer in the valley of the Ancient Ones. I was back among the lands of the mesa. These lands I had come to call my home. Opening my eyes, I could see the marks of the spirit wind...this spirit wind that had come over these lands of our people.

All around me were the changed faces of the Earth Mother. For many of the little ones had been moved by the force of this spirit wind. Moved to another place where they could be offered more to learn from. More of those events that would come to them so that they too could complete this great circle of life and return to the Great Spirit once again. Standing up, I began shaking off all that had gathered over me…all of these small ones who needed to return to the face of the Earth Mother where they could learn. Finishing dusting myself off, at least as much as I could, I looked over to the place where the village was and began walking to it. I did not know what I would find, but since this spirit journey had finally begun for me, I did not want to stop it from being.

Part 2

▼

CLOSER TO THE FLAME

Chapter 4

▼

SPIRIT OF A SHARING FRIEND

Walking back to the village. I could see a face come to me. It was the face of the one called Calling Thunder…the one who had come to me on this day…come to me with the sharing that it was a good day to ask for answers. Seeing his face come to the front of my thinking mind, I held the knowing that he was waiting for me to come to him once the spirit vision of the Ancient Ones had traveled its course of being. However, before I would travel to meet with this one called Calling Thunder, there was one I would see before. The one I had grown up with on these lands of the mesa. The one who had been prepared with me for performing these great quests for the Earth Mother - Cheeway.

Entering the village, I could feel the life that had been residing here for many generations…these many generations that our people have been allowed to share this land with the Earth Mother. Walking in the path that was between the buildings, I could see many of the leaves of the last growing season piled by the corners of the houses that had been built so close to this path I was traveling on. There were a few of them that were being tossed around by the small wisps of wind that were still here. These small reminders of the place they had come from was the spirit wind…the bringer and carrier of all things of the air.

Continuing to walk in the direction of the house Cheeway was in, I could see there were many of these small leaves that were being blown in little circles. Little circles that were being taken out from their corners where the buildings would meet and into the dirt path I was traveling on. As I would watch them, I remembered what Grandfather and Two Bears would often tell us. Those speaking words they had been willing to share with us when both Cheeway and I were of short seasons. "When you will see these small ones…these small ones of the leaves of the past season… when you will see them and they are being led out into the open spaces in small circles, then, little ones, then you will have the knowing that this is a good time for you to ask questions to the spirits of the land.

"As it is with all life, there is a time for doing and a time for playing. And these spirits of the lands…these spirits of the lands of the mesa, they are not any different. They too wish to have this time that is for them and the many things they will wish to do. Those things that will bring to them a great joy in doing.

"Also, this is the time when they are relaxed and are not so busy with the tasks they all have to perform. When you will see these small leaves being played with…when you will see them traveling in small circles over the lands, then you will have the knowing that this is the time when the spirits of the land are playing. And while they are at play they will take the time to hear those things you will have a need for.

"They will have this time of listening because they will not be so involved with the many things that are usually being required of them. When you will see them playing with these small little leaves…then will be the time when you will be allowed to speak to them. This will be the time when your spirit will be allowed to touch them with your requests.

"And, little one, this will give to you another path of requesting. A path of requesting that will be in addition to the one you have been holding with you. That path we had shared with you…the path that allowed you to travel up through the tree child and have them hold your requesting up to the spirit wind. This spirit wind who would carry them to the spirits of the land as well as the Earth Mother if she is needed."

Looking at these small ones traveling within these small circles as I was walking to the place where Cheeway was…this was giving to me a reminding. It was a reminding of the many times that Cheeway and I would see these spirits of the land playing. And, how we would always try to jump into the middle of these small circles of wind they would make. I was remembering how we would always feel as if we were one of them when we would do this. When we would try and follow their path of playing by running in the middle of these small circles they would make. Looking over this, I could feel those memories fill me. Fill me from my within place.

As I rounded the next corner of the houses, I was taken out of this place that had been shown to me. I was reminded that this was the now time…this now time where I was at. And, as I looked up from the place I was traveling through, I saw that I had reached the front of the house where my best friend, Cheeway, was staying. Standing on the outside of the land that was around it, I sent my picture thoughts into it. Sending my picture thoughts of my wanting to be invited inside was considered a very polite way among our people. This was considered to be polite because of the ones who would live here and the spirits that would also be here. Those spirits who were members of our spirit family that had come to offer to them their assistance.

It was not long before someone had come to the door and invited me in. Thanking them, I looked to the place where I knew Cheeway would be. One of his favorite places was a couch. And in this house…this one house where he had been invited to remain until his spirit journey would begin. He had been blessed with yet another luxury of this life path. The couch was next to a large window. And under the window and on the couch was Cheeway. Looking at the place where my best friend was laying, I could see that he had placed a great smile over this face he was wearing. A smile that shared with me that he felt as if he had all things in this world that he needed now…a smile that gave to me a great comfort. A great comfort because this gave to me the knowing that he was being well cared for. And for this I was very grateful.

"It is good to see you once again, my brother," came the beginning of the speaking words from Cheeway.

"It is good to be here with you once again, Cheeway," was my response. Looking over to where I had found a comfortable place to sit, Cheeway looked at me with a knowing in his eyes. It was a knowing that I had seen many times before. Those times when he was forming his speaking words from something that had been shared with him…from something that had come to him from the within place…this place where his spirit resided.

"I have the feeling that you have been shown a great lesson, Speaking Wind," was his continuing of speaking words.

"Yes I have, my brother. But tell me, what gives to you this knowing?"

Looking at me with a larger than usual smile over his face, he said, "I have seen the wind cross over these lands of ours. It was not the normal wind though. I held the knowing that it was the spirit wind that had come to us. And it had come from invitation. This is what had given to me this knowing, Speaking Wind."

"Cheeway," I said sitting up rather straight now. "Just because you have seen the presence of the spirit wind over our lands. What would give to you the thinking that it was I who had called it? This could have been done by a good many of our people who have also been prepared by the path of the spirit."

"But this was not the case was it, Speaking Wind? It was not the calling of another. It was the calling of you, my brother," came the response from Cheeway. "And I will tell you this, Speaking Wind. I will share with you now that in all of the seasons I have been traveling in this life path with the Earth Mother…and from all that I have seen from those of our people who have been prepared with this knowledge…there have been none who have ever been able to call on this spirit wind as you have. At least none that have come to cross my path.

"Perhaps it is because this is your spirit totem or it is because you carry with your calling a signature that I have come to recognize. But for whatever reason I can tell when it is you who is calling to the spirit wind. I have always been able to tell this thing, my brother."

Finishing his speaking words to me, Cheeway lay back against the couch once again. I could see that he was trying to retrieve as much energy as he could…the energy that would not seem to remain with him for long periods of time. And, I could see that there was much he wanted to share with me on this day…much that he wanted to have a knowing for…this knowing from what had taken place on the lands of the mesa.

And, for this understanding of what it was he was asking of me…this asking that did not have to come to me from his speaking words, I did not mind. For this one…this one who had and will always be my best friend, I would not mind sharing with him any of those things that he had the believing in…those things that his believing told him that he would have a need for. Looking over to the place where he was, I smiled to him and said, "Would you like to know what happened to me then, my brother?"

"Oh yes, Speaking Wind. I would like this very much," came his response. "You see, I told you that I held the knowing that it was you who was calling on this day. I told you that the spirit wind will always carry with it your face's signature over itself when he will answer you, didn't I?"

"Yes, Cheeway, you did share this with me. And, you are very correct," I responded to him. I could see that this recognition to him gave a good face for him to wear. It was a face that he had placed over himself for both of our benefits. For him, I could see that this face was a form of knowing. A form of knowing for him that not all ability had left him. And for me this face was sharing with me that he was still willing to learn. Still willing to learn for this last season that had been given to him...this last season of his life path with the Earth Mother.

"It is good to see you have not lost your eye for such things, Cheeway," I responded to him. These speaking words carried a great weight of joy to Cheeway. This I could see from the look he had placed in his eyes.

"Thank you, my brother," came Cheeway's response. "It is just that sometimes...these times such as the one that I am in now...this last season with the Earth Mother, many are not willing to allow you to continue to be who you are."

"To where are you leading me, Cheeway? I am afraid that I do not have the clarity of vision. This clarity that allows me to follow your speaking words."

"Well, it is just that when one like myself is in this last season of their life path...I have seen that the ones who have been made aware of this time...the ones who have shared much with me, they are no longer willing to accept the fact that I am still living."

Taking a deep breath into himself, Cheeway continued. "I am made to feel as if there is nothing that I can do for myself any longer, Speaking Wind. These times that I am in I am feeling like I am being held a prisoner."

"Are there those among you who you would like me to keep away, Cheeway?"

"Oh no, Speaking Wind. It is not that," came his hurried response to me. "I am only sharing these things with you so that you will come to a place of understanding. A place of learning from these things that I am now going through."

"Just as it has been when..." I could not carry these speaking words to Cheeway. Suddenly my throat became very dry and my eyes were getting their wetness.

"Just as when we were of the short seasons and still learning from Grand-father and Two Bears?" Cheeway picked up where I had to leave off.

"Yes, Cheeway, this is what was on the front of my thinking mind."

"Very well then; we will continue with these things that I had been will-ing to share with you. Then, after I have been willing to take this time for them, then you must take the time with me to share what took place on the mesa just a while ago.

"Is this an agreeable portion of sharing, Speaking Wind?"

"Yes, Cheeway, yes, this is a very agreeable portion of sharing, my broth-er," came my quiet response.

"Very well then. I will continue. You see, Speaking Wind, when one is at this last season of traveling their life path with the Earth Mother, then there are always going to be those who will not want to let you go. And, there will always be those who see your leaving on this greatest of spirit journeys as a time that is very short for them. A time that is very short for them that is left to share with you. And, for them they will take this last season and try to pack an entire life path into it. This results in their not being able to leave you alone. Do you realize just how long it has been since I have been able to go to the bathroom alone?"

"Well, now that you mention it, Cheeway, this is not one of the subjects that I would have spent a lot of time thinking on. But please tell me. How long has it been since you have been alone in the bathroom?" I responded, trying to hold a slight urge to laugh within me. I knew that this had to hold a great weight of importance to him. From the seasons that we have been together, Cheeway was one to always hold his time in the bathroom as something of a sacred ceremony. At least that is what I could remember of him. There had been many times when Grandfather, Two Bears, and myself had been made very late by this peculiar trait of his. And, now that he was not even being given the privacy to spend his time alone in there, well, I knew for him this was almost a catastrophe. Nevertheless, I let him continue. I knew that he would make his point clear in a short time…a short time now that he had taken the necessary preparations of setting this situation up for me.

"Is there something coming to the front of your thinking mind that is funny, Speaking Wind? I could use a good reason to laugh now; that is, if you would wish to share it with me."

"No, Cheeway, there is nothing that I am laughing about. Not that is anything that is worth sharing at this time," came my somewhat chocked response to him. "Please continue with what you had begun with." Even though I did not like to keep this from him, I knew that he would not have reacted in a good way. Not at this time when he was willing to share in this way with me. However, I was very thankful to my spirit within for sharing this with me. I had begun to fall into a deep place within me. And, this feeling of laughter being held within me was keeping me out of a dark hole. A place that would have brought no benefit to either Cheeway or myself.

"All right then. If you are sure you want to hear this, Speaking Wind."

"Yes, Cheeway, I am sure that I wish to hear these things that you are willing to share with me."

"Well, as I had begun. There have been so many of our people around me in this time that has come…so many of them who have come here to visit…so many who have come here to share. And, when they see that I do not hold onto my energy as well as I once did, then they are confused. They do not have the knowing of what it is they can do for me.

"And it is from this confusion that has come over them that they seemed to have learned another way…another way of sharing with me. In a way, my brother, they are trying to make up for all of the time and sharing that they feel they did not do…those things that they could have done when there was time for them to do so. But, now that this time has been cut so short, well, they are trying to make up for all they feel they could, or should have done with me. They are trying to make up for all of this by doing for me now.

"And, I will tell you, Speaking Wind. This is something that is not sharing. It is not the kind of sharing that we have been prepared with. The kind that has been shared with both of us by the teachings of Grandfather and Two Bears."

"So then what have you done to ease this, Cheeway?" I asked, still sitting straight.

"Nothing, little brother."

"Nothing? Cheeway," I said, leaning over in my sitting position a little, "those things that you have just shared with me. They gave to me a picture of you. And in this picture you were not comfortable at all. And you still lie there and tell me that you are doing nothing? For this I do not have an understanding, Cheeway. Perhaps you would be willing to share this path with me."

"Of course I will," Cheeway responded, as he adjusted himself a little on the couch. "Do you remember what Grandfather and Two Bears would often tell us? Those things that they would take the time to share with us when times like these would come? Times such as the one I have just described to you would be?"

"There were many things they have shared with us, Cheeway. Many teachings and openings that we have come through. Which of these many are you referring to now?"

"The ones that share with us that all things that have been and all things that are yet to be are now. These are the teachings that I am now referring to, Speaking Wind. Do you have a remembering for them?"

"Yes, Cheeway. I do have this remembering for them."

"Well then, this is where I would wish to lead both of us on the back of my speaking words. That is, if you will be willing to travel with me for awhile."

Looking back to the place where Cheeway was sitting, I could only nod my head in an up and down motion. A motion that would share with him that I was willing to travel with him. This knowing that I could share with him now and without breaking the silence I had gone into.

"Very well then, my brother. I will begin." Taking another deep breath in, Cheeway stretched himself out a little…then let it out. As he did this, he took a moment to look into the direction of the lands of the mesa that were available to him. This view that was so well portrayed by the large window he was laying next to. Looking at this action he was doing, I could see that this was his way of filling himself with all things that are. I could feel this filling of himself with those things; and as I would feel them, I began to see them come into their own life from within me as well.

"The times that are on me now, my brother…well, they are filled with a sense of shortness. This has come to me because of the spirit vision that I have been given…the spirit vision that I will share more completely with you when we will travel into the lands of the Jemez. But for now, there is only one part of it that becomes important to those things I am now willing to share with you.

"This is the part that has shown to me that the time for my life path is over. And because it is over, there are many reviewing pictures that have been coming to me. And, my brother, one of them has been to share with you these things that I am now about to. I do not have the knowing of why, Speaking Wind. For it must not have been so important for me to hold this knowing. I only have the knowing that they will be necessary for you in the seasons that still lie before you. In those many seasons that have yet to be born to you. Those seasons when you will begin this great quest of sharing with many all that has been shared with us.

"You see, my brother, this event that has come to me…well, it has not come only to me. It has come to you, as well as others too. What has been shown to me from the teachings of the silent brotherhood. These things that are coming to me now in this time of the reviewing time…they are sharing with me those same things that had been shared with both of us in those many seasons past.

"I can see now. I can see how this event that has come to me…this event that has placed its mark over me that my time is now ending. Well, this has brought on the back of its spirit picture a knowing that I am not the only one who will learn from it. That all those who I have been close to will have learned a great lesson from this as well. And it is from this place of knowing that I can share with you that I do nothing for all of these actions that have been offered to me. Those actions that have not given to me any solitude at all even in the bathroom.

"I have come to the place of knowing, my brother, that there is no thing that we will ever do…that there will not ever be a time when we will put anything into action that will only affect us. And this is the simple part of the knowing that has come to me.

"The more difficult face of this knowing came to me when I was shown how those same actions that not only affect my life path…how and why they affected the others around me as well. And I will tell you this, Speaking Wind, this face…this face when it showed itself to me gave to me a great awakening from within. An awakening that I knew would benefit my spirit growth greatly.

"When Grandfather shared with us that all that has been and all that is yet to be is now, I have seen what his meaning in those speaking words means, my brother. I now hold this knowing and I will tell you that this is a face of truth that you would do well with.

"In all things that we will do...those things that we will come to do in the seasons of our life path...they will be for the most part done away from this time that we are now sharing. What I am sharing is this...that for all actions that you will take in this day...in this time that we are in...well, they will usually come to you from an action that has taken place in your past or they will take place from an expectation that is in the future. The future that is still unseen by us.

"What all of this means, Speaking Wind, is that for all actions that many of us will make...and these actions include thoughts as well as deeds...they will only be a symptom of what was or what is yet to be. However, most of the decisions that we will come to make, they will not be resident in this time that is the now...this now that we have come to call the present.

"Because of those many things that have been left undone by ourselves, well, they will leave us with a very uncertain future. That is, we can only know what will lie ahead of us to the same degree of completeness that we will have come to know the past...the past of all those events and actions that have created things to happen.

"And, if this is not difficult enough to keep up with, Speaking Wind, we will also have to hold a complete knowing for all of those things that our actions of the past have created over others...on the ones who had come to be in the way of our actions way.

"Look at it in this way, Speaking Wind. When you will drop a small pebble into the middle of a calm lake, do you not see how the ripples that are created by this action will reach even the furthest sides? This then is how our actions come to affect others. It is a ripple in the time that we are making these actions take place that will spread out to many...to those many who are not even close to us."

"And this is a part of those things that we will have to hold a knowing and understanding for, Cheeway?" I asked, looking rather dazed.

"Yes, Speaking Wind. If we are to come to the place of a complete understanding of the past, then we will have to come to a place where we will be allowed to see all of those pieces of life that have been affected by our actions...all of the life that has been affected from those things that we took to do ourselves in our past seasons.

"When this will be…then there will be a complete understanding of the past events. Those past events that have presented themselves to you that you took the energy of acting on. And, it will be at this time when we will receive the face of knowing for what has become of them. When we will hold onto this face of complete knowing and the understanding that will come from it. That will be the time when we will have the eyes of seeing into the seasons that are yet to be born to us. And, we will see what they will bring because we have come to know our past and what it has done so well."

"Cheeway!" I said, placing both of my hands on my knees. "Do you hear what it is that you are saying?"

"Yes, my brother, I do. Can you?" Cheeway responded to my speaking words.

"To even attempt to do such a thing would be an impossible task…a task that would not bring anyone to a place of knowing or understanding, Cheeway. It would only bring them to the place of the dark shadows. Those same dark shadows that are to be found on the path that leads to the right…this path where so many of the others travel.

"And, Cheeway, even if one were to be able to do such a great feat, then to what purpose? What would they have learned? They would become so involved with seeing all things that have taken place in the past that there would not be any more time to see the present. I just do not see where this is all leading to, my brother," I said, leaning back in the chair that was at the foot of the couch.

"Oh, but you see more than you are giving yourself credit for, Speaking Wind…much more," Cheeway said, holding a small but very bright light in his eyes. "You can see the futility of doing such a thing…such a thing of trying to make everything so well known and understood. But this was not the point I was leading to. Let me continue if you will allow me."

"Very well, Cheeway. I only hope that you will arrive at the place we are going soon."

Cheeway looked at me with a smile over his face. This was a smile that I had seen many times before. In those many seasons we had passed together. It was a smile that was giving to me the knowing that he was about to make his point…this point that had been so long in being formed. However, from all of the seasons that we have been together, I was holding in the front of my thinking mind that this was very normal for Cheeway. And having this knowing come to me allowed me to sit back and patiently wait. To wait for him to reach this destination he wanted me to see.

Chapter 5

▼

SPIRIT OF SEEING

"You are right, my brother. You are very correct when you will share those speaking words with me. Those speaking words that say to do such a thing would only take away from this learning. From this learning that we have all entered this domain to perform.

"And, my brother, you are just as correct when you share with me that to do such a thing will take away all of the time that is in the present. And take it away for no beneficial reason, at least any beneficial reason that we who travel on the path of the spirit can see. However, there is one part of this face that you are not seeing. This part of the face that is still hidden from you is the one that will allow you to see why this has taken place. Why so much time is always being spent in living from the past while looking to the future.

"All of this has come to me on the back of the spirit vision that had been shown to me…this spirit vision that had been brought to me by the spirit of seeing. You see, Speaking Wind, the only time in one's life path when they will be required to live from those events of their past, well, this is the time that I am in now…a time when the Ancient Ones are coming to me and asking me to review…to review all of those things that I have been willing to perform in this domain. In a way, my brother, it is like being asked to look over all that had come to you once again. To look over these things and see if there is anything more that you would wish to work on while you are here. And, even though there are still limitations on what things can be worked on…because of the time limitation, well, there will certainly be other things that can be accomplished. However, if one will not be willing to only review their past seasons with the Earth Mother but to live in them, then they will not have the ability of being in the present. In this present where there will be the now that I am willing to share with you.

"It has always been the case with so many who come to travel this domain to look upon all that had come to them with regret…with the regret of not having done something or many things another way. Many who will enter this domain will come to know this face that I am willing to share with you, my brother. And for many of them, well, they will depart this same way. Many of them will depart without ever experiencing the now and present. And I will tell you, Speaking Wind, this is the only place where any lessons are to be learned."

"Cheeway," I said, sitting rather straight now in my chair. "What is this face that comes to them?   This face that shares with them that to live in the past will give to them the answers they are looking for? Has this come to you yet?"

"Yes, Speaking Wind. This has come to them from the way that they were brought into this domain of the Earth Mother's. While they have entered in the same way that all will, they will come to the place of believing that all that has been done for them when they were very young…that these are the same methods they will employ for all things they will do…all things they will come to perform in this domain of the Earth Mother's.

"Think of how a small child will receive many things when they will cry for them. And if they will not get them, then they have come to the place of knowing that if they will pretend to be hurt or to give hurt to another…that the ones who are their parents at this time…that they will give into them. And this will get them what they want.

"If you will look on the face of the parent during this process, then you will see they will not have the clarity of vision for those things they are doing. Those things of giving into the small children they have been given to raise. They will not see that they are doing them any harm. But, from the far vision, this far vision that comes to the ones who will travel on this path of the spirit, they will see it.

"And what they will see will be that while the parents are easing their own bad feelings of denying their child those things they want, they are not seeing that they are reinforcing those same things they will some day turn around and wonder why the child acts the way it does as it becomes the adult. This adult that is still getting the things they want in the same way. At no time, when this child was little did it ever have to earn what it had received. And because there was no work involved in getting those things it wanted, then there was no feeling of accomplishment. And without this feeling of accomplishment there can be no appreciation.

"It is from the appreciation of those things that are made available to us that will allow us to arrive at the place called understanding. This place of understanding that will allow us to see the face of all things that will come to us with the lesson they are bringing.

"And, my brother, it is this understanding that we will come to the place of knowing how to return to the ones who have given for what they have given. This is the process of attaining the balance in the life path, Speaking Wind. And these are some of the teachings that Grandfather and Two Bears have left us.

"For us, my brother, this has been something that we have been prepared for...these preparations that have come to us from the teachings of our people. However, for the child, this child that has grown from the parents that have given to it, this child that had grown into their adulthood with the knowing that they only have to cry their needs loud enough and they will be given. For these they will not ever come to the place of having the eyes and ears of the spirit opened for them. They will not come to this place. Because for them, it does not exist. For them, it will not exist because to arrive at this place...this place that is to be found on the path of the spirit, they must first have the appreciation for what they have now. This appreciation for all they have already been given before they will be given more.

"The path they must learn to travel will be one that will require a great effort on their part. A great effort that is so far from all of those things they have done to now that they will not be able to see how they could ever arrive...how for them to do such a thing would ever be possible. Even when they will look around themselves and see others who have found the way, it will not enter their thinking minds that they too can also find this way. This way of being in the present for all they will do.

"Instead of thinking on how they too could arrive at this, they will rather look at the ones who have become successful in their life path. The ones they can see who are making good decisions and all that has come to them is accepted. And they will think that there is something they have missed in those things of the past...in those parts of their life path that have already passed them by.

"It is from this place of believing that you will see so many of the oth-ers...the ones who have not yet learned of the path of the spirit. That so many of them will always be seen doing the wrong thing. They will be making the wrong decisions and taking the wrong direction. And not only for themselves, but to all who would come to listen to them. All who would be close enough to them to also be caught up in their lost path.

"They do not have the knowing that all they really need to do is to cross over. To cross over from the path they are traveling. This path that is lead-ing them to the left. And simply jump over to the path that will lead them to the right. This same path that will eventually lead them to find the path of the spirit.

"However, they will not do this. And, as they will continue to see oth-ers who have seemed to found their own way, they will continue to look to those events of their past for any kind of a clue to why they do not have such satisfaction in their life path. They will continue to travel on this path that is leading them to the left and the great sadness. This, they will do rather than trying to jump across to the path on the right. This path where they will find all of the answers they are seeking.

"Now, for these same ones, these ones who are traveling on this path that is continually leading them to the left and further away from the path this is on the right, they will soon come to a place of knowing. A place of knowing that will share with them that all of these efforts they are making are taking them nowhere.

"When this will come to them...and I will share with you that it will... just for some, it will come sooner than for others. That when they will ar-rive at this place and see that all of their efforts have only led them to a path with an empty end, then they will look around themselves at those who are near. They will look at them and in an effort of trying to hide their miser-able failure to them, they will call their attention away from the end of this path they have been following...this path that they will not want anyone else to know of. They will not want another to know of this end because to do so would be to show themselves as a failure. And, this is something that would only add to their already miserable feelings within them.

"So, it is an effort on their part to first cover up this mistake of theirs. And in this process, they will make great efforts to keep others from dis-covering this same thing for themselves by keeping their attention drawn away from this path. This path that they once held the believing in that it held something for them. That they could find at least some of the answers they were looking for on it.

"And, in the beginning, they will only try to dissuade those others from seeing what it was that they had found at the end of this path. But, as they will soon discover, those efforts will not be enough. Those same efforts that they had used in the beginning will have to be increased in their intensity if they are to keep their secret away from the others.

"And, my brother, this then is when the controlling of others first begins to appear on this path that leads to the left. This is the grounded foundation they feel they will have to keep others in control at all times. For in their own thinking minds, if they cannot control others then they might find out what they had found at the end of this path they have been traveling. And, it could become very embarrassing for them.

"This, my brother, is also the foundation of the reasons the ones with the white skins could not allow our people to live among them in the beginning of their coming to these lands…if they had left us on the lands we had come to call our homes…if they had not tried to kill all of us by locking us all away. They held a great fear of those things that we have come to know as the face of truth.

"Even this knowledge that is shared with our own, this knowledge that there are two paths to travel and how to tell the ones who are on the path to the right or the path to the left, all of this became a threat to their own secret way of life. So they have devised many faces of fear to those who would not listen to their controlling ways, Speaking Wind. They would keep those of their own kind from coming to a place of understanding by not telling them those teachings truths that would assist them. And those things they would place before them, they knew if they would not have the understanding, the understanding that would allow them to walk them and see them for what they were…to see things as the offering of lessons that they were, then all of the rules they would convince them to live by would carry with them a great face of fear…a face of fear that would keep them from discovering their own truth. The truth that would allow them to set their own spirit free within them.

"However, for the ones who have ever come to the place of knowing this freedom to travel within. They are the same ones who will not ever again give in to the controlling of another. They will become the strong ones on the path they will travel. And they will become the great threat to the established way of life among the outsiders.

"This is what was shown to me in my spirit vision, Speaking Wind. This is the reason that not many will ever come to know the meaning of those speaking words we had been prepared with: "All…that has been is, and all that will be is now.""

"It was shown to me, my brother, that it is better to forget all that you have come to know from the past. That it is better to give up all that has come to you from a false sense of beginnings if that beginning comes to you without the understanding of these speaking words I have been willing to share with you. That the purpose of this life path is to remain in the present. For this is where all of the lessons of value and truth reside. They do not have any weight in those events of the past…none that will assist you in coming to the place of being…this place of being who and what you are.

"However, from the path of the others, this path will share with you that there cannot be a present nor a future if there is no past to learn from, I say to you, Speaking Wind, that there can be no present while there is a past that holds you to it. That there can be no future without a present. I have been my own fire, my brother. And this fire has brought me to this knowing…this knowing that I have been willing to share with you."

Listening to these speaking words that my best friend had been willing to share with me…they were giving to me a good face to wear…a face that was bringing to me a great knowing as well as a blessing. It was a knowing that for all that we had been prepared with and for…that even though Cheeway was not going to be allowed to share this path of offering these teachings and wisdom that had been given to us, that he had learned to understand those things that we had been prepared for and with. And, it was this knowing that gave to me a great peace.

It was a peace for me to have the knowing that he would not have to wait long at the great spirit waters' edge before he would be taken across… across to the waiting place where the other members of our spirit family were waiting for both of us to return…this waiting place we had come to call our temporary home…a temporary home until we could complete our great circle of life and return to the Great Spirit once again. The blessing was filling me. And it was this same blessing that was filling Cheeway from the look that he had placed over his face. I was being shown that this face of truth that had been shown to both of us…this face of truth that had come to both of us from the speaking words of Grandfather and Two Bears…that they were still traveling with both of us…that they would continue to remain with our spirits even when it was time for the last season's preparation…this place on the path of the spirit that Cheeway had come to now.

However, there was a place on the path of leading that Cheeway had shared with me…a place that gave a great rise to my within place. It was his sharing of the flames that he had been able to pass through. These flames that somehow seemed very familiar to me. These flames he had shared with me…could they have been the same ones that I had been shown in the spirit vision on the mesa…those same flames that were appearing to me from the path on the right? For all of the seasons that Cheeway and I had been allowed to share together, there had been no thing that had ever been withheld from the other. And, I held the knowing that this would not begin now.

"Cheeway," I said, including an inquisitive tone in my speaking words, "you mentioned the passing of flames. And I would like to know more of this event that you have been willing to share with me. Would you be willing to make such an effort, my brother? It would give to me a great assistance in coming to the place of understanding what was shown to me in my spirit vision."

"Of course I will, Speaking Wind. I will share with you this face that has come to me. But you too must be willing to share with me those things that had come to you…those things that have come to you in this spirit vision that was announced to me by the passing of the spirit wind."

"Very well, Cheeway. However, when I too can see this face of truth… this face that is worn from passing through the flames, then I will have a better understanding of what had been shown to me. This event that had come to me from the Ancient Ones."

"If you both would not mind, I too, would have a great need from this sharing that is coming to both of you," came a voice from behind both of us. Turning our heads, I could see that it was the one who was called Calling Thunder. The one who had shared with me that it would now be a good time to ask for assistance…this same asking of assistance that had opened the path to the spirit vision that had been presented to me.

Chapter 6

▼

CALLING THUNDER

"Of course not," came the speaking words of both Cheeway and myself at the same time.

"Please have a seat. There is plenty of room in the other chair next to me," I said pointing to the place where he could sit.

"If you do not mind, I would much prefer to sit on the earth floor that is in this room," came the return of the one called Calling Thunder. "It is always better if one can maintain contact with the Earth Mother when they are discussing those things that are from her."

"Very well," came the speaking words from Cheeway. "However, for this sharing I will remain on the couch. For me it is much more comfortable."

"I understand, little one," came the comforting sounds of Calling Thunder. "This is not a reason for one such as you to move from your laying position among any."

However, before any eyes had come on me, I was also taking a place next to Calling Thunder on the floor of the Earth Mother. And, as I was taking my sitting position, I was also coming to remember those same speaking words that had been shared with me by Grandfather and Two Bears. Those speaking words that shared with me that it was always a good thing to keep your contact with the Earth Mother. That is unless there was just no other way.

"It is good to feel the face of the Earth Mother under us is it not, Speaking Wind?" came the beginning of Calling Thunder's speaking words to me.

"Yes, Calling Thunder, it is good to feel this face that has given to us so much already." Looking over to the place he was sitting, I continued, "I had forgotten how good this feels. For the longest time I have been traveling with the others…those who are not of our people, nor our lands. And for this time, I have become so used to sitting on chairs and couches…that

I had forgotten how much we all need to feel our contact with the Earth Mother."

"I too, have been traveling with those others," came the return from Cheeway. "However, for all of those long seasons among them, I did not have the luxury of sitting on chairs and couches. I had been on the face of the Earth Mother for the last twenty-two years and I have shared my share of sitting with her.

"For all of those times, Speaking Wind, I will now trade this place with you."

Placing a large grin over his face, Calling Thunder looked over to the place where Cheeway was laying and held his eyes with his own. "Do not have a place of concern for this time, little one, either of you. These seasons that you have been away from these lands, they have only been to prepare you for those things you both had been willing to prepare for."

"It was only a preparing?" came the questioning voice of Cheeway.

"Yes, little one. This was only a preparing," came the speaking words of the one called Calling Thunder. "Why does this give to you such a face, Cheeway?"

"I have such a face because of the speaking words you have been willing to share with me," came the reply from him. "You mean what I have shared with you about the twenty-two years of preparing?"

"Yes," was Cheeway's reply.

"And this causes you to feel left out now, doesn't it?"

"Yes, Calling Thunder. This causes me to hold a great weight to my face and heart now."

"This should not, Cheeway," was my reply to my best friend.

"Speaking Wind, before I held this knowing that has now been shared with us by Calling Thunder, I held the feeling that all of those things I had been able to do held a purpose to them. But now, now that I can see the face of truth in what he has been willing to share with me, well, I too can see that those past seasons have been presented to both of us in a path of preparation…this path that was preparing the both of us to begin this great quest for the Earth Mother.

"And, now that I am in the last season of my life path, I hold the feeling that all I had done… that all I was working for is for no use to me or to you. I hold this feeling because I have the knowing that what I had prepared for will not be accomplished. Not by me and in this domain I have been allowed to travel."

Finishing his speaking words to me, Cheeway turned his head to the floor. I could feel the heaviness that was coming to him from where he was. And I also held the knowing that there was nothing I could do for him either.

With this knowing coming from my eyes, I turned to look at this one called Calling Thunder. And, as I turned to look on him, I could see that he had followed my feelings much faster than I had been able to see them. He was already forming his speaking words to Cheeway…these speaking words that would bring to him a knowing…a knowing that would lead him to understand the why of all that had come to him.

"Cheeway," came the speaking words from Calling Thunder. "Do you remember the time that has been shared with you from Grandfather and Two Bears?" Lifting his head from the downward position, Cheeway looked over to the place Calling Thunder was sitting.

"Yes, yes, I do remember those speaking words that have been shared with me. And I can see the great number of sharings that have been held between us. Which one are you looking at?"

"None in particular, little one," came his response. "I am looking at all of them perhaps. And, I am looking at them in this way for a reason. Can you see this reason, Cheeway?"

Looking at Cheeway, I could see the same face as Calling Thunder could see. And, from the look that had come over it, I could only see a blank stare…a blank stare that was coming from him.

"I do not have a knowing of where you are trying to take me, Calling Thunder. Can you be more specific?"

"Of course, Cheeway. This I will do. When you and Speaking Wind were of the short seasons on the land of the mesa, there were many teachings that were shared with both of you. And, for the most part, these teachings came to you from Grandfather and Two Bears. Are you following me to this point, little one?" Calling Thunder asked.

"Yes, yes we are beginning to see those things you are willing to share with us," came the combined speaking words from both Cheeway and myself.

"This is good. Because what I am willing to share with both of you will be of great assistance. I have held many councils with the two of them. And, I can share with you that they had come to the place on this path of the spirit of knowing. This place of knowing that had shared many wonderful teachings with me.

"The most important teaching we had come to know during these times was when anyone would take the time to look at those things that they did. Then would be the time when they would be the weakest. This would bring to them such a place of vulnerability that even the spirit of illusion could pass through...pass through and cause this one to fall back onto the path of illusion. This same path that holds nothing for any of us."

"I am not sure what these speaking words bring us, Calling Thunder," I said, looking directly at the place he was sitting.

"It is this, little one. When any of us will take the time to look on all of the achievements we have done, this will usually bring to us a good face to wear. But it is also a face of short duration. When we will look at those things that are still ahead of us, then we will look on ourselves for the strength and duration that is needed from our spirit. And, this is also a face of short time for us.

"You see, little ones, all that we will do and all we have yet to do...well, these are not important to look on. They are not important to look on because they are only fleeting pictures anyway."

Looking over to the places where Cheeway and I were, Calling Thunder could see that we were still not grasping those things he had been willing to share with us...these sharings that had come to not only himself, but to Grandfather, and Two Bears as well. These speaking words of sharing that would remain alive within this domain were being offered to both of us. Offered to both of us to hold in our within place.

But I could see from the look that had come over Cheeway's face that he did not hold the understanding of why. Why he was being shared with in this way. In this way now that he was in the final season of his life path. Once again, looking down to the earth floor that was under us, Cheeway said, "Calling Thunder, I do not hold the knowing of why you find it necessary to share such things with me. With one such as myself who does not have another season left to be in this domain."

"Then I will explain, little one. I will explain if you will allow me to continue," came the return of Calling Thunder. "Cheeway," Calling Thunder began, "tell me why you hold this face before this sharing with you. Is it because you can feel the temporariness of your life path or is it that you are only looking on yourself and can see nothing else?

"Be honest with yourself now, little one."

Sitting up a little from his lying position on the couch, Cheeway looked rather shocked with this approach…with this approach that had come to him now.

"To share in speaking words that carry a weight of truth to you, Calling Thunder, I cannot say the reason of why. This reasoning you have asked of me. All I can share with you now is that it is that it is and nothing more."

"Then lay back and listen, Cheeway. For these things that I am now willing to share with you will hold a great weight. A great weight of understanding not only for what they will bring to you now, but also to carry their clarity of sight for those things you have been preparing for. You see, Cheeway, you are not finished yet."

As these speaking words came from the mouth of Calling Thunder, they seemed to hit Cheeway straight in the chest. So straight and strong that I could see their force knock him back. Back to the laying place he had begun from.

Then, turning his head from Cheeway, Calling Thunder looked over to the place I was sitting. "Tell me, Speaking Wind. Is the reason that you are not willing to listen more carefully to these speaking words I am willing to share with you…is the reason for this because of your brother? Or is the reason you are not willing to listen to them more openly and acceptingly because you are placing yourself before all other knowing? I will ask you to answer me honestly, little one."

"I cannot say, Calling Thunder. There has been so much take place to me in these last few days that I am not sure of where I am. I can only say that you are correct in this question you are asking of me. You are correct in what you see. But in truth I cannot give to you an answer. Not this answer that you are asking of me."

"How close you both have become in these seasons with the Earth Mother," came his response. "I can see now how good it was to find both of you here at this same time. That both of you have a great need for this sharing. This sharing that is not only of our people but this knowing that is continually being shared with us by the Great Spirit as well. So, for this time of sharing, I would ask of both of you to sit back and listen to me openly and acceptingly. Listen well…now is the time."

Chapter 7

▼

MY FACE OF CONCERN
FOR WHAT WILL NOT BE

"Listen well, little ones. For what I have to share with you is very important," Calling Thunder began. "For you, Speaking Wind, this sharing will assist in carrying you to the higher places. Those higher places you will need to live in so that you will be able to succeed in this great quest for the Earth Mother.

"And for you, Cheeway, these things that I now share with you, they will assist you in performing this great quest for the Earth Mother as well."

Looking at the face Cheeway had placed over himself, Calling Thunder could see a look of disbelief that had come over him…a look of wanting to tell his situation once again to Calling Thunder. However, this was also a look of great respect for this one who was willing to share with us now. And because of this respect for the old one, Cheeway was remaining very silent…very silent and without the intent of listening openly to what was being offered to him. Seeing this look covering his face, I held the knowing that Calling Thunder also held this same place as I did for Cheeway. And, in the speaking words that followed, I was not at all surprised. At least not at all surprised for the speaking words that would be given to Cheeway. But, there was no way that I could have been prepared for what would be shared with me.

"Cheeway," Calling Thunder began. "Why do you wear a face for me as you would for an old and forgetful man? Do you not have the knowing that these things I share with you now wear the face of truth?"

Cheeway did not break the silence he was in. He only looked over to Calling Thunder's place of sitting with a look on his face for him and me to see…a look of surprise. "Come now, little one. Have you not traveled long enough with Grandfather and Two Bears to know that when one who has traveled this path of the spirit as long as I have…as long and has understood those things that have been offered to him…do you not have the understanding that speaking words are not needed? Remember, little one, remember that time is short now. This short time that has come over all of us has not allowed us to keep to the customary protocols we once did. And, it is with this knowing that I am now willing to enter your within place. Enter this place of your spirit without being invited. I do this because it is necessary. It is necessary because you still hold onto the face of your believing that nothing more will be."

Looking over to the places where Cheeway and I were sitting, Calling Thunder held one hand out to each of us. One hand out to each of us with his first finger pointed to each of us. As he did this, there became a sudden heavy stillness in all of the air we could feel…a stillness in the air as if it too were waiting for a sign. Within just a few heartbeats, there was a sudden blackness that was filling the sky above us. I knew this to be more than the calling of a storm by the children who lived here. I knew this because when I reached this house to enter, I saw the sky was completely clear. And a clear sky from all directions meant that there would not be the chance of any storm reaching here in less than one-fourth of a day. But now the sky was blackened out and it had not been more than an hour since I had entered this house…this house where my best friend, Cheeway, was resting. Also, there was no announcement of an approaching storm by the spirit wind. And, this was filling me with a great concern for this event…a concern that was shared by Cheeway as well.

Then, there was a sudden blast of white light…a great blast of white light with an immediate clasp of thunder. This came to both of us so suddenly that it nearly knocked us both out of our chairs. But looking over to the position where Calling Thunder was sitting, it did not affect him. Still, he was holding both of his hands out with the first finger pointed at both of us. "This is the totem that I carry, little ones. And my spirit totem comes now to share with you that I do not speak alone. That it is not me who you are listening to now. Not me, I have not existed for many seasons." Hearing these speaking words come to us brought a great look over our faces. It was a look that I had not felt before and from the face Cheeway was wearing, I could tell he had not either.

The darkening sky over us coming without the calling of the spirit wind was already quite a shock. And then came the white lightning followed by the clap of a great thunder call. And, all of this that had affected both of us greatly, all of this did not seem to move this one called Calling Thunder in the least. Then, looking at us, he shared with us that he had not been Calling Thunder for many seasons. I am sure that if either Cheeway or I had been able to run out of the house at this time we would have. However, we had become weighted to our positions from having so much come to us so quickly. Seeing this look that had come over both of our faces, Calling Thunder smiled at each of us. Then he continued.

"Cheeway, " he began, "look to all of these speaking words that I am willing to share with you in this way. See them for the weight that they are. Not the way that you would have yourself come to believe them.

"I say this to you because you are at the place where your vision has become clouded by your thinking thoughts. These same kinds of thinking thoughts that are showing to you that you do not have much time left in this domain of the Earth Mother's. I tell you this, little one. I tell you that you are not ending a journey. But you are just beginning one. And it will be a journey that will be in assisting the Earth Mother greatly in performing those things that you said you would do with her."

"But how is this possible, Calling Thunder?" came the trembling speaking words from Cheeway. "How is it possible for me to continue to do those things for the Earth Mother. Those things that Speaking Wind and I have prepared for. How can this be when I will no longer be here?"

"It is because it is, little one," Calling Thunder returned. "And for you, Speaking Wind," Calling Thunder said, keeping both of his hands in the same position of pointing to each of us. "You will soon encounter the spirits of the flame...those same spirits that have shown themselves to you on the path to the right...this path that was shown to you by the Ancient Ones of our people. By the spirit vision that had come to you from them."

"So this is a part of what was shown to me, Calling Thunder? This was what was shared with me by the Ancient Ones because I will soon be traveling these flames as well?"

"Yes, Speaking Wind. This is holding the face of truth for you," was his response. "But now I wish to share with Cheeway. For what lies ahead of him is also great. What is yet to be seen by him. For what will soon come to him he will need these sharings that I wish to share. Otherwise, he will find that the necessary preparations that are needed by him…these things that he must still learn while he is in this domain…that if he will not come to understand them, then he will not be allowed to continue.

"Cheeway, look at me for a moment," came the beginning of his speaking words. "Do I look any different to you now? Any different now from what I did those many seasons ago? From those times when we all had the opportunity of sharing on the lands of the mesa?"

"Well, Calling Thunder, I must say that there is not any difference that has come over you. And, in seeing this, I must say that this creates a difference over you. But it is not a difference in change…it is a difference in looking the same," Cheeway began.

"And for this that you see of me, little one, is there a reason that has come into your thinking mind?"

"No, Calling Thunder. For this seeing I do not have any speaking words. Only that in by remaining the same in the way you look that this is the change I can see. And the reason that I share this with you, Calling Thunder…this reason is that what I see over your body part…these lack of changes that normally come to all who pass many seasons…that this lack of change is what appears to be different on you. Different on you because there does not seem to be the wear of many seasons on you."

"Then what you are sharing with me, little one…these speaking words are very good. They are very good not because they do me a great compliment. But they are very good because they will share with you the importance and great weight of truth in those things I will share with you. As it is with all sharing, little one, when one will share with you, then this sharing becomes valid when you will see this in the one who is offering the sharing. This will be the confirmation that is needed by all who will be willing to listen.

"When one will have the understanding for those things they are willing to share, then it becomes apparent because they will carry all of the attributes of those things they are willing to share with you…all of those things that will come from them. They should have been understood well enough for them to have lived by.

"It is when one will share with you…when one says they are willing to share with you and they do not exhibit any of those things themselves… then you will have the knowing that for all they will tell you…that they will only have come to know the words but they have not yet reached the place of understanding them. This understanding that is needed so they will attain the wisdom to use them as well.

"And, little one, this is why it is so good to have you see this in me now. It is good because I can see the eyes and ears of your spirit have been opened for you to see such things in another. And, it is good because as you will see these things in me, they will clear a path of understanding for you to know their weight of truth. The weight of truth they hold within them…this weight of truth that you too will come to know if there is the willingness of acceptance for them.

"You see, Cheeway and Speaking Wind, I have not called on my spirit totem to show you what I could do. I have called on him so that you might see that I am not just another crazy old man…one that you will listen to with the customary courtesy but with none of the acceptance for those things I am now willing to share with you.

"This was what was in the front of my thinking mind. And because there is so little time in the seasons that are already on all of us…so little time for us to begin this great task for the Earth Mother, there was not enough of it left for you to come to know me better. It is time, little ones, it is time to begin what we have given our word to the Earth Mother we would do.

"Now, Speaking Wind," Calling Thunder said, looking directly at the place I was sitting. "I wish for you to give the same attentiveness to my speaking words that Cheeway will give as well. These sharings that he is to be given on this day will be just as important for you. For you and all of those things you will have placed before you to perform."

Returning my gaze back to Calling Thunder, I could only sit and nod my head in an up and down motion…one that would allow him to have the understanding that I was in complete agreement to all that he was sharing with both of us. And, I could see from the look that had come over the face of my best friend, Cheeway, he too was of the same mind as I was. That he also had become just as attentive and was more than willing to listen to all that this one called Calling Thunder would offer to us.

However, the front of my thinking mind kept running to a place that I needed to look. It was a place of wondering…wondering when I would get a break from all that was taking place with me. When I could find some quiet time. From the early part of this day, I had been taken to the between place…this place where the Ancient Ones were residing now with this sharing of the speaking words of Calling Thunder. And still I had not heard Cheeway's description of what he meant by his walking the flames. And this was a great need for me I was feeling.

"Do not hold a worry, Speaking Wind. This meaning of walking the flame will be brought out in my speaking words to both of you. And, I tell you in truth it will be very accurate," Calling Thunder began. "Once again, little one, you must allow yourself to know that there is just not time for me to perform this going to your within place and hearing those things that are coming to your thinking mind in the usual way. It is as I have said…there is no more time for any of us to be polite. Not now. Not now because my seasons for me are over as well. And, there is still so much more to share with the both of you."

"You too are in the final season of your life path, Calling Thunder?" I asked, looking as if someone had beaten me over the head.

"Yes, Speaking Wind. This brings to you a feeling of another loss, does it not?"

"Yes, yes it does," I responded. "Tell me something," I said, sitting a little better on the face of the Earth Mother.

"What is it?"

"Am I to be the last of all our people to remain? Or am I only feeling this because there are so many who are near me that are leaving?"

"Little one," came the somehow pleased response from him. "If you could be sitting in the place where I am now, you could see just how funny you really are."

"I did not mean for this to be funny, Calling Thunder. I really hold this meaning very close to me."

"Then listen carefully to what I am willing to share with the both of you. For in my speaking words to you there will be great wisdom. As well as those answers that you are looking for." Turning his attention from me, Calling Thunder looked over to the place where Cheeway was laying. I could feel a great weight fill this room. It was the same kind of a weight that had come over both Cheeway and myself many times when Grandfather and Two Bears would begin to share a great truth with us. And, from looking over the face that was being worn by Cheeway, I could see that he was feeling this presence of the heaviness as well…this feeling of the heaviness that comes when the Old Ones are present…the Ancient Ones of our people and they have come close so that they might be heard so that they might share.

Looking back to Calling Thunder. I could see that these feelings were being shown to me…being shown to me that I was on the right path of seeing…shown to me in the same way that I would often see them on the faces of Grandfather and Two Bears when they too would move over from themselves and allow the Ancient Ones to enter. The ones who had for as long as our people could remember been willing to share with us the path of the spirit…this path of the spirit and those events that would be needed by all of us. Events that would be presented to us so that we could come to a higher level of understanding for all they would share.

And now, now looking over the face of Calling Thunder, I could feel the heaviness of the air becoming very thick and as it would do this, I could see him taking on many faces of changing. Faces that I knew were not of him…faces that were of the ones who had long since passed from the need of this domain…from having to enter here to learn anything more. I held my breath as I was observing these changes fill our air, our room, ourselves. I held my breath and called to all of my spirit's strength to assist me in hearing those things that would be shared with us on this day. These speaking words that were soon to arrive through the corridors of time itself…these speaking words of the Old Ones that were being offered to both Cheeway and myself.

Chapter 8

▼

WHEN I AM, I AM NO LONGER

"Cheeway, these speaking words are for you and for what you will need. For those things that you will need to complete before you will come to us," came the beginning of the speaking words from Calling Thunder's mouth, but I could hear they were not of him. Within the sounds of these speaking words he was now sharing, there was a kind of an echo…the kind of echo that would come back to us when we would yell into one of the great stone caverns that were on our lands. And, while it was something similar it was not the same. For within the sounding of these speaking words that were coming from Calling Thunder, there was also a feeling of great love and belonging carried on their back. A love and understanding for all that is, that has been and is yet to be.

Sitting in the presence of these speaking words, I could not move. I did not want to move. I only wanted to become a part of them. A part of all they were carrying to both of us. A part of this love of understanding that they were a part of. Suddenly, my thinking mind went back to a place in the seasons of the past…a place where Cheeway and I were sitting before Grandfather and Two Bears. They had taken us both to the lands of the mesa. More specifically, the spirit ledge. This was a time when they were sharing with us the meaning of calling…of hearing the calling voices of the Ancient Ones.

I can still hear them sharing with the both of us. "When you will hear the calling voice of the Ancient Ones, little ones, this will bring to you a face of great fear. However, as it is with all things that will come to you, there can only be fear when there is no understanding. And it is this lack of understanding that so many will become trapped with. Trapped into believing that there is a good and an evil.

"However, I tell you both this. There is neither. There only is. And with this knowing kept in the front of your thinking minds, there will not come to either of you the face of fear, this same face of fear that allows others to be controlled. You see, when you will travel the path of the spirit, this path that we have taken great effort in preparing both of you with, then one of the first thinking thoughts that will come to you…the first things that will cross you when an event will present itself, you will not find the face of fear in this. Rather, you will look carefully at this event. You will look into this event carefully and look for what it is that you are being offered. What you are being offered to learn from.

"And when the ones who do not yet know of this path of the spirit, when they will not have the same knowing as you both have been prepared with, they will look on the face of all things they do not have an understanding for and see this face of fear come to them. For them there will be no other way. And because of this, they hold themselves open to the control of others, the ones who, like them, are also traveling on this path that leads them to the left…to the left and the place of the great sadness.

"However, for what will come to you for each time that you will find the strength of your spirit to do this, for each time you will find the strength of your spirit to see these events that will present themselves to you, you will not see through the eyes of fear, but the eyes of seeing. Then there will be more and more presented to you.

"When the Ancient Ones of our ancestors will see that you are gaining insight into these offerings from these events, they will be pleased. And as they will see you begin to grow from a little seed in this domain, they will share with you more of those events that they see you have a great need for…those events that will bring to you a higher level of understanding for yourself and all things that are around you.

"It will be in this same way, little ones. In this same way of having events come to you that you will soon find the Ancient Ones will no longer be the far away strangers to you. For when they will see that you are ready…that you have done all of the necessary preparing for what they are to share with you, then they will come. Then you will feel all life that is around you become heavy with their presence.

"And this heaviness of their presence comes to you from their being… from their having become no longer…no longer the one they once were but having become that which is all. When you can come to know them by their face, by this face I have been willing to share with you, then listen. Listen to all that will be presented to you. For those things that will come to you will be all that you will have the greatest of needs to know…the greatest of needs to understand…and, the greatest of need for the wisdom that will soon come to you. This wisdom that will allow you to use what you have learned."

Hearing these speaking words of Grandfather's and Two Bears' come to life within me once again, I held the knowing for all that had come to me on this day, for all that had come to both Cheeway and myself. I could feel that this presence that was forming itself into the heaviness of the air around us. That it was not being centered into the one who had come to give us his assistance. This one called Calling Thunder. And, looking over to the place he was sitting, I could not help but feel the presence of Grandfather and Two Bears as well…their presence that had been so strongly missed by Cheeway and myself over these many growing seasons of our life path.

Now, as I was becoming used to this presence that had come to us, I could see from the face that had come over Calling Thunder that he was about to continue…about to continue with his sharing with Cheeway and myself.

"Cheeway," began the echoing of the speaking words from Calling Thunder, "you have come to a sad place, little one. It is a place where many are stopped from this progress that we have come to learn from…this progress that has made itself available to all of us so that we learn from it.

"However, this reason you have come to this place is very simple. That is, if you will be willing to listen to these speaking words with an open heart."

Looking over to the place where Cheeway was sitting, I could see that this look of listening had come over his face…this look I had seen come over him many times before. Those times when we would sit for long periods listening to those things that Grandfather and Two Bears would be willing to share with us.

"You have come to this place of the sad face, little one, because you have forgotten to remember those things that had been shared with you…those things that had been presented to you to learn from, those same things that were offered to you so you could come to the place of higher understanding.

"As it is with all who are within this domain, Cheeway, there will come to them many events…those same events that will allow them to have a great opportunity. An opportunity of being able to work their way through them in order to attain a higher level of understanding.

"However, there is something that many will come to believe in. And this believing they will encounter will be far from the face of truth they are seeking. Far from those places they wish to travel. They will come to look on all of these events that will come to them as one would look at themselves when they are traveling on the path that leads them to the right…this path that will lead them to no where…no where but the great sadness that is at the end of their journeys.

"They will come to look at all things that are within this domain only as they will appear to them. And, it is when they will have this kind of a seeing eye…this is when they will come to see the face of sadness. This same face of sadness that you are now wearing over yourself, little one. You see, Cheeway, when an event will come to you…an event that will come to you with the face of lesson over it, then, there are many who will look on this kind of learning as something that is only for them. Only for them because the eyes they are used to seeing through only show them this part of themselves. And, this can even take place for those who have come to know their way very well on this path of the spirit. This same path we have all taken great effort in preparing you with.

"However, when we will come to you with a lesson to offer, when we will allow you to come to the place on this life path you are traveling with the Earth Mother, then we do not only see you as the only traveler…as the only one who will have a great need. When we will see the place where you are traveling, we also see the places others are traveling as well. And, it is from seeing them as well as you that we will come forth with another event…with an event that will hold a great lesson for you.

"Even though you have been the one who has decided on all of these events that will be offered to you, little one, we are the ones who will hold the gate open or closed. This gate that will either hold them back from showing themselves to you or this gate that will allow them the freedom to travel to the place where you are.

"However, with so many of our people who travel this life path…so many of them who are not seen well by many…not seen well by many because they have entered this domain of the Earth Mother's other people and other places, then we see that this is the time when there is also a great need for them as well.

"It is through this great need of theirs that we do what we do and how we will do them, little one. It is during this time of the long shadow. The season of the ending of this age for the Earth Mother when so many will have returned with great quests to perform for her. Quests that will, when accomplished, allow her a much easier entry into this new age she is standing at the doorway to now.

"It is as you have been told, Cheeway," continued this sharing of the speaking words by the voice that I knew was not of Calling Thunder. "These things you have been prepared with in those long seasons past…those long seasons that have passed when we were there to assist you. But, as it is with so many who travel in this domain, you too forgot to remember, Cheeway. You too lost the knowing of the time of the great long shadow season that is now over the Earth Mother. And it is from this place that we wish to share with you that you need to look into yourself. Into yourself much deeper than you have been doing.

"You see, Cheeway, you have been wearing this long face over yourself because you have been looking at yourself through the eyes of the others… the eyes of the ones who have not yet learned their way to the path of the spirit. And it is from this kind of looking that you have lost your way…lost your way of being able to see with the clarity of vision that you need."

"Looking through the eyes of the others!" came the immediate reply of Cheeway. "I have been looking through the eyes of the others you say! Calling Thunder, I cannot believe that you have said this of me. Why, you who has known Grandfather and Two Bears for so many growing seasons on our lands, why do you say this to me when you know well the path I have been willing to travel. Tell me, Calling Thunder. Tell me for I hold a great need for your answer."

Looking to Cheeway, the face that had come over Calling Thunder did not change. In fact, there was nothing at all that changed on him. He only looked into Cheeway and said: "We are not Calling Thunder, Cheeway. Have you not seen this yet?"

"Grandfather?" came the startled reply from Cheeway.

"Grandfather. Grandfather, is that you?" I followed up with the speaking words of my own. Looking over to the place where Calling Thunder was sitting, I could feel the presence of more than he…of more than any whom I had come to know in this life path with the Earth Mother. However, there was something that was very familiar to me, but something that was not, as well. It was like reaching out to touch an old friend one who has shared many seasons of their love and understanding with you. And, when you would touch them, they would be the same but not the same.

Looking over to the place where Cheeway was sitting, I could see that his thinking mind was also filling…filling with the same kinds of thoughts that were flooding mine. Silently, Calling Thunder turned his head to where he could see both of us. And as he turned it, we could feel a love of understanding pouring from his every pore…a love of understanding that until now neither Cheeway nor myself had experienced. This kind of love that had only been shared with us by the speaking words of the song legends we had been prepared with. But now we were living in the middle of it. And, as we were living with this love of understanding, we were coming to a place of understanding it more.

"When I am, little ones, I am no more," came the peaceful and warming voice of the one called Calling Thunder. "This is who I am no more…this one who is sharing this face with you. It is I but more than that, I am all.

"Does this give to you a knowing, little ones? It should. It should because this has always been a part of your preparation. This is the most basic part of the path of the spirit…this place where one will be no more. This place where one will be set aside to allow their self to blend with all that is…to blend with all that is but still be in possession with their own identity.

"This is the path that has been shown to both of you. And it is on this part of the path of the spirit that you will come to know that when one will have begun their great spirit journey, that they have not left. They have not left at all. For if you will allow yourself to become the all you are, then you too will find the comfort in those who are no longer in their shells. Then you too will come to know their face of the spirit and hear their assistance that is willing to come to you.

"This is no great secret, little ones, this face that I am now willing to share with you. For all that has been is with me now and I am a part of it because I am no longer. Keep these speaking words in the front of your thinking minds, little ones, for they will be of great assistance to both of you.

"For you, Speaking Wind, it is a path that you will come to find your comfort on. For it will not be in this domain that you will have a great amount of time to do this. The quest that is before you will be a great quest and it will also require you to hold true and strong to the spirit who is you. You would do well to remember this, Speaking Wind. This is how we will be better able to offer you the assistance you will have a great need for.

"And for you, Cheeway, you will have a great need for this knowing as well. Do not think that just because your seasons in this domain are finished that you will only go home to rest? For if you will hold this face over yourself, then you are not holding the face of truth. You are holding the face that will lead you to discover something that is completely different from what you only thought you were looking for.

"You and Speaking Wind have been well joined. As you have been joined many times before. However, from the path of the need in this domain and in this time, there will not be room for the two of you to continue your life path in this form together. And this is why we have heard your request to enter this side of the spirit family…this spirit family who is willing to assist the Earth Mother in her great need. However, from the time you will enter this side, you will not begin your spirit journey home. Not until Speaking Wind will come to join with you and the others who are going to assist in their way from this side…from this side that I am now speaking to both of you from.

"For you, Cheeway, when the time comes for you to lay aside your body part, then your part of the great adventure will begin. For when you will no longer be a part of this path you have come to know, this path that has allowed you to travel on the two legs, that will be the time when your assistance to Speaking Wind will truly begin. When you will come to this time, little one, then your brother will have the greatest of need for the assistance you will then be capable of sharing with him.

"However, Cheeway, now you must come to understand what it is you have done…what you have done to your thinking mind and your spirit from within you. These lessons must be learned while you are still in body. While you are still breathing the air of the Earth Mother herself.

"You have this great need to overcome the lessons that are giving to you the pain and the long face you are wearing now, little one. This is the only way that you will be allowed to cross over to your brother in his time of need…in his time of needing the assistance you will be capable of giving to him.

"Grandfather and Two Bears are ready. And, they have been giving to both of you their assistance. But neither of you have learned to listen yet. And this is why you must both come to the place of understanding now. This is a lesson of great power for both of you. Listen well to our speaking words to both of you, little ones. They will carry you far…they carry the weight of truth to them."

Chapter 9

▼

THE SPIRIT OF ALONENESS

"As both of you have been prepared with the teachings of Grandfather and Two Bears, you are well aware that when any spirit will enter this domain…this domain that is the Earth Mother's…that they will immediately be taken over by this spirit of illusion. And as this spirit of illusion will come over all of you, there will be a great sleep come to you…a great sleep that will not allow you to see anything for what it is. But a sleep that will only allow you to see things for what you think they are.

"As this sleep continues over each of us, we will be found following many voices. But they will not be the voices that are calling to us from the spirit side of the spirit waters, little one. These voices that we will be following will be from this side…from this side where both of you are still traveling. But this is normal for one who is still wrapped in their sleep of illusion…this sleep that not many have ever come to awaken before it was their time to cross the great spirit waters.

"From the many who we have been observing from this side, little ones, we have seen that most of those spirit families who enter this domain do not ever wake up. Most of them will exit this domain of the Earth Mother's in the same way they had entered. They will exit asleep from the veil of illusion and will not have ever come to a place of waking at all. They will not awaken until they will look on the faces of their spirit families. And these same members of their spirit families will come to ask them why. Why they did not choose to leave this sleep of illusion behind them and learn from the lessons that were being offered to them…offered to them from all of these members of their own spirit family.

"We can see that this much has been set into the front of your thinking mind, little one. However, what has not come to you so clearly is that one can always be covered once again with the veil of illusion. Even with a part of it when they will begin to take their eyes from the path of the spirit. And, Cheeway, this is what has happened to you. This is why you wear such a long face before us now. Cheeway, you must not come to the place of believing that once you have come to begin your spirit journey…the journey across the great spirit waters…you must not come to the believing that once you have left this domain that all of your work has stopped.

"If you will hold onto this, then you will have a great surprise for you when you reach the other side…this other side that we are now speaking to you from. This may have been the path many have been able to take in the seasons of the past, little one. But this is not the seasons of the past. In fact, this is the most critical season of all. And, not only for the Earth Mother, but for all who would ever wish to enter this domain that is hers to learn from.

"It is because of the importance of this time, Cheeway, that you will not have the time to return to the waiting place. Not at least until this passage of the old age is over and all of the children are assured of being able to stand on their own once again. Remember to keep in the front of your thinking mind, Cheeway, that it is during this time that you and Speaking Wind have entered that so many events will be taking place…events that are being offered to all who will be willing to accept them with the face of lesson on them. But for all of the ones who will not be willing to accept them, these events will only have a great face of fear over them. And it is because of this face of fear that will come over them for so many that our work in this time becomes so important.

"It will be as it was in the closing of the last circle of life for the Earth Mother. As she will enter this new age from the old one, there will still be many weights attached to her…these weights that come to her from all of those things that are carried by others…those things that they carry with them that hold no truth to them…those things that also carry no under-standing for them and what they will do.

"It is because of the way they will see this life path of theirs that makes what we have to do here so important. They will look at all of these events that will be entering this domain through their eyes of fear. And, when they will see that they cannot run from them, they will panic. And it is this panic that will cause more disaster to take place…more disaster than would have normally come here naturally.

"Also, Cheeway, keep in the front of your thinking mind that for those who travel the path of the others, the ones who have not yet found their way to the path of the spirit…that they will hold a great fear to all things they cannot control. And, for the ones who will travel on this path of the spirit they will hold a great respect for all things they will come to understand.

"And this, little one, this brings us to the place of our sharing with you. You have been holding onto the face of leaving, Cheeway. You have been holding this believing that when it comes time for your body part to rest that this is when your life path with the Earth Mother will be over. However, we tell you that this is not truth that has come to you. The face you are looking on is one that belongs to the false spirit of illusion…this false spirit that has attached itself to you because of your weakness…this weakness that has come to you from thinking that you are alone.

"You are not alone, Cheeway. And, this is one of the reasons that we have returned to both you and Speaking Wind. It is to share with you that you are not alone. Whenever you will feel the loss of something, then the spirit of aloneness will come to you. And riding on the back of this spirit is the face of illusion. This face that will bring you to a place of feeling this loss so greatly that you will only have the eyes to see that you are alone.

"Remember, little ones, your life path does not end with the passing from this domain. It is just the opposite. All of us are still here and waiting for you to accept our assisting to you. And soon, Cheeway, you too will be here so that you may assist your brother in the seasons ahead just as we will. However, from all of these events that we bring to you now, Cheeway, these are those same events that you had entered this domain of the Earth Mother's to learn from the beginning. And, from the time that you sat in council with the Earth Mother, both of you had planned them to be done in exactly the way they have been given to you.

"But, little one, since you found that your seasons with the Earth Mother were soon to be over, that was when you had stopped yourself from learning anything at all. What you had done was to place yourself in the most secure place you could find. And that place was one that did not allow you to continue to learn from all of the events that were being offered to you…those events that would have allowed you to continue with your growth of your spirit within you. And as we saw this come to you, we held the knowing that this was not good…that this was not good because you were stopping yourself from doing what it was you had come here to do.

"To those who have learned the path of the spirit, Cheeway, to the ones who have found their way but because of an event that had come to them…an event such as the one that has now come to you…when they will fall away from this path of the spirit, we say that they are now traveling with the spirit of aloneness – this spirit who keeps them in the dark side of the path they have fallen into.

"And it is this spirit of aloneness that has been telling you that all you have been working for is over. And, that there is no need for you to try to accomplish anything further…because to do so would only be a waste of your time. And the time that you have left to enjoy those things of this domain are limited.

"However, little one, we have come to share this one who is called Calling Thunder to tell you that this is not truth…that you have been deceived by these false spirits. These same false spirits who will find their end in any case when the Earth Mother passes to her next age. And we share this with you because it carries a great weight of truth to it. That no matter what is done, Cheeway, the Earth Mother will have to pass into her new age. And this is something to which she does not have a choice in doing.

"And when she will pass into this next age of hers, then all of those false spirits who are with us now, they will pass away into the nothingness that they have come from. You see, Cheeway, these false spirits, these same false spirits who have had you listening to them, they do not hold this truth to be the same for them. For in their minds, they hold the believing that if they can stop all who have entered this domain from doing those great quests for the Earth Mother, then the Earth Mother will be too heavy with all of her weights from those things others hold onto them without the face of truth to them. They hold the believing that this weight will be too much for her to enter this next age of hers and she will have to remain in this one for all times.

"These false spirits see this to be the truth. But, as it is with all they represent, they are holding onto things that carry no weight to them. They are holding onto this believing as a fact. But we share with you that it is not and their time is soon coming to an end. It is because they are not seeing this face of truth, Cheeway, that they are holding onto you. Holding you away from those things that you have come into this domain to perform.

"However, as it is with all things, they could not have attached themselves to you without your permission. And because you have given them this permission to enter, it can only be by your actions that they will be forced to leave. You see, Cheeway, as it has been shared with you by the teachings of Grandfather and Two Bears…that it is only the now that is important to live in…that when one will take the time and effort that is required to travel this life path and spend all of their time looking at the past or looking at the future, then they are not allowing themselves to share their time and efforts with anything that is.

"For them, all life exists as it once was or as it is yet to be. But in either case, little one, they will not ever come to see that they are in the now. They will not have the knowing of what it is like to live in the present. And because of this they will not come to see the lessons that they have come into this domain to learn from.

"You will know them as your turn comes to cross the great spirit waters, Cheeway. You will know them because they will be the ones who appear to be completely lost. Completely lost and holding their heads downward because they have spent a complete life path here and hold nothing at all in their arms and hands.

"You on the other hand, Cheeway, you have begun to fall away from this path of the spirit from the picture the false spirits have been showing to you. They have been showing you many of those things that you have found comfort and joy in…the seasons that are of your past. And they have been filling all of the places where there was room in telling you that all of those wonderful things you had been looking forward to…those things that could have been in your future, that they are no longer available to you…that this is something that is just not possible for you to get to.

"And as you continue to listen to them, little one, you have found that there is no longer any room in your thinking mind for anything else. No more room for you, Cheeway. There is no more room for you because you have allowed these things of the false spirits to fill you up.

"We will share this with you, Cheeway, so that you can truly see the face of truth that is before you. This face of truth that has come to you so that you may learn well from it. And we tell you, little one, in order for you to have the means of assisting this one who is called Speaking Wind, these lessons will have to be learned by you before you come to join us. Otherwise, you will have to sit beside us and not be allowed in assisting in any way…assisting either your brother in those things he will have ahead of him or assisting the Earth Mother in entering this next age of hers.

"In order to be of any assistance, Cheeway, you must be willing to learn while you are still here in this domain. Do not become weighted down by those false spirits who are trying to keep you from doing those things they have seen for you. This is their wish…we do not hold the believing that it is yours.

"Look at it in this way, Cheeway. Perhaps it will be easier for you to follow the direction of our speaking words to you. Try to remember what it is like for one who suddenly becomes very ill. Becomes so ill that they are no longer able to do any of the things they have once found joy in doing. When you will look on them, you will see that they are no longer living in the past. When you will look on them, you will see that they are not living in the future. When you will look on them, little one, when you will have the eyes of the spirit do this looking for you, what you will see is that they are remaining in their present.

"And, this is regardless of whether they have learned to find more comfort in their past or their future. When they will have an illness come to them and they will only want to get rid of it, then it is natural for them to stay in the present. For it is only by their staying in the present that they will be allowed to find those things within themselves that will allow them to get better.

"You see, Cheeway, before one will have this ability of getting better, then they will first have to come to accept the fact that there is something wrong with them. And in order to come to this place of knowing there is something wrong with them, they will have to look at themselves in this present that we should all remain in. This present that holds so many of the answers to the things we are seeking for.

"However, this something that is wrong with them, it is not what they will come to look on at first. It is something they must have a knowing for. Something that is much different than many have ever come to know. And, this is where we will continue with our speaking words for the benefit of both of you, little ones. These will be the speaking words that will share with you what to expect from this place. From this place that is on the path of the spirit."

Chapter 10

▼

THE SPIRIT IS CALLING

"We are aware that both of you have seen many cross the path you have been willing to travel, little ones. Many have seen great illnesses and Cheeway's illness is not any different than the ones you both have seen. This must be kept in the front of your thinking minds for what we are about to share with you.

"You see, little ones, when we will look at someone else...someone who is not very close to our circle, then it is very common not to see them for who and what they are. This is very common because they are not close enough to you so that you may come to the place of thinking they can affect your path. And this gives to many the face of detachment for them and those things that they will have come to be bothered by.

"However, when something that is great...something like this illness that has come to Cheeway, then this becomes a completely different matter. It is now something that is affecting you and the path you travel. And, now it is something that carries a great weight to it...a weight that you too can feel, Cheeway. And this weight that is being felt by you, little one, is also being felt by Speaking Wind.

"We are sharing this simple truth with both of you so that you will come to the place we wish for you to be...a place where you can see how to look at those things that have come across your life path...how to look at them with the face of truth and not the face of involvement or detachment. When there will be one who is not within your circle, little ones, it becomes very easy to say 'Oh, how sad for them', or 'I am glad this has not happened to me' and then walk past them and forget all about it.

"But we tell you both. There is a great lesson in what has been offered to you. And it is this offering that can assist you greatly if you will only look upon its face as something that is...as the something that is the eyes of the spirit.

"But when something like this will happen to one who is traveling within your circle, then you will not look upon it as something that you can walk away from. You will look upon it as something that is also affecting you as well. And this weight that you will carry with you…this weight that has come to you from this knowing, well, it does not share with you the face of truth either. Rather it shares with you the face of caring. And this face of caring has emotion to it. And you both have learned what the face of emotion carries with it. It carries all things that can be felt by you as being something more than what they are. And it is from this face of emotion that stops you from looking upon this event and seeing it for what it is. It is the emotion that does not allow you to know that there is a great lesson being offered to you.

"Look at both of these situations that we have been willing to share with you, little ones. When you will look at both of them, you will see that it does not matter how close or how far you have been to the one who has encountered an illness. It does not matter because in both situations, you have not been able to see what was being presented to you.

"From the situation that was removed from you and the circle you travel in…from this one you would only look on the face of the one who had a great illness and feel sorry for them but also grateful that it had not happened for you. From the situation of the one who was traveling in the circle you had formed, you were filled with emotion…an emotion that would not allow you to see far at all. And for sure, you would not be able to see the face of the lesson that was being offered.

"Now, little ones, keep in the front of your thinking minds that in both cases, there was emotion. In the first case, this emotion came to you in the way of seeing how fortunate you were for not having this same illness of the one who was a stranger to you. But nonetheless, it was an emotion for you to follow. If this were not an emotion, then you would not have felt sorry for this person…this one who was not close to you at all. And in the second case…the one we have been willing to share with you about Cheeway's illness…well, we do not believe that you need our assistance to see that there too is a great emotion that is filling both of you for this.

"So it is, little ones, that when we will see something that will come to us with the face of lesson to it…then if we will look upon it with the emotion that will come to our surface, then we will not be able to see it for what it is.

We will not have this clarity of vision for what is being offered to us. And, when there is no clarity of vision then there is only groping in the dark of emotion for those things…this groping around like one who cannot see…like one who can only feel but not know the reason why.

"And this is the place we wish for both of you to be at this time of our sharing, little ones. It is this place where we may now share with you what our ancestors have long called "The Spirit Is Calling." It is from this place of "the spirit is calling" where we will be willing to share a great truth to both of you. And it will be from this truth that you will both begin to see what it is that is present before both of you now.

"When the spirit first enters this domain of the Earth Mother's, there is a great sleep of illusion that is placed over it. And it is from this sleep of illusion that we have come to know the place called the sleeping children. This place of the sleeping children is what brings us to explain how one will look on another when they have encountered a great illness. And because they are still asleep, they will not see the face of lesson that is being offered at this time. They will only see the face of sorrow or emotion…both of which will not allow one to work through anything…only to feel sorry for themselves or another.

"However, as you both have been prepared for by the teachings of the silent brotherhood, you have the knowing that to look at any part of life through eyes such as these is to open the doorway to those false spirits. To open this doorway very wide so that they will be allowed entry to your within place. And it will be in this within place where they will remain very busy keeping you from knowing your spirit. This spirit who is in truth you.

"Because we are lulled into this sleep of the illusion, little ones, this is the reason that so many others will only see all that is life only as those things that affect them. As those things that they can touch, feel, or hold. To them, little ones, this is their reality. They do not see nor do they recognize anything more. Now when one will look at the teachings of the silent brotherhood, they will come to know that only the ones who will learn to travel on the path of the spirit will have the understanding of how untrue this concept is. This concept of needing to hold, touch, or feel something before it can come into your reality.

"The ones who travel on the path of the spirit, they have the eyes that share with them that part of this world of the others. This part of their world that exists in their reality is in truth so very small…so small when compared to the rest…the rest of those things that we have come to know as the face of truth…this face of truth that is held on the path of the spirit.

"Think about it, little ones. Can you touch your spirit? Can you see it? Can you feel it? But you know that it is there because you have learned to live with it. And when you will learn of the waiting place, the Great Spirit, and how our spirit families are in a great circle of life in returning to all that we had come from, this also cannot be seen, felt, or touched. And it would stand to reason that those who travel the path of the others…the ones who have not yet learned their way to the path of the spirit, it would make great sense if they did not have a believing in such things wouldn't it? After all, the Great Spirit cannot be held, touched, or felt.

"So when you will place this in the front of your thinking minds, ask yourself this. Why then do so many of those we have come to call the others…why do they spend such great amounts of time in their form of prayer for such things? For these kinds of things that they cannot see, hold, or touch. Why do they even try to consider them when none of these values fits into their world? The truth of the matter is this, little ones. They do not want to take the chance that it is not real. This is why they do these kinds of things.

"And it is for this same reason that you will look to one who has taken a great illness through the eyes of emotion, little ones. It is not that you really feel so sorry for them. You are in truth afraid that if you do not show them sympathy, then this could happen to you. And, that is the reason so many wear the long faces when they are ill or when they will see another who is. It is not that they are trying to assist them in getting better. They are just afraid that if this one who is ill leaves them, then they will be left alone. And this is the second reason for them looking on them or themselves with these eyes of emotion. Just as the others do…these others who have not yet learned their way to the path of the spirit. They and both of you look but you do not see.

"We tell you both this, Cheeway and Speaking Wind, that when one will receive an illness, great or small, the reason this will come to them is because their spirit is calling to them to learn something. Something that has been offered to them but they did not take. The spirit is not slow nor is it in any way short of understanding. It is only through this combination of the body and the spirit that so much has to be learned before there can be understanding.

"And, when the learning is not adhered to by the body part, then the spirit sees the shortness of the seasons it has been given to travel its life path here…this life path in this domain where only here it can learn from. It sees this shortness of time and becomes frustrated with the body part of ourselves for not being willing enough to work its way through these events…these events that it has been offered to learn from.

"So it is the calling of the spirit that will first bring to you small illnesses. Light ones at first but greater the longer you will not be willing to listen to its calling voice to you…this calling voice to you to let you know that you are missing great opportunities."

"Is this then what has happened to me?" came the questioning voice of Cheeway. Turning my head to the place he was laying, I could see a great heaviness that had come over him. One that I knew to be from these things that had been shared with us by Calling Thunder or the ones who were now within him for this blessing to us.

"No, Cheeway," came their response. "The reason that this great illness has come over you is because the number of seasons you have been given are over. They are over and it is time for you to join with us on this side of the spirit. This will be where you will find the remainder of this path you have chosen to travel to be. It is with us now, little one."

"So then, why would you be so concerned by my not learning to see the lessons that are being offered to me?" was Cheeway's response. And as was very usual for Cheeway, he had once again taken the defensive to those things that had been offered to him…those things that had been offered to him but had made him uncomfortable with himself. Uncomfortable with himself because what had been shared with him was true and he could see it.

"Tell us, Cheeway, are you not willing to assist your brother in this great quest for the Earth Mother?" came the penetrating voice from the one called Calling Thunder. Returning his look back to the place Calling Thunder was sitting, a great questioning look filled Cheeway's face, I could

see. A look that I had come to know meant he did not have a full understanding of this question that had been asked of him. A look that I had
seen many times over him when he was using all of his energy to hold
back a questioning defiance. One that had come to him from not having an
understanding of what someone had asked him to do. And now this look
was over my best friend's face once again.

"Of course I will wish to assist my brother in any way that I can, Calling
Thunder. I will assist him even from the other side of the spirit veil…this
other side that I will soon be on. However, I do not see why I must continue with this learning of those things that are still coming to me…not
now that this time has come over me…this time that is the preparing.

"So, Calling Thunder," Cheeway continued, "tell me why those who are
with you now see the importance for this."

Chapter 11

▼

PREPARING FOR THE RETURN

Looking back to the place where Cheeway was laying, Calling Thunder placed a large and warm smile over his face. It was a smile that was carrying with it a feeling of acceptance. A feeling of acceptance that was sharing with both of us that he had reached the place of understanding…this place of understanding why neither of us held a better understanding for those things that were being offered to us.

"When we will share with you in this way, little ones, it often comes from a higher place of understanding," Calling Thunder continued. "One that is within your reach but it is also a level that requires much work on your part to attain it. This comes through us because we see you for what you will become. For those things that you have within your grasp but many times have not yet learned to extend yourself to them.

"Now, Cheeway, this question that you have asked of us, this question of why it is necessary for you to continue to learn from these lessons that are still coming to you, in truth, little one, the answer is very simple. And in this same truth you both have heard this answer before…this same answer that has been shared with you from the speaking words of Grandfather and Two Bears.

"However, as it is within this domain that is the Earth Mother's, there are many things that are not remembered. And they are not remembered because of the lack of need for them. The need you still have while you are in this domain, Cheeway, is great. It is great because of the blessings that may be granted to you while you are still among the others in this domain. Even though you have been shown that this is to be your last season with the Earth Mother, you will continue to have a great quest to perform. And this will be the same quest that both you and Speaking Wind have been prepared for when your seasons were short.

"However, what was not shared with you is this, little one. You will be undertaking this same quest as your brother, but it will be from this side of the spirit veil that you will find it…this side where many of us have now returned to, little one. Do not keep in the front of your thinking mind that the only place where this great quest of awakening all of our people will take place is on this side. For if you will do this, then none of the preparation that has been offered to you will make any sense. And, if it does not make sense to you, then what value will all of your efforts hold for you.

"You see, Cheeway, there is no thing in this domain that is ever offered to another that is without its reason. And this great quest that has come to you and your brother, well, it is not different. However, from the time that both of you have been preparing for this awakening of your spirits, the amount of preparing for both of you has been rapid. And the reason for this rapid rate of preparing is because there is not as much time left in this age of the Earth Mother's as either of you think. Her time is running out and what must still be done is great.

"We have the knowing that both of you hold the understanding of this time and these seasons of the long shadow. We see this in your colors of understanding that surround both of you. We have shared with both of you before…in the times that our presence was felt from the speaking words of Grandfather and Two Bears. And those things that we had been willing to share with both of you, they are upon all of us now.

"Cheeway, we can see that what you feel is the same as one who has been prepared to run a great race for all of their seasons. But when the time will come for them to begin this race, they will be pulled out of it before it has begun. And to think in this way is not correct.

"The assistance that is required of you is greatly needed. But it is greatly needed on this side. This side where so many of us are waiting to begin our part in assisting the Earth Mother. There is not a great need of having so many on the side of the spirit veil that you are on now. For if this were the case, there would not be much room for the ones who need to learn at all. Our numbers would be so great that we would only find ourselves getting in the way.

"In time, little one, you will come to understand why you are needed on this side with us and your brother, Speaking Wind, is needed here…at least for a while longer. Remember well, little one, it is in this time of the Earth Mother's when all of the members of all nations will have returned. All of them have been returned now and are waiting to be awakened from their sleep of illusion…this sleep of illusion that all who enter this domain are placed into.

"And, there are only a few of those who will be the callers in this domain. The callers to those who have returned to return their assistance to the Earth Mother for all they have been allowed to learn from her in the many life paths they have walked. However, in order for the callers to become successful, little one, there will have to be great assistance from this side of the spirit veil in order that they may succeed in this part of the great quest. This assistance will come from others, such as yourself, who will have held them in the deepest parts of their heart…ones such as yourself who will have the knowing of trust for them and them for you.

"And, Cheeway, this is to be the greatest test for you…this great test that must be willingly accepted by you. And it is in the willingness of continuing to learn from all of the events that will be presented to you in this your last season with the Earth Mother. You see, little one, you are preparing for the final part of this long journey you and your brother, Speaking Wind, have begun. This journey is now coming to the place of beginning. But in order to begin it, you must both be prepared equally so that the needed assistance may be made available…this assistance that you will be able to provide. You and so many others who are even now waiting for this beginning to take place on this side.

"However, Cheeway, in order for you to be allowed to travel from this side of the spirit veil to the one that your brother will still be on, this will require from you all of the efforts that you can make. All of these efforts of coming to work your way through all of the events that are now being presented to you. For it is only in the succeeding of this work of these events while you are still here in this domain that will be the only doorway that will be made available to you. This doorway that will be made available for you to enter in and out of so that you will be able to assist Speaking Wind for those things he will have a great need for.

"And each of these doorways is significant to these events that are now coming before you to learn from. For each of these events that you will now learn from, there will be an additional doorway that will be made available for you. An additional doorway that will allow you occasional entry into this domain you are about to leave.

"It is only by coming to understand and learn from these events that you will have this privilege, little one. If you will not be willing to take the time and effort of learning from these events, then there will not be any path for you to follow. And for all of the assistance that will be needed by Speaking Wind, you will be powerless to give him assistance for. So it is, Cheeway, that for all of these events that are now coming to you…coming to you in this your last season with the Earth Mother…they have come to you in a way that will assist you in coming to overcome all of those things that have yet been unworked. Those things that you and the Earth Mother had designed for you so that you could learn from them.

"And, little one, this is the reason that I share with you that you should continue to learn from them. To continue to learn from these events that are coming to you now just as if you did not know this was the last season of your life path on this side. There are still a great many things to do, little one. And, if we are to be successful in this great quest for the Earth Mother, then it must be by the effort of all of us. All of those who are on this side of the spirit veil as well as the ones like us who are on this side.

"Do not forget to remember, little one, that you had been given this knowing for a reason. This knowing that you are now in this last season of your life path. You see, Cheeway, there are not many who are given this knowing. And, the reason they are not given this is very simple. We have seen so many of them give up on their learning. It is as if they see their only purpose as being one of waiting for the inevitable end to them. And with this in the front of their thinking mind, they believe that they are waiting for a bus to arrive…this bus that will take them back home.

"However, from the teachings of the silent brotherhood, we have found that this is not to be the case. That in the last season of one's life path, that this will be where the greatest of lessons will come to them from. These lessons that had been missed before but are now being offered to them as a second chance of learning from them. And this is the reason that so many of those you will see in this last season of their life path will wear a long face.

"Most of them will look at all of this learning that is being made available to them from the wrong set of eyes. They will look at all of these second chances of learning as something they no longer have the time to complete. As something that is out of their past and nothing more than a memory. However, we will tell you this…that when one is in their last season of the life path with the Earth Mother, that this will be when they will be allowed to make up for all of those things they had not done. To remember how to learn from all of the events that had come to them in all of their past seasons.

"And when this will take place, this is one of the times when all of their spirit families are permitted to give to them assistance…assistance that will allow them to work through all of these things quicker and more thorough than they had ever been capable of doing before. It is not that they feel sorry for them. Not that because their time is so short that this happens. This will take place for all who enter this domain of the Earth Mother's for one reason alone. And this reason is to allow them to have one more chance of learning from those things they had originally entered here to learn from.

"But because of the shortness of time that is left to them, if they are to become successful in achieving this learning, then it must be with the assistance of the ones who are members of their spirit families. This is necessary because they cannot do this alone. We have not seen any who would not welcome this opportunity, little one. We have only seen those who have not yet learned to see the face of these lessons of opportunity that are being offered to them.

"You see, little one, it is common among the others, the ones who travel on the path that leads to the left. It is common for them to have a believing in so many things that are not from the truth. A believing in them so great that they have spent many seasons in leaning on them…many seasons leaning on them but only to find that when it is their time of being depended on that they are nothing more than the shadows of dreams that they are made of. Shadows that will not give to them any of those things they are in need of.

"So for them, little one, for so many of these others, disappointment has become something of a sure ending to all things they will encounter…disappointment in all things they will hold in a high place. So it is that when this time of the last season will come over them, they will not see it as a great opportunity of learning for them. They will only look upon it through the eyes their path has trained them to use. They will look upon this last season on their life path as only a sad reminder of all those things that had gone before them…those things that bring to them a great sorrow.

"And it is from this looking at them in this way that they will not ever come to the place of seeing these lessons and opportunities that are being offered to them for what they are. It is because of this that they will not have the believing that to continue to learn from them will assist them at all. For from all of the conditioning they have received, they will come to believe that any effort that they will extend in this time will be not any different for them than they had come to know…that this time is not different for them. And, if they will continue to make any effort of understanding even now that they are in their last season of their life path, that these efforts will bring to them another sadness and disappointment. And this they do not want any more of. They have now come to the place of being that shares with them they have had enough of this.

"So for the outsiders, little one, the ones who have not yet learned the path of the spirit, their last season with the Earth Mother is usually kept a great secret from them. If it were not, then they would go through all of these things we had been willing to share with you. And this would not be good, would it?

"However, Cheeway, you will not be like this will you," came the questioning voice from this one called Calling Thunder. Looking over to the place where Cheeway was sitting, I could see that he had lowered his head into the direction of his lap. I could also feel a knowing accompanied with its understanding filling him as well.

Looking up from his downward place on the couch, Cheeway said, "This is something that I will do no more."

"Good then, little one. Then we may continue to assist you in preparing for your return to this domain. And this is good."

"Yes," came the return from Cheeway. "Yes, this is good."

Chapter 12

▼

THE FLAMES THAT HIDE

No sooner had the speaking words from this one called Calling Thunder finished echoing through this small room we were all in...just before the silence fell to the four corners of this room, than he looked over to the place where Cheeway was lying and continued. I could see from the look that was filling Cheeway's face that he truly wanted these speaking words to stop. I could see this from the face he was now wearing for Calling Thunder. It was a face that had been shared with me many times before...many times before when we would be feeling the weight of the speaking words of Grandfather and Two Bears. I was filled with a feeling of compassion for my best friend. But I also knew that from the teachings that had been shared with both of us that this was very necessary. Both Cheeway and I had been prepared with the teachings that when one of the old ones of our ancestors or many of the old ones would share speaking words to us, that they would all be shared with us for a specific reason. And this reason, even though it would not be apparent to either of us in the present, that when the time would come for us to have a great need for them, that they would return to their life from our within place once again.

And, from what both Cheeway and I could see from this one called Calling Thunder, we held the knowing that this was not he who was sharing the speaking words with both of us on this day. But Calling Thunder had taken a leave of this time and place so that he would allow the Old Ones entry into this domain...entry into this domain so that they could share their speaking words with us directly. Looking over to the place where Calling Thunder was sitting, I could see a definite change that had come over him. It was a change of color as well as density in the room we were occupying with him.

When we had first begun to share on this day, Calling Thunder was of the same color of skin as were Cheeway and I. And, the air in the room had been lifted to a lighter level from the cleaning of the storm that had just passed. But now looking at him, I could see that he seemed to be glowing with a bright color of white. And, it was not coming from him by any light that I could see. Rather, it seemed to be coming out of him. It seemed as if Calling Thunder had been shedding a white light from every pore of his body. And this was giving to him a glowing appearance…one that could not be mistaken by any who would be close enough to see it. I knew that this would often take place when one of the ancient ones would pay a visit through another in this domain…pay a visit so that they could be heard directly for those things they were willing to share with us. And I also held the knowing that when they would enter another, one who would be willing to share with them for a short time, that there would also be a slight heaviness to the air that was around them.

However, from the weight of this air and from the brilliance of the color of white that was coming from him, I could see that it was not only one of the ancient ones; but there were many who had entered this form of the one called Calling Thunder…many of them. And I was also receiving a picture of Grandfather and Two Bears as well…a picture that I knew was not coming to me from my within place…but a picture of them that was coming to me from the presence of those who were now with Calling Thunder. And this was giving to both Cheeway and myself the knowing that we were to listen very attentively to these speaking words that were being shared with us…to listen to them and learn to look through the face of emotion to see what was being offered to both of us. However, even with this knowing, I could see the weight still crawling over Cheeway. But it was a weight that he knew was necessary. For within this weight, came those things he needed to see for himself…see for himself these things that were coming to him for him to learn from.

So, lying as comfortably as he could on the couch, he continued to look over to Calling Thunder and listen to what was being presented…presented not only to him but to me as well.

"We share now with the both of you, little ones," came the beginning of another set of speaking words from the one we had come to know as Calling Thunder. "We are willing to share with both of you those things that have come to the front of your thinking minds…those things that have held both of you in their path…those things that you have come to see and know as the spirits of the flame."

Looking over to the place where Cheeway was sitting, I saw that he was returning my look to him…returning a look to me that was a mirror image of all those things that were going through my thinking mind as well. When we both heard these speaking words come to us from this one called Calling Thunder, it was as if the ones who had come to reside within him could see those things that had been placed before both of us…those things that had come to me from my spirit vision and to Cheeway from those events that he had encountered…those events that had come to him that allowed him to share with me that he had come through the flames. Those same flames that I held a great question for.

Now the ones who had come among us and through Calling Thunder…now they had come to explain these things with us. And, this came as a great surprise to both of us. It came as a great surprise to us because we did not realize that these things had been known by any one besides ourselves. However, it was a re-reminding to both of us that we are not ever alone – that there is always life around us. And where there is life there is teaching.

"What you have seen in this spirit vision that was shared with you, Speaking Wind," the speaking voice began, "this was what was and is still waiting for many who will travel the path of the spirit. This is what is waiting for them, but it is not always something that they will enter…enter to learn from. We were also present when your brother Cheeway shared with you that he had passed through these flames. And it was from his speaking words to you that there was an immediate connection. An immediate connection from what you had seen to what he had told you about…about his having passed through the flames."

"We will tell both of you that what you have come to know of these flames, that you have not begun to learn from what is there…from what is there and what is being offered to all who will encounter them. You both will be very pleased to know that for all of the preparing that has taken place within each of you, that you have both encountered the spirits of the flame more often than you have believed. The only difference is this, little ones. This difference in the ways that you have encountered the spirits of the flame has been through understanding. While the others who you have encountered, they have done this with the face of fear. And as you have been shared with the face of fear, so it will come to all who will not have had a sufficient level of understanding for themselves and those things that are around them.

"Let us now look at what brings us close to these spirits of the flame. What brings us close to them and what will cause us to see them for who and what they are. As many will travel on this life path with the Earth Mother, little ones, they will find many things that will come to them. However, not all of the events that will be presented to them will be understood. And this lack of understanding comes to them because they do not know who or what these spirits of the flame are.

"For them, they will only have a great fear of them. A great fear because they know that whenever they will come to them, then there are always great changes that will take place to them. It is because of the lack of understanding that all of these changes that will come to them will always be seen through the eyes of fear. And it is because of this fear that they have decided not to take the time to understand what has happened.

"We will tell to both of you that it is only when one will come to the place of understanding that they will no longer be filled with fear. Only then will they have the eyes of the spirit that will be allowed to see. And until this can take place for them, they will have to learn to look past themselves, little ones. And this is what has been such a wonderful blessing for the both of you.

"Your blessing has come to both of you from the speaking words of Grandfather and Two Bears. And it is from this basic understanding that both of you have been able to travel as far as you have on this path of the spirit. However, now that the time for the great awakening has come over the face of the Earth Mother, you will be in great need of additional understanding for what you will be carried through next. In order for both of you to have the level of understanding that is needed in this time for the Earth Mother. And, Cheeway, this is going to be the same in the place you will be arriving at soon, as it will be for your brother, Speaking Wind, who will remain behind."

Pausing for a few moments from these speaking words of sharing, this one called Calling Thunder looked over to the places where both of us were sitting. Both Cheeway and I knew what it was that was taking place. We were being followed. Followed from our within place to see where it was that we had come to. Where we had been able to arrive at on this long path we both had decided to travel…on this path of the spirit. However, as I was feeling the presence of more than one within myself, I could not come to a place of remembering when I had ever felt such a presence within me. Even those times when Grandfather and Two Bears had allowed themselves to enter, there was not ever this kind of a feeling for me. Now with the entry of the ones who were within Calling Thunder, I was feeling their presence. And this was such a combined feeling of the familiar as well as the unfamiliar that I could not find a place within me that would share an understanding. An understanding of why this was taking place now and in this way.

However, from the teachings of the silent brotherhood, since I did not have any feelings of hardness, I continued to sit in my place and wait for an explanation of this. To wait for the continuing of the speaking words from this one called Calling Thunder or from those who were now within him to share their reasons with me. Suddenly, there was a large smile that had come over his face. It was a smile that I knew was for the benefit of Cheeway and myself. It was also a smile of continuation…the continuation of those speaking words that were being shared with us.

"Keep in the front of your thinking minds, little ones," he continued, "that there is virtually no difference on either side of the great doorway. This great doorway that keeps you in this domain separated from the residing place of the ancient ones…this same residing place where we are speaking to both of you from.

"We are familiar with all of those song legends that have shared with you that the difference is great. But we will tell you with the speaking words of truth that there is no difference. No difference but one. From the times of the great separation from the Great Spirit, there have been many truths that have been shared on both of these sides. And, if you will look to these things we are now willing to share with you, you will both come to the finding that truth does not change regardless of the place you are. The only part of the truth sharing that has any change at all to it will be those speaking words that will be used to express it.

"And it is from these truths that we are now willing to share with you the reason why there is not any difference from this side of the great doorway to the side both of you are currently on. Those same spirits of the land are as prominent on this side as they are on yours. But as both of you have been able to see, there are not many in your domain who are either willing or capable of seeing them.

"There are also the same events that will come to us on this side of the great doorway as they will come to both of you on your side. But, as you will look at the many who will cross your paths, you will have seen that not many will ever come to the place of seeing them for what they are. For the truth they carry with them in their lesson offering.

"So it is, little ones, that the same path of the spirit rests with us on this side of the great doorway as it does for you. But the one great difference is this. We who reside on this side…this side where we too offer our assistance to the Earth Mother, we are not as limited in those things of seeing as you are. On this side of the great doorway, there is no spirit of illusion; and all that is of our spirit, it remains with us.

"When we will see an event come to us, little ones, we will have the eyes and ears of the spirit to see and know it for what it is. Unlike those who are in this domain of the Earth Mother's…those who will first have to look their way through the emotion before they will be capable of seeing what has been offered to them. You see, little ones, when you, Cheeway, say that you have been through the flames and you, Speaking Wind, say that you have seen the flames that are residing on the path of the spirit, what you have experienced and seen is truth. For there are many flames on this path of the spirit, but they are flames that are not understood by many.

"And it will be this understanding that we will present to both of you. However, you must be willing to keep in the front of your thinking minds that it is not necessarily the flame that is the topic of understanding…it is what resides behind them. This is the true measure of understanding them."

"So it is not what is obvious to us when we will first see these spirits of the flame, Calling Thunder?" I asked, sitting in a very straight position.

"This is the face of truth, little one," was his response. "Many who will have been presented with the face of the spirits of the flame…they will become very frightened of it. However, as it is with all things, Speaking Wind, for those who do not hold the understanding for those things that are presented to them, they will only see the face of fear and will fail to understand that there is a great lesson that is being offered to them."

"But, Calling Thunder," came Cheeway's following up to those speaking words, "when I had gone through the flames that I was willing to share with Speaking Wind, I could only see the hurting that I had gone through. At least, as I was traveling through them. But once I had come out on the other side of them, well, I was filled with a great peace…a great peace for those things that I had been weighed down with before I had gone through. Is this what you are sharing with us now? Is this what you are speaking of when you say we do not hold an understanding of what resides on the other side of them?"

"Yes, Cheeway, this is the direction of where we are wishing to travel to. But it is not the destination that we will eventually share with both of you. Do both of you remember the song legend of the arrow?" came the questioning speaking words from Calling Thunder.

"Not in this way…in this way that you are sharing them with us," was my response.

"Well then, this might help the understanding to Cheeway's statement," Calling Thunder continued. "When one will see the face of an event come to them…this face that will carry with it a hurting, they will only be concerned with this misunderstanding of the hurt. They will not see through this emotion to look at the lesson offered. As they will encounter this kind of an event…this kind such as the one Cheeway has been willing to share with us, they will only be aware of the hurting that has come to them. This hurting that has come to them from the event or events they had encountered.

"You see, Cheeway, it is not the passing through the spirits of the flame domain that is bringing to you this hurting. For all that they are, of all that they have been given dominion over, is without any hurting at all. What you were feeling was the hurting of passing through those events that had come to you. Those same events that had been weighing you down because of the lack of understanding you held for them.

"And it was when you had begun to pass through the flames that they were burned away from you. Which allowed you to come to the place of understanding for them in a way that allowed you to let them fall off from you. It was this process of understanding them, little one, that had caused you this pain…this pain that you once believed was the hurting of the spirits of the flame."

"But this pain that I had felt, Calling Thunder, this pain that had come over me – it was so real!" Cheeway returned. "It is not that I do not hold a believing in the weight of the speaking words of truth you are willing to share with me. But as both my brother and I have been prepared with, we must each come to a place of understanding…this place of understanding for ourselves that will allow us to not only believe in something but to understand it as well. And, this is where I am speaking to you from now. This place that shares with you that I do not have an understanding that will allow me to accept this explanation without a better knowing."

Looking over to the place where Cheeway was sitting, Calling Thunder smiled, then continued. "This is the why of the song legend of the arrow, little one. It is to share with those who do not yet have the understanding of what is being held for them behind the flames…this great lesson that we will have offered to us. And, it is also a way of coming to a better place of understanding for those things that had come to us in the seasons past or the ones we are now in. As we have shared with both of you, all events will come to us with an important lesson to offer. And, all of them have come to us in exactly the right time and place.

"This is to say that we have already designed them to come to us long before they have been given life in this domain of the Earth Mother's. It is when we are sitting in our council with her, this council that allowed us to ask her for permission of entry into her domain, it was at this time when both the Earth Mother and our spirit decided if we could learn those lessons we needed from this domain. And, it was also at that time when we designed them not only how they would come to us but when.

"So this is why we say to both of you that all that had come to you so far in these seasons of your life path…that all of those events that have crossed your life path…that they have come to you in exactly the time and way you had intended for them. However, as all who will come to enter this domain, they will be placed into the sleep of illusion…this illusion that will not allow you to see things for what they are but only for what you would wish for them to be.

"And so it is with all of these events that have been designed by you. Designed by you so that your spirit could learn from them in this domain. But, when they will come to you while you are even partially asleep, you will not see them for what they are. You will only see them as either something that will cause you fear or hurt. And both of these feelings come to you through the face of illusion, not understanding.

"So when Cheeway will share with us that his passing through the flames caused him to feel the hurt, we will share with you that this hurt was not from the flame but from the emotions that he had been carrying around with him. Those emotions that had come into him like the arrow will do when one is hit with one. When the arrow finds its mark into you, little ones, it becomes like an event that has hurt you. And, in truth there is not much difference. For the emotion that will cause you pain and hurt is just like the arrow that finds its way into you. It will cause you a great hurt and you will see the leaking of the blood of your life pouring out of you from its entry.

"However, with the arrow you will realize that to leave it in will cause your pain to continue. And if you will leave it within you, there can be no healing take place. This healing that will allow you to be as you were before the arrow found its way into your skin. So realizing that there will be pain associated with the pulling out of this arrow…a pain that will most likely be just as hard if not more than when it first entered you, you will hold the knowing that this is something that you must do. That you must take this arrow out of you even if it does cause you pain.

"So, holding your mouth tight, you pull on the other side of this arrow until it is out. Then sitting back and getting over the pain, you are comforted with the knowing that for all of this effort there can now be a healing. A healing that could not take place if you were to have left the arrow in. And so it is with the emotions that will come to us that we do not understand…these emotions that will also carry with them a hurting. A hurting just like the arrow did when it first found its mark within us.

"But the difference is this, little ones. The arrow you can see, but the emotion leaves no outward visible trail. And because it does not leave an outward trail of its presence, many will fool themselves into thinking they can just ignore it and no one will notice. It is this kind of thinking that carries them into this place of inaction, little ones…this place where they have felt the hurt of the emotion enter them; and this entry has caused them to feel a sorrowful pain in their life path. And, it is from being included on this path of the others…this path that does not allow one to show they are hurting without being thought less of, that will teach them what they will next do.

"This thing they will next do is to try to hide the face of this hurt that is with them. This face of hurt that has come to them from this entry of the emotion they do not hold an understanding for. You can see them, little ones, as you will continue to travel on this life path with the Earth Mother. And, Cheeway, you too will continue to look into this side of the great doorway. To look and to see these things we are now willing to share with both of you. For we are sharing them with both of you because each of you has a great need to come to understand them. And, as it is with all life path travelers, each of your needs is different from the other.

"Now, as you will look to those who would cross your path, little ones, you will notice that many of them will seem to walk stooped over and many of them will not be of the best of health. However, this is all for a reason. And this reason is that for all of the events that have come to them on this life path of theirs...all of these events have come to them first with the mask of illusion. And it is this mask of illusion that we have come to know as the emotion.

"This emotion is what comes to us first. And it comes to each of us as a means of testing our strength of the spirit. This strength of the spirit that will allow you to work your way through the emotion and see the face of the lesson that you are being offered. And, little ones, it is from this emotion that we must work our way through that has become the face of the flame...these flames that you, Cheeway, have felt as if you have traveled through and those same flames that you, Speaking Wind, have seen in the Old Ones' spirit vision to you. It is when we have learned to work our way through the emotion of all these events that are being presented to us, little ones...it will only be then that you will see what is hidden behind these flames that you speak of. Only then will you see the face of truth for yourself.

"And remember, little ones, when any who are still in this domain of the Earth Mother's...when any of them will see this face of truth, then they must keep in the front of their thinking minds that this truth is only for them. It cannot and must not be forced onto another. For another does not have the same needs as you do. They do not have the same needs for those lessons that your spirit does, and they do not travel your path nor do you travel theirs. "But as it is with all things in this domain, you are always free to share those things that have come to you on this path of the spirit…those things that have come to you with their face of truth…and, those things that you have reached a level of understanding for. To do anything more than this, little ones, is to attempt to control them. And, you both have been sufficiently prepared enough to know what this will bring to each of you.

"When one will attempt to control another, then all of the lessons that should be coming to them, they will come to you. And they will come to you in addition to the ones you have designed for yourself to learn from. Think over this, little ones. Do either of you really have any more room to work through more lessons than are being given to you already?

"However, we wish to continue with the explanation of what has happened to the others, the ones who have not yet learned their way to the path of the spirit. As we have shared with both of you, there have been many of them who have crossed your life path. And, you have each seen them for they seem to carry a great weight. But this weight does not come to them from anything that can be seen. For it comes to them from not having taken the time and effort of working their way through their lessons…these events that have come to them. For them they have not yet learned of the secret that is being held for them behind the flame…behind these spirits of the flame that we have seen a great need for each of you to learn from.

"These others, the ones we are speaking of who have not yet learned that there is more to them than what can be seen from the outside, for them all that is in reality is only what can be seen, felt, or held. To ask any of them if there is more to their reality is to ask them a foolish question. They will look at you with the look of one who is far above the place where you are and tell you that there is not…that the only reality in their life is what comes to them that can be seen, felt, or held.

"However, from the teachings that have come to each of you from Grandfather and Two Bears…the ones who have prepared both of you so well on this path of the spirit, you realize that this is not the face of truth. But it is only the face of one who is still sleeping in their sleep of illusion…this same illusion that does not allow any of them to see things for what they are, only for what they would wish for them to be.

"As each of you have learned from the teachings of the silent brother-hood…as each of you have seen, there is only one out of one thousand things that can ever be seen, held, or touched that will come to any in this domain. To think of it in any other proportion would be to speak in the sleep of illusion.

"Look at them, little ones; listen to all of those things they will say. You will hear them speak to those who are near them of believing in things that they cannot see. You will hear them telling others that to have faith in something that they cannot feel is all right. You will hear them tell these others that to ask for help from an unseen source is natural. But when you will ask any of them to share with you their reality, well, it will always come back to you in the same way. They will tell you that their reality is only made up of those things that they can see, feel, or touch. And that anything more is only to be another dreamer in this life…a dreamer who will not ever accomplish anything great…either for themselves or for anyone else for that matter.

"So it is not difficult to see why so many of these others who you will see in the seasons of your life path seem to be so very lost. And, in truth, little ones, they are. On one hand they hold the believing that if they will have faith in those things they are wishing for, that they will come true. But on the other hand, they do not believe in them at all. They do not believe in them because they are not within their limits of reality.

"Is it any wonder why all of those things they have been asking for do not come to them? But they do not come to them because there are none who are willing to offer them the assistance they are in need of. They do not receive them, and this is the face of truth that both of you must come to understand. When any who is within this domain of the Earth Mother asks for assistance…assistance to come to understand those things that have come to them…those things that have come to them in this life path they are traveling…those things that have come to them that they do not understand the why of, well, they will always be answered. They will always be given this assistance they are seeking.

"However, for them to see what it is that is being presented to them, they will first have to hold the understanding that where they are stand-ing…that this standing on the path of the others will first have to change. That they will first have to come to the place of knowing that there is more to the reality of this life path than only for those things they can see, hold, or feel.

"And if they will not have the accepting for this knowing…the understanding that there is so much more to themselves and all life that is within this domain than what can be seen from the outside, they will not have the eyes and ears of their spirit opened for them to use. And unless they will see through their eyes of the spirit and hear through their own eyes of the spirit, they will not ever come to see what all is being offered to them. And for them, they will hold onto the believing that they are not being answered. They will not understand that all that they are asking for is being presented to them…they just do not know how to look for it or how to see it.

"So to them, little ones, as they will see these many events that will be presented to them, they will not see them as something that is for them to learn from. They will only see them as being something that is getting in their way. However, because they are still locked into their sleep of illusion, they do not have the knowing that there is anything more to these offerings that are coming to them than an inconvenience…an inconvenience that is causing them to feel many things.

"Remember, little ones, remember that behind the flames lie all of these answers that one will seek. But before they will see this answer, they will first have to pass through the flame. And to the ones we are now speaking of, this is a frightening thing for them to think on. So they continue to look on the face of these events that are coming to them as some kind of a personal injury to them. And it is always a kind of injury for them that will cause them to see it as one that will make them look small in the eyes of the ones who are near them. Those who have been taking a great pride in telling them what is right…what is wrong…what is good…and what is bad.

"And it is these others who are telling them so many of the things they should be doing…it is they who are just as lost as the ones they are trying to fool. However, when any who are on this path of the others…this path that is comforted by the sleep of illusion, they cannot afford to have another see them in a weakened state. A state that would share with them that they are hurting or that they do not know what to do with any situation. And this is what will first cause them to see the need of ignoring these great lessons that are being offered to them. This is the reason that they will refuse to see them for what they are bringing to them.

"They will find more comfort in pretending that they are not bothered by these events that are being presented to them...these same events that they and the Earth Mother had designed for them to learn from. But the more they will ignore them, the more they will cause them to feel the heaviness of their emotions...these emotions that are being carried on the front of all lessons...on the front of all events that come to all who are in this domain. You see, little ones, it is when one of the others will see one of their own becoming weak...weak either from a injury to their body, or even worse, from an injury to their emotions...it will be then they will see them in another way...in a way that will no longer allow them to keep the position among them they once held.

"For when they will see this outward expression of this carrying of hurting emotion over them, they will not be filled with an understanding. They will be filled with the face of one who does not want to see this in anyone. They will not want to see this in anyone because they too carry this hurt with them as well. And, if they do not show theirs to others, then any one who would do such a thing, they must be very weak and cannot keep any position of authority among them.

"The path of the others is filled with such things, little ones. And it is from this continued weight of emotion that will come over them that will make them walk with this weight showing eventually. Even if they will not admit they are hurting, through the emotions that will come to them in time, they will feel its weight. For as more seasons of their life path will pass them by, this emotion will gain in weight and size. And, it will come to rest on the very top of them. This is what will cause them to begin their stooped over walk. And with the passing of even more seasons, its weight will bring to them many illnesses as well.

"Also, little ones, the path of the others...this path that is held not only by the veil of illusion but the same path where the spirits of the flame do not come to any...this path will only give to those who appear to remain strong and unbending all of these emotions that are continually pressuring them. It is almost as if these others...these who have not yet found their way to the path of the spirit...as if they are trying to breed out any of the weakness that they will see in another. And their reward for this will be to give to each of these strong ones a position of authority. One that will make them feel very good in the beginning but one that will not allow them to grow through their spirit at all. And, when the time will come to them for the last season's review…this same review that you are now going through, Cheeway, there will be many tears of the water spirit fall from their eyes.

"For in this last season of the life path…this last season when those who have been assisting them or trying to assist them in their life path quests… they will show to them what they have become. But, more important than that, they will show them what they could have become. And they will see a great distance between these two faces that have come to them.

"It is at this time when they will no longer be capable of looking away from all of those events that had been presented to them…presented to them so they could attain a higher level of understanding for themselves. It is at this time when all of those emotions that they had been carrying with them will come to the front. And it is in their coming to the front of their thinking minds that they will see the beginning of the spirits of the flame. These same spirits of the flame that will come to all before they will be allowed to leave this domain that both of you are in now.

"However, if they had come to see that there was another path they could have traveled…the path that is always right next to the one they had been on…and this path we have come to know as the path of the spirit, then they would have seen a better way for all of those things that had come to them. A better way of seeing them for what they were and what they had to offer rather than simply looking away from them…looking away from them so no one else would see that they had feelings.

"But, little ones, this is what is held on this path of the others…this path that does not lead anywhere but to the great sadness. And, for the ones who will travel on it, they will not ever come to understand that all that is coming to them is for their benefit so that they may attain a higher level of understanding…this higher level of understanding that will eventually lead their spirit to the next higher place and one more step closer to the Great Spirit.

"So it is that they do all they will ever come to do either for someone else or because of someone else. But it is not ever for themselves that they will do these things. And because of this, they remain locked into their small but endless little circle of life. For them, little ones, they will not ever hold the knowing of what it is that lies behind the flame. To them this flame that will come to them only bears the great face of fear…this face of fear they see not only for the flame but for all things they do not understand.

"And the greatest harm they can do, they have done. They have not ever come to know who and what they are. You see, little ones, it is not as bad a thing for one to lead others. It is not bad because all of those others have allowed themselves to be led. So, when you will look at it in this way you can see that there is always freedom of choice. Not only for these others but also for all life.

"However, the great sadness will come to them when they find in their last season with the Earth Mother that they had not learned themselves. But for all of the seasons they had been given in this domain of the Earth Mother's, they had only come to rely on those who were around them. And all of them will undoubtedly disappoint them in time.

"So when you will see them passing by you, little ones…and you will see how heavy they will walk in this domain, do not feel sorry for them… only understand that all of those things they have done have been done by them of their own choosing. That it is always the individual who will have the last say in what they will do and who they will become. Remember, little ones, and put this in the front of your thinking minds. That what the flames hide from you is you."

Finishing these speaking words, the ones who were with Calling Thunder seemed to be looking around the room. Both Cheeway and I were following their eyes as they would go from one thing to another. As they seemed to be reading them just as they had been reading us before. It was almost as if they were making sure that all of those things that were in the room with us were being able to keep up with their speaking words as well. And just as this thought had crossed into me, Calling Thunder continued.

Chapter 13

▼

TO PLACE MYSELF FIRST

"As one will travel closer to the spirits of the flame, little ones," came the speaking words of the ones who were now with Calling Thunder…those same ones that we held a recognition for but at the same time did not, "as they will come close enough to see or to at least feel them, they will see a great change come over them, a change that will not be believed at first but one that will later be accepted by them and the truth that it bears. One of these great truths that they will come to find on this path, little ones, is to place themselves first…to place themselves first in all things they will come to see, know, or do. And we share with you that this truth holds the great weight of truth within these speaking words…this great weight of truth that has been placed within it by the Great Spirit.

"However, from those who we have come to see within this domain of the Earth Mother's…those who are still residing within their sleep of illusion, we have seen how grave this choice is for them. And, the difficulty they have in coming to place themselves before all things is that it makes them feel vulnerable."

"Calling Thunder," I said, sitting very straight in my position, "why do you say that this makes others feel vulnerable?"

"Why do you say that it does not make them feel this way, Speaking Wind?" came his response to me.

"It is just that both Cheeway and I have seen many of these others who have crossed our life path before. We have seen not only the way they are in the present but also we have come to the place of understanding why they act in the way that they do. And, for all of these observations we have seen of them…for all of those reasons that we have found within them, well, I just have not seen this reason of vulnerability. I have seen another reason. One that has carried a great deal of understanding for me and this way that they will always place another before them."

"Then, Speaking Wind," came the reply from Calling Thunder, "would you be willing to share this reason with all of us who are with you on this day?"

"Yes, Calling Thunder, I would be willing to share this with you."

Looking over to the place where my best friend, Cheeway, was sitting, I could see a look that had come over his face. It was a look that I had seen many times before. One that had been placed there when both of us were of the short seasons and still living with Grandfather and Two Bears on the lands of the mesa. However, this look that had now come over his face, it was more than one of casual concern for these things I was about to embark on. It was a true concern for what I was willing to share. And his reason for this concern for my actions, for these speaking words that I was now willing to share, was because he, like me, was aware that this was not only Calling Thunder that we were sharing with. Both he and I knew that the ones who were now within this one called Calling Thunder were the Old Ones. The same ones who had been giving guidance and direction to our people for as long as we had been drawing breath from the Earth Mother.

It was with this concern of respect for them that had caused Cheeway to share with me this face of his. And, it was this concern of respect for them that was causing me to ask these questions and to share my believing. If I was not willing to ask, I might not ever know. These were the continuing speaking words that kept coming back to me on this time of thinking. These were the speaking words that were echoing through the long corridor of the past. Those times when Cheeway and I were still with Grandfather and Two Bears.

Keeping this in the front of my thinking mind I decided to continue.

"Calling Thunder," I began. "From all of those things we have seen from the outsider, our teachings have shared with us that the ones we call the others...the ones who have not yet learned the path to the spirit...that they hold many things to them...things that do not hold the weight of truth in them. And, it is from this lack of truths that can be found within their believing that they are very frightened to look closely at them or even at themselves. Are my speaking words finding an acceptable place within you?"

"Yes, Speaking Wind," came the response. "We are finding this direction that you are willing to take us acceptable for now."

"Very well then, I shall continue. It is from this knowing...this knowing that the path of the others...those of whom we are sharing speaking words with...that this path they have been willing to travel does not allow them to look closely at things...closely at those things that are close to them. And, from this knowing that they are not willing to see themselves for who and what they are...that they are not willing to do this because they are afraid of what they will find...afraid that they will find that there are not many things with them that hold any truth to them at all. Well, this is the beginning of the reasons that they are so willing to place another in the front of them. And this necessity has been included into their religions as well. Many of them are taught that when one will place another in the front of them, well, they are doing the right thing – that by doing this they are bringing themselves closer to their own spirit. Even though none of them would know when this would come to them if it did, they continue to do this anyway. They continue to do this because they fear more the possibility of it being true more than they fear the possibility of it being untrue.

"So it is, Calling Thunder, that so many of these others continue to hold another in the front of them. It is not that they understand the importance of this; they just fear that if they would not do this that it could be very bad for them. Have these speaking words come close to those things you wanted to share with us?" I asked, sitting back a little in my position on the floor.

"Close, Speaking Wind," came the return to my speaking words. "Close but not correct," Calling Thunder said, looking deep into the eyes of both Cheeway and myself once again. "When you will look over these speaking words that you have been willing to share with me, you will find that there is a great hole in them...a hole that has come to them from the lack of understanding. However, this understanding has not been present in this domain for many seasons. And for either of you to have no holding onto it, well, this is merely the mark of the times that have been with you." Looking over to the places where we were sitting, Calling Thunder placed a warm smile over his face. It was a smile that was for our benefit. A smile that was sharing with both of us that all things were as they should be. And these speaking words of his were not to bring us a long face as much as they were to share with us.

Seeing this recognition come over us, Calling Thunder continued, "Remember, little ones. Remember to keep in the front of your thinking minds that the path of the others is nurtured by the body part of one's self. And because it is more controlled by the wants of the body, it is only safe to say that it is a very self-serving path indeed. A path that will not have room for any feelings of responsibility for one's actions to come back to them. This path has been traveled by so many for so many seasons of generations that it has become a believing for them...a believing for them that it is better for them to hide from themselves than it is for them to learn.

"What we are sharing with you, little ones, is a great truth for this domain. And it is a truth that has been set into motion by the Great Spirit and given to the spirits of the flame to hold dominion over. This truth that has been set into motion is one that will make one feel as if they are passing through the flames of destruction. And for those things that they carry with them it is truth. For these spirits of the flame will cause all that has been gathered onto you that does not hold truth to fall away.

"However, from the place where so many of the ones who choose to travel the path of the others, they continue to hold this believing that it is better to not look at themselves. They hold onto this believing because they are in truth afraid of what they will see. And it is this way of thinking that has brought them to this path they now travel...this path that will not share with them anything of learning from their within place.

"You see, little ones, for the most part, they are so filled with this fear of looking at themselves and seeing what is there that they will place a great effort in not doing such a thing. And this effort that they will place is explained by themselves as performing something that is not selfish or fearful in its intent. This is their way of convincing themselves to see things for what they would like for them to be. This is their way of remaining within the sleep of illusion and not having to see anything for what it is. For by this way of thinking for them, it allows them to hear many words of agreement from those who are around them. Even though this has nothing to do with speaking words of truth for them, they feel better if others will agree with them and those things they will do.

"So it becomes very important for them to have this agreement of the ones they are near. This will give to them the illusion of being correct in what they have decided is best for them to stay away from themselves. So in an effort of not having to look at themselves, they have come up with a process that will not make them look bad or to carry a long face for what they are doing. They have come up with the illusion that it is better to place another before you for all that you will want or do. To them, this gives the outside appearance of doing the right thing. After all, when you will only look on the surface of such a deed, well, it would appear to be a very good thing indeed.

"It would seem to the one who would not look deep into this action that there are a group of individuals who are trying to become unselfish in those things of their life path. That they are placing another before themselves and to only look at the surface of this, it does appear to be good. However, let us look a little deeper into what this kind of an action is bringing about. Let us go into this action so we will see below the surface…to look below the surface to see what this truth is bringing to all who will embrace it.

"When you shared with us the speaking words of your understanding, Speaking Wind, those speaking words that shared with us the reason for the others to feel so strongly about placing another in the front of them, you were close but not correct. And, little one, the reason for this was that you did not have the ability of seeing behind their actions. From the place you were looking at them from, you could only see their actions and hear their words to you on this matter. However, we will share with both you and Cheeway that this is much deeper than either of you have come to believe…deeper and necessary for each of you to hold an understanding for this kind of action on their path.

"You will both need this understanding. And, not only for this but for many things they will have with them. Those who do not yet travel on the path of the spirit, it is because of this 'Season of the Long Shadow', little ones. Because we are now in this last part of the old age of the Earth Mother's that we are sharing with you now…that you are in such great need of this understanding. In those many distant seasons when our people traveled this domain, there was much more time for them to arrive at the same place we are asking both of you to get to. And this need for this speed is because of the shortage of time that is available to all of us.

"So, little ones, let us now go into the meaning of this action of the others…this action that allows them to believe that it is much better to place another before them in all things. As we have shared with both of you, this has resulted from those who have traveled the path of the others, not wanting to look at their own face of truth…this face of truth that is the cover of their own spirit. And it was because of this that so many of them were looking for a way to justify their actions…their actions that would always seem to take all attention away from themselves…to take it away from themselves and focus it onto another.

"This kind of thinking for them resulted in sharing with those of their own kind that it was better to place another before you. To set yourself behind their needs. And in this way they would be assured that they were being very righteous in all that they would think and do in this life path of theirs. That if they were not to think of themselves, they would surely be filled with the thoughts of those who were around them. And, by doing this thing they would be more assured of being pious and not falling prey to any evil that would come to them.

"However, even their premise was begun from a false start. This starting of their thinking begins with the believing in anything being evil. And it is from this kind of thinking that has added weight to those things they have asked so many others to follow…this concept of evil existing in the same way for all who are with them.

"You must place in the front of your thinking minds, little ones, that there is no such thing as this evil. This thing called evil by the ones who do not have a path of the spirit. To them this evil is another way of controlling those who are close to them…another way of making them feel so much fear that they are afraid of not doing what they are told…afraid of the consequences of thinking and doing on their own. As both of you have been prepared with from the teachings of the silent brotherhood, you remember that there is no good, no bad, and no evil. There only IS and this can only apply to yourself. Fear and evil are the same thing, little ones.

"What gives to them their weight of existence is the lack of understanding one will have when they will encounter them. For those who travel the path of the spirit, they will only see these things as events that are being offered to them. Events that when learned from will increase their level of understanding for themselves and all things that are near them. The ones who travel the path of the spirit have the knowing that it is only when there is no understanding for those things that will enter your life path – only when there is not an understanding for them – that there will be seen on them the face of fear or evil.

"Those who travel on this path of the spirit hold the understanding that for every event that will come to them, that it is perfectly timed and placed for them to learn from. And the only thing that will stand in its way of being learned from is the distance between the lesson and themselves. What fills this distance is emotion. And emotion when it is not understood can do many false things to the thinking mind. And for the others, the ones who are telling those who are near to them that they will be safe from all evil in the world if they would place another in the front of themselves, they are the ones who are still caught up in this emotion…this same emotion that precedes all lessons.

"We know that this emotion is strong in the realm of illusion. This illusion that keeps so many from seeing things for what they are. We also hold the knowing that this emotion comes to all as a test…a test of the strength of the spirit…a test by the ancient ones to see if you are willing to accept this face of the lesson that is being offered to you…if you hold the seeking spirit and the desire to work your way through this emotion, so you will be able to see clearly.

"However, for the ones who have not yet found their way to the path of the spirit…those who are still caught up in this falseness of the emotion… they are the ones who are also afraid of seeing themselves or having any other see them for who and what they are. And when you will combine all of these things we have been willing to share with you…those who they have convinced to follow them and those things they will tell them, they are also of the same kind of thinking mind. They too are afraid of being seen by themselves or others for what they are.

"For all who travel on this path, we are sharing with you. All of the ones who will get caught up in this emotion…they have this problem because they have not yet learned to understand that these things they have been so afraid of are in truth being offered to them to learn from. Being offered to them so they will have the ability of raising their spirit to the next higher place…the next higher place on this long circle of life back to the Great Spirit.

"You see, little ones, it is not the thought of being very good that has given such a weight to these others that makes them believe it is for the best to place another in the front of them. This is not the reason that this kind of thinking has lasted so long with them. The reason for this kind of thinking is that they will not have another look at them too closely for those things that they are of and those things they will come to do.

"When one will place another in the front of himself, the first thing that will take place is that he will no longer be in any place of learning. They will not be in any place of learning from any of those events that will come to them. And the reason for this is very simple. When there is another who is now standing before or in the front of you, it is they who are taking all of the emotional onset of those events that are trying to come into your life path...those same events that bring with them the lessons you should be willing to learn from.

"So, in the first place they are placing themselves in a position that is far from being affected by their own lessons. And they are allowing the one who is being placed before them to go through them for them. This is somewhat like hiring another to do your work for you. But in this case there is no work or growing for the one who has done this thing...for the one who has placed another in the front of themselves.

"And, for the one who has allowed themselves to be placed in this position, they too have placed another in the front of them. And this has resulted in them going through all of the emotion of another's lessons and another going through the emotions of yet another's lessons. None of which have been designed or needed by their own spirit.

"When you will look at all of those who have come to the place of believing in this...believing that to place another in the front of themselves and their needs, well, you can see how little is accomplished by doing this. There is very little growth and very little understanding. And this is the weight of truth that we are sharing with both of you on this day.

"You see, little ones, unless one will place themselves first in all things they will be or do, there will not be any learning accomplished for them. And, without learning there cannot be an increased level of understanding for themselves. And, without this there will be no wisdom for them to have...wisdom that would have allowed them to use their understanding from those lessons to continue to grow their spirit.

"It is only when one will be willing to place themselves in the front of all things that they will be able to learn from those lessons they themselves have designed. Those lessons their spirit knew had a need for long before they entered this domain of the Earth Mother's…from the teachings of the silent brotherhood…those teachings that both of you have been prepared with. You will remember that it is a time when our spirit will come to the Earth Mother to petition her for a life path. That it is at this time when we will sit in council and make the determination of what it is that our spirit may gain from a life path with her.

"Both of you will also remember that it is at this time when our spirit, with the assistance of the Earth Mother, will design all of those events that are needed. Those events that are needed by our spirit so that it may advance to the next higher place on this long journey back to the Great Spirit. And, as we will have come up with this designing of these life path events, we will, as we are still in our spirit form, see how well they all fit into those things that we need. From this place of designing and timing all of those events that will be needed by our spirit, we will then be placed with another of her children. And this child is our body part.

"However, as it is with all of those who would enter when this union is made with our body part, all of this knowing and understanding that our spirit carries with it, all of this is to fall silent for a time. For some it will be longer than others. And for others it may not ever come to them at all. And the reason for this is because when we will join with this body part of ours it is then that we are lulled into the sleep of illusion…this sleep that we must all wake from before our eyes and ears of our spirit are opened for us once again…opened so that we may see things for what they are and not for what we would wish for them to be.

"And, little ones, until this time and place are reached by those who would enter this domain, all will see each of these events that have been designed by us for us. They will only see them as they will come to them as something that will bring them a great inconvenience or pain or hurt. They will not hold the understanding that these are all of the things that they designed for themselves on this life path to learn from. They will not see the need that they will have for them. And it is because of this that they will not have a good face on them when each of these events will come to them…come to them to assist them in learning.

"Because of this, little ones, so many of them will not be willing to endure the time and effort of looking through the emotion that precedes each of these events. Because of this, they have come to believe that they have arrived at a place that is much easier for them…easier for them to be than to have to work through so much for these events that have come to them. And this place they have come to believe is so much easier is the one we have been willing to share with each of you on this day. That place is to put another in the front of you and keep yourself behind. These speaking words that we are willing to share with you carry the weight of truth to them. Place this in the front of your thinking minds, little ones.

"When you will place another in the front of you, this means that you will be telling yourself that all of those things that you will do and say, that it will be either for them or because of them. But in any case it will not be for yourself. This results in you living all of the seasons of your life path for this time that you are keeping another in the front of yourself. That all of these seasons you will go through will be done in a way that will not allow you to grow at all. While this other one is in the front of you, you will say to yourself that any and all effort that you will make, that all of the bad feelings of going through something, that all of this is for them…for someone else and not for you.

"When you will be in this place, little ones…when you will be in the place of placing another's wants and needs in the front of yours, then you will indeed be making a sacrifice. But it is not the kind of sacrifice that is in the service of others. It is more of a sacrifice that is giving up the potential growth for their being in the front of you. And this seems to be the path of least resistance in the beginning.

"However, as the passing of more seasons will come over you, there will be another observation that will come. It is an observation that results from those actions that you have taken. Those actions of having another fill the front of all that you will do and say. And, little ones, in the beginning, this will seem to be the path of least resistance. But as the seasons of the life path pass by there will be a great change in the way one will look at this process…this process of taking this path of the least resistance.

"When one will first set out on this path, there is a great amount of excitement over them. This excitement will come to them in the way of showing that they will not have so much to contend with. So many of those things they once felt they were doing battle with are no longer coming to them. And for this, they are very thankful. However, they have not yet learned to see that all of these things that had been coming to them…that they were events that had been designed by their own spirit…events that were being presented to them so that they could learn from…learn from once they would take the time and effort of working their way through the emotion that was being carried on the front of them. So in this beginning, they do not see that the one they have placed in the front of them is taking all of these events on their behalf…taking all of these events but gaining nothing from them other than the inconvenience of having them come to them. And, while this process is still new to them, they will only feel the goodness of not having to contend with all of those things they were trying to get away from before. They will begin to feel very accomplished in this beginning…accomplished in having been able to keep those things away from themselves that were bothering them.

"However, this time does not last very long. And in less than a handful of seasons, they find themselves holding a feeling of missing…a feeling of missing something but this something is un-named by them. So they will continue to look over themselves trying to see what it is that is making them feel this way. And the more they will look over themselves and all that is around them the less they will discover. The less they will discover what it is that they are feeling this missing for: the face of truth that is coming to them, little ones…this face of truth that is over the feeling of their missing something. It is that they are no longer participating in their own life path. They are no longer taking place in any of those events that have been coming to them. Those same events that are being offered to them to learn from are the same ones that are being offered to them to allow them to feel the life within them.

"You see, little ones, when one will place another in the front of them they will not have stopped living in this domain. Not in the same way as one would look at another crossing the great spirit waters. They will however stop their participation in those things that take place in this life path that allow them to feel as if they are a part of it. By placing another in the front of themselves, they have very effectively caused themselves to be taken out of the life path they had designed for themselves to travel. They have taken themselves out and put another in its place. Now, as some of those others had seen from their past seasons, this feeling of missing was a very real portion of this placing another before them. And, as the seasons passed them by, they came up with what they thought was a good solution for this missing.

"The solution to this was to have the one who was going through this missing have another place them in the front of their needs. And through this process, they would have many of those events that were meant for another come to them. In this way they would feel as if they were still a part of something and would not have to contend with those things that were in truth meant for them to do. So it is, little ones, that so many of those who travel on the path of the others will come to do these things, they will feel as if they are certainly going through those events that fill their life path. However, for all of their efforts and time that are spent on doing these things there is none of it that is benefiting them at all. As you will look over them, these others who are continuing to remain on their path and still in the sleep of illusion, you will see many of them going through many events and learning processes. However, not very many of them if any at all, are meant for them.

"All of those things they are going through are the events and lessons that are meant for another, meant for the one they have been placed in front of. And because they are not meant for them, they will not benefit from them at all. And, neither will the one they were originally meant for. So as you will look over the path these others are traveling, you will see great movement. You will see much action taking place on it. However, so little of it is of any value to those who are going through it, little ones. So little of all their efforts that they are willing to make while traveling on this path will ever be returned to them. And the reason for this is that none of those things they are working with are meant for them. These are not the lessons they are in need of. These are not the events their spirit needs to learn from; they are doing the work of another and another is doing the work of them. And with so much motion taking place, and with so little being accomplished, then this feeling of missing that was being concerned by them…this feeling of the missing no longer becomes the issue for them.

There is another step in their path that is soon to come for them. And that step is one that is called frustration. But it is a frustration that is not seen as they being the cause for it is seen in another way. But this way is not surprising because, as it is with all they will encounter, they are still seeing through the eyes of illusion. For they are still locked into this sleep of illusion. As they will continue with these efforts on this path of the others…this path that does not lead to anyplace but the great sadness…they will feel the weight of all their efforts…these efforts that have been made by them in confronting those events that had come to them…those events that were meant for another to learn from but are now coming to them because they had placed another in the front of them.

"While they will feel this great effort that they have been making on this path they are traveling. They will soon come to the place of seeing that for all they had been willing to do there is nothing coming back to them. And this will give to them a long face to wear. This will give to them a long face to wear because they can begin to see they have nothing in their hands for all of this work they have been performing. And still, there are so many more efforts that are being requested of them. As the next stage of this path comes to them, they will at first only feel the tiredness for all of it. However, as more seasons will pass by them and they will not see any relief for them – nor will they find anything being returned to them for all of this effort – they will begin to look around themselves to look for what it is that is causing this to take place for them.

"Now keep in the front of your thinking minds that they are still in their sleep of illusion. This same sleep that does not allow them to see things for what they are but only for what they would wish for them to be. And, as you will keep this in the front of your thinking minds, little ones, you will be better able to follow what we are willing to share with you next. When those who are traveling on this path of the others, this path that leads to the left, they will feel the great weight of tiredness fill them. And they will begin to become very frustrated by not having anything for themselves for all of their efforts. With this in the front of them, they will begin to look around for the cause of these kinds of things happening to them. However, the last place they will ever think of looking is within themselves.

"You must remember how we shared with both of you that this lack of willingness by them to look at themselves – that this is what had caused them to follow this path in the beginning. And, to think that they would now begin to look at themselves, well, this is not good thinking. They will look around themselves to gather some kind of information that would share with them why these things are happening to them. But they will not ever come to look at themselves - this place where all things begin and are completed.

"They will look around themselves and they will see those who they have placed in the front of themselves. These will be the ones who will come to the front of their eyes. And, these will be the ones on who they will now begin to focus their attention on. And these will be the ones who will ultimately be blamed for them feeling the way they do. Up to this place they have traveled, little ones. This place where there are many events that seem to be coming to them in spite of their having another to be placed in the front of them. They will begin to wonder why there is so much they are still feeling…why there are so many feelings of emptiness that are coming to them…with having taken such a great amount of effort in keeping themselves out of those places. With all of their thoughts of placing another in the front of themselves and their needs and desires, they will be looking for their reward for those actions they have taken…this reward that has been told to them will come when they will perform such an act of placing another in the front of themselves.

"However, when there will not come to them any such reward, when they will only feel the emptiness of no thing that is coming to them, they will begin to wonder if they have done something that is not entirely correct. And this kind of thinking will be perceived by the others as something that is very dangerous. Dangerous because if it is continued to be looked at, then this one who is caught in thinking in this way will eventually come to see themselves through their own light of truth. And this is something that those who travel on the path of the others – this is something that they do not want.

"Remember to keep in the front of your thinking minds, little ones, the difference that we have been willing to share with you…this difference that makes these two paths so different from each other. That the path of the others – this path that leads to the left – that this path is ruled by the wants of the body and fed by the emotions. Neither of them will travel to anyplace that holds value to the spirit. And that the path that leads to the right – this path that both of you have been prepared for – that this path of the spirit is led by the spirit and fed by the spirit. Now, with these things in the front of your thinking mind, perhaps you will be more likely to follow these speaking words that we are now willing to share with you.

"While these who will come to the place of wondering if there is something that they are not doing that is right for themselves – when they will come to wonder if they should look within themselves to find an answer, this will cause those who are in places of controlling on this path of the others to see them in a way that would bring a great disruption to all who are traveling with them. They will see them in this light because in truth that is what they are doing. In truth, these others who will not want them to look within themselves and begin to question those things they are doing, well, this too is true in their eyes as well. They will see this one or these who would attempt to go within themselves to look for answers and they will not see them so much as the enemy. But they would see them as someone who could possibly change the balance of those things they have come to believe in…as one who would enter their speaking words that would bring a great fear to the faces of those others who are traveling near them. To those who have a form of authority on this path of the others – this path that will lead to the left – they will see this potential action of the ones who are attempting to look within themselves as something that it is not…as something that will cause more harm than good to those who are on this path with them.

"However, as we have been willing to share with you before, little ones, those who will travel on this path of the others – they are all still trapped in the sleep of illusion. This sleep that does not allow them to see anything for what it is. And this case of the ones who are trying to look within themselves, this is not any different. They will see this effort of the ones who are looking within themselves as something that will bring many to the place of going through another frustration and another hurt. And, in the front of their thinking minds, this is something that must not be allowed to continue. As we have been willing to share with both of you, the ones who will make all of these efforts of stopping another from traveling within themselves - they will not be doing this out of anything but a caring for those things as they will see them. We cannot hold this so much against them because we have come to know that they cannot see…that they cannot see any of those things that are being presented to them for what they are. And this is because they are still sleeping in the great illusion. They have not passed those tests of the spirit that would have brought them into the light of their own spirit...into this light of their own spirit that would show to them this path they travel.

"While we may feel sad for them, little ones, we must not carry this feeling of sadness with us for very long. Otherwise, we will become in the same way that they are. We too will be caught in this illusion's path because we will have been trapped by this same emotion that holds them. But to them, to the ones who will try to save so many from having these feelings of badness they have gone with before, they will hold onto the believing that the only way of ending this kind of thing will be to hold all away from this place that leads to the within. To keep them from looking to those places where in their minds all of the problems and hurting reside. They will hold with them the believing that whenever they have been in a place that was too close to those things that are still held within them. That this was the only time when so many of the bad feelings would come to them. That this would be the time when they would no longer feel as if they were in control over those things that they would see and do.

"However, the sleep of illusion shares with all who are trapped within it that this concept of control is something that only they can culminate – that they are the only ones who are in control of all things. And when things go out of control, that this is a sign that they are not looking at them correctly. So it is, little ones, that when those who travel on this path of the others, when they will see one who is attempting to travel within themselves, they will see one who is about to make a great mistake. A mistake that will take them to a place of not only bringing themselves to a place where there is pain and suffering but also to a place where they will no longer hold a control over them...a control over those things that they would have them do and say. And, while they will see this begin to take place in another, there will be great efforts in sharing with them that this is not the correct thing for them to do. That by their going within themselves, they are only bringing onto them bad things...things that are only left into the imagination.

"They will make a great effort of telling them to believe them in those things they are sharing with them...those things that reality is only in those things that can be held, felt, or seen. And that all other things hold no reality for them at all. Nor do they have any business working with them. And looking at those things that have come to them, this one who was going to make the attempt of looking within themselves, they will hear those words that had come to them from the ones they have given a position of authority to on this path they are traveling. They will listen to the words that have been given to them and they will see that there may be something in them. That the reason they are willing to listen to them is their own fear of the unknown.

"Remember, little ones, when you will ever see anything that will be seen by you as fear, do not run from it. Stand strong with your spirit and look at it for what it is bringing to you. And the way this will take place is when you will have within you the strength of your own spirit that will allow you to see through the emotion that is being carried on the front of it. When you will look through the emotion of all things then is when you will see the face of truth come to you. This face of truth that will show you the lesson you need to learn from.

"However, when the ones who are still trapped within this sleep of illusion, the ones who are continuing to travel on the path of the others, they will not see those things in the same way. To them, just the thought of hurting or being in a position of not having control on those things they will do, will be enough to cause them to see a great face of fear for themselves. And, it is from this face of fear that they will react to those things that have been told to them by the ones who are near them. And they will listen in a way that they will convince themselves that this is indeed their face of truth. Then they will come to believe in it. So it is when they will begin to feel this spirit of loneliness come to them. When they will feel the surprise that will fill them from having done what they had been told and still having these feelings come over them. They will begin to look over themselves and first try to see what is taking place…taking place within them. But that will be the time when they will begin to hear those speaking words of the others come to them. Those speaking words that we have been willing to share with you that tell them to look within themselves is not the right thing to do.

"That it is not the right thing to do because they will only find those things they are trying to keep away from…those things that will bring to them bad feelings and faces of fear. And without the needed levels of understanding that will only come to one who is willing to place themselves first in all things, they will not see anything different from what they had experienced earlier. It is because they do not have this level of understanding for themselves and those things that are near them that they will do this, little ones. And it is from this lack of understanding that they will only see the face of fear on all things that will be presented to them. They will not see any other face because for them there is none. And it is from their remembering and continuing to see these faces of fear come to them that they will make all of their efforts in hiding from them. But in truth, little ones, they are only hiding from themselves. For those lessons that are being presented to them are from their own spirit. They are those things that they still have holes within themselves for. And it is from those holes that they have that they feel so much from these events that are being presented to them.

"So, as they will listen to the voices of the others, the ones who will tell them that it is of no avail to look within themselves, they will first feel as if they are being helped by those shared words from them. They will first feel as if they are correct and when they will have this first feeling they will try to convince themselves that nothing at all is their fault…that nothing is their fault but it is the failing of another. And, this is where they will begin to look on the face of the one we have shared with both of you before. This is where they will find the face that will always come to those who will place another in the front of them. You see, little ones, when they will listen to the voices of those who are near them, the ones who they have come to believe in and listen to, they will hold onto a false believing within themselves. This believing comes to them when they will accept this concept that they have been told of…this concept that what they are feeling is not their fault as well as the one that has been told to them that tells them there is nothing to be gained by looking within themselves. For there is nothing to be found there nothing at all except for the feelings of fear and badness.

"However, as both of you have been prepared with from those teachings of Grandfather and Two Bears, you know that this is not true. You have been prepared to see through this emotion that these others have been caught up in. This emotion that comes to them from the sleep of illusion they are still caught up in. So they will look around themselves to try and find the one who is responsible for making them feel so bad. The one or ones who are responsible for making them feel this spirit of loneliness that has come to them in a filling way. And, when they will look around, who do you think their eyes will first fall on? They will fall on those they have been placing in the front of themselves. The ones who they were trying to do the right thing for.

"And, when their eyes that they are born with fall on them, they will immediately feel a great anger for them. And this anger will come to them because they will see them as one or ones who have not kept up their end of the bargain. You see, little ones, when they first placed these others in the front of them, it was done in a way that was false to begin with. Even though they were believing in those things that were told to them…that to place another in the front of all your needs and wants was a good thing to do. That by doing this, they were affirming a place for themselves in the after life of their own kind. What they have done is as far from the truth as one can possibly be. What they have done is like hiring another to do your own work for you. And, when you find that all of this work is not being done then you will feel as if you have been let down greatly. And this feeling of being disappointed by them is great. It is so great that when they will see them, when they will see them at this time when they are looking for another to place this blame on, they will only see them as the ones who have been hurting them. They will see that for all they have done for them, for all they have given of themselves for them, that this has not worked. And this is what gives a great fire to the anger that is rising within them.

"So, with the combined feelings of loneness and this feeling that someone else is responsible for them feeling these things, they will center all of this on the one or ones they once felt a great closeness for. They will not accept any of the responsibility for themselves. And this is where they will center all of their emotions and bad feelings onto these who they had placed before themselves. And when this will take place we tell you that it will complete another circle…a circle that is only to be found on this path of the others. And it is a circle that is to be found when one will allow themselves to be caught up in the emotion of those things that will come to them.

"Remember what you have been prepared with, little ones. Keep it well in the front of your thinking minds and you will not fall into this trap. Remember that for every lesson and for every offering that will be presented to you, that on the front of it is a great space. And this space is filled with emotion. For those who cannot see this they are destined to remain caught up in it. They are destined to remain in those small circles that we have been willing to share with you. And they are destined to be very much alone with all of their fears and uncertainties. For them there is no other path they could follow. To them this is the path to their reality. So it is, little ones, when they will come to listen to those things that will come to them…those things that will tell them that there are none of these feelings that are coming to them that are their fault. They will always follow this path…this path that we have been willing to share with you. Their destiny is one that will be without many long feelings of truth. Their destiny will be one of continually reaching and grabbing for all of those things that they will see…those things that they will see will always be in the way that they see them when they are held by another.

"You see while they are caught up in this circle of the great illusion, this great illusion that will come to them in the face of emotion, they will continually be caught up in looking at all those things another will have with them. They will not ever be able to look at themselves to this place that is within them where all of their treasures lie. And as it is with all things, when any will be in a place of not feeling good with themselves about those things that another will have, they will look much better to them than those things they hold. And they will do all they can to get them anything. This is what has taken place with the arrivals of the new skins. Those who had come to our lands and have continually grabbed all they could see from our people. Their path is one of great sadness as well, little ones. It is one of a great sadness but it will not be fully seen until they have reached the end of their seasons in this domain of the Earth Mother's. When they will be standing in the waiting place…this waiting place that is across the great spirit waters. They will be confronted with all of the members of their spirit family and they will ask them why they bring nothing back from this domain with them. They will tell them that they were given many opportunities to assist the Earth Mother and all of her children. And they had all of those talents that would have allowed them to do this. And they will have one question on the front of their thinking minds. Why?!

"When they will try to answer their spirit family – when they will try to tell them why their arms and hands are empty from any blessings from this domain – they will find no answers to give them. No answers except that they did not make the effort of looking within themselves for those truths. For those truths that their spirit was more than willing to share with them. And this will give to them a great sadness. It is a sadness that comes to them when they will see how wasted their time in this domain had been. And how they had not only let down their own spirit family…this spirit family who had been trying to get them to see those things that were being offered to them for what they were but they will feel as if they let themselves down greatly. But now it is too late to do anything about it…too late now. But in order to make up for this they will have to return to this domain. And before they will be allowed to do this, the Earth Mother will have many requirements for them to fulfill…requirements that will not be easy for them. But those requirements will have to be done by them before she will allow them to enter once again…to enter and hopefully make up for all that they had missed the first time.

"Now, little ones, when you will come back with us to the place where another will place one in the front of them. Keep in the front of your thinking minds of something like a car being built. We have seen this thing they call the assembly line. This place where there are many people who have one specific thing to add to this car as it will pass them by. And, when all of those thing that need to be done, when they are all done in the proper place and the proper time, there will be a good car sitting at the end of this assembly line. And when another will look on it they will have a good face to wear for all of the work that was needed was done and the result is something that was desired. Now, when you will think of how many are used to listening and believing in those words from the others, those words they have been telling them for many generations that it is the best and most noble thing to place another in the front of all your needs and desires, then we can share with you what takes place in the picture form of the assembly line.

"Let us say, Speaking Wind, that you hold a specific function of placing a tire on one side of the car and that Cheeway has the function of placing the steering wheel on. And let us say that both of you are in places that are different from the others…those others who also have their specific function of placing these things on the car as it will pass by them. Now let us say that you have been willing to place Cheeway in the front of you…in the front of you for all of those things that you hold a need for and that Cheeway has placed another in the front of him and so on and so on until all of those members of the assembly line have done this thing. Now, when you have placed Cheeway in the front of you and Cheeway has placed another in the front of him, and, when all of the others have placed another in the front of themselves, then what will correspond to this will be that this piece of the car that you hold…this piece will be placed into the place where another has been assigned.

"By placing your piece of the car in a place where another's should have been is the same thing in a more picture way of sharing with both of you what will take place by placing another in the front of you for all things. Now, when you will carry this down to the rest of the assembly line…think of what this car will look like when it is finished. Think of what it will look like when it comes with your tire in the place of Cheeway's steering wheel and Cheeway's steering wheel in the place of someone else's part.

"Would you be willing to buy this? We do not think you would be willing to do this, little ones. But this is the same concept that many who have been traveling in this domain of the Earth Mother's are returning to the waiting place. This is how they are looking. Basically, this is what they are doing when they will place another in the front of themselves. They have given up on accepting those events that are coming into their own life path. And they have given this responsibility to another to work through. And this other has given up their own responsibility of working through their own events and has passed them on to another.

"In the end, little ones, in the end when all of their seasons have been completed in this domain, they will have the feeling of being put through many events for their seasons. But for all of their work there was nothing accomplished nor learned. There was nothing accomplished or learned because they were not doing the work that they needed from their own spirit. They were busying themselves with doing the work of another. Of one who had nothing at all to do with the advancement of their spirit and eventually to learn who and what they were. So they leave this domain in the same way as they had entered it. They leave with the same need for all of those lessons they entered here to learn. And we tell both of you that this is not a good thing.

"Now, when you will place yourself first in all things that you will do and say, when you will do this you are not being selfish nor are you being unfair to any other. What you are doing is being true to yourself and you will be in a place of learning to work through all of those events that are being offered to you…those events that have been designed by your spirit and the Earth Mother when you were sitting in council with her asking for entry into this domain. Keep in the front of your thinking minds, little ones, that when an event will come to you, any of these events, that there will always be presented to each of you the forefront of emotion. And, this emotion comes to you as a forerunner of the lesson that is being offered to you."

Chapter 14

▼

LESSONS FROM THE EMOTION

This one called Calling Thunder took a few moments to look over the faces that Cheeway and I were wearing. This was not an unfamiliar process to either of us. And this was not familiar to either of us because we had become so used to Grandfather and Two Bears doing this in those many seasons of our past with them. However, from this looking that was coming over each of us there seemed to be something much different coming to us from it. It was as if we were standing in a great crowd of others of our people and they were looking on us. Looking for those things they had been willing to share with us and to see where they would need to touch our own spirit next…where to touch those places that needed touching… those places where we would be in a place of seeing with more clarity those things that were still to be shared with us.

As I caught the face of my best friend, Cheeway, out of the corner of my eyes, I could see that he too was feeling this same thing as I was…that he too was being tapped on the spirit for this learning. And, there was another thing that I could see in this face that Cheeway had placed over himself. It was the lack of concern for his time that was remaining with the Earth Mother. The colors of his weight were not showing to me that this was a cause of great concern for him any longer. And for this I was receiving the comfort that I needed…this comfort that was sharing with me that my friend would be all right now.

"Emotion by itself, little ones, has nothing at all to teach anyone," Calling Thunder began once again. "It is much like having a fire to cook on but not having any of the food to prepare. However, from those things that we have been allowed to see in this domain of the Earth Mother's, we will share with you that there is indeed a great lesson to be learned from the emotion that will always be carried in the front of each event that will come to you.

"This emotion that will show the face of truth to those things that will be presented on each of your life paths. Keep this in the front of your thinking minds, little ones. Keep with you while we will be willing to share that there is a great difference between the two paths…these two paths that we have been willing to share with you before. These same two paths that have been shared with you before by the speaking words of Grandfather and Two Bears…as well as from the teachings of the silent brotherhood.

"And, it is from both of these paths that we will share what this face of emotion will share with all…share with all who are traveling in this domain of the Earth Mother's. The two paths that we will share with both of you from are the path that leads to the left…this path that is led by the body and fed by the emotions; and, the path that leads to the right…this path that is led by the spirit and fed by the spirit as well.

"Now, when the event will come to you, little ones, it does not always have to be one that is great in nature. It can be as small as stubbing your toe on the end of the table. However, realize that for any event that will be offered to you there will be a price you will have to pay for its lesson…a price that will be paid for this lesson that is being offered to you and this path you have been willing to travel.

"Remember to keep in the front of your thinking minds that there are many truths to be found on this path of the spirit. And many of these truths will be re-reminded to both of you by the spirits of the flame. However, we will come back to this in time. But for now, remember them.

"We have been in this domain for many generations, little ones. And we have been in the places that are on both sides of the great doorway…this great doorway that keeps separate the side that we are now on from the side where both of you happen to be now.

"And, from those things that we have seen, we will share with both of you that many of the same laws that have been set into motion for you by the Earth Mother will also apply to us as well. This is the speaking words of truth because those things that she has set into motion have come to her from the Great Spirit. And, the Great Spirit's laws are for all things and all places.

"So keep in the front of your thinking minds that if you will consider one of these great truths or laws to be unfair, if you will see them with this kind of seeing while you are still traveling in this domain of hers, realize that this has come to you by not coming to a place of understanding for yourself and those things that are around you.

"And, when you will not have the sufficient levels of understanding for yourself then there will not be much that will come to you with the seeing of clarity for it. Many who will come to this place, have been holding onto the believing that once they will leave this domain of the Earth Mother's, this domain that they will have come to consider to be unfair, that they will no longer have to put up with these things that they see as unfair when they will leave.

"However, when they will come to leave this domain that is the Earth Mother's, and they will not have attained the levels of understanding they will need to see those same laws on this side for what they are, then when they will arrive at the waiting place, they will see how good the Earth Mother was to them. They will come to find that these same laws are the same on this side but there is not the same easiness here as the Earth Mother allows there.

"So when you will come to see an event that will come to you, little ones, an event that will come to you covered with the emotion of illusion over it, come to know that those things you will need to do while you travel with the Earth Mother will assist you greatly. It is by coming to the place of understanding those things that will take place that will give to you the clarity of seeing that is needed…this clarity of seeing that will also assist you greatly on this side of the great spirit waters.

"Now, when one will have an event come to them, they will first encounter the emotion of illusion that covers it first. And whether this one is on the path that leads to the right or if they are on the path that leads to the left they will always have to work their own way through this emotion of the illusion before they will be allowed to see the face of truth…this face of truth that is being offered to them by this lesson.

"We will tell you that this emotion that is covering this event is from the great sleep of illusion because for the ones who are traveling on the path of the others, this path that has no sight of the path of the spirit, for them they will only see this emotion that covers this event and they will see it from their sleeping eyes of illusion.

"Keep in the front of your thinking minds that when one is trapped inside of the sleep of illusion, that while they are there, there is not any other way of seeing other than seeing all things for what they would wish for them to be. And, while they are seeing in this way they cannot see that there is a great offering coming to them…an offering that is coming to them but with a price to pay. And this price that is being asked of them to pay is to do their own work and get through the face of the emotion so they will be able to see what it is that is now being offered to them.

"However, for these sleeping ones, they will not ever come to the place of seeing this event or any others for what they are. And it is because of their sleep in the illusion…this sleep that does not allow them to receive the understanding that they will need to see otherwise…that they will continue to see all things for what they would like them to be."

"And as they will continue to use these eyes of the illusion, their entire life path will pass them by. Pass them by and they will find at the end of it that they have learned nothing at all of themselves or any of those things they had come here to learn.

"However, when they will see this event come to them, it is because they do not have the understanding within themselves to see this as a great opportunity that is being offered to them. Instead, they will only see this event come to them as something that will give them harm or hurt in some way.

"So, when they will have these events come to them, these events that come to them in many ways they will either run from them or turn and fight them, they will do these things in hopes that if they will do so they will go away from them. Then they will not have to deal with them anymore. And, little ones, this kind of thinking only comes to one from the spirit of illusion. This same spirit that holds all of us in his sleep until we can learn how to wake ourselves.

"Think of it in this way. For one who is traveling on this path of the others, this path that is leading to the left, let us say that an event has come to them…an event that will be given a face by us…a face so that you will be better able to see what it is we are sharing with you. Let us say that you are still a small child and there is a bully at the school you attend. There are many days that this bully will pick on you and make you do things that you would not want to. Now this poses a problem for you. One that seems to be larger than you are. So, for what it is worth, you will take this problem home to share it with your parents.

"When you begin to tell your parents about this bully at the school. They both look at you and ask you what you would want them to do about it. And, amid all of the frustration that fills you, you tell them that you do not know and that is the reason you have come to them. It is because your parents do not see this issue through your eyes…those eyes that you have been looking at it with. They smile at you and say that all bullies are just a bunch of big babies. That all you will have to do is to hit them one good one and that will be the end of it. Looking at them, you as this small child do not have any other frame of reference than to believe in those things they have been willing to share with you. And in some kind of a state of stupor, you smile back at them and go off to your room…to your room where you will think over those things that you have been told.

"However, when you will get into your room, you come face to face with the stark reality of things at the school and this bully. This person is much bigger than you are and you wonder if all those things your parents have told you. You wonder if just by hitting them one good one they will come back on you and beat you up. As this night of worry progresses, you do not find any solitude from those kinds of thoughts. Even those things that you have used to play with to take your mind off of those things that weigh you down do not work. So, spending a restless night in your bed, the morning finally comes. And it comes without an answer that is suitable to you. An answer that will share with you what you are risking for trying to hit this bully one good one and then they will leave you alone.

"At the morning meal, your parents reaffirm to you that those things they have been willing to share that they are true and all you have to do is to hit this bully very hard and stand your ground. So, for lack of anything else to do and with no other experiences to draw from, you look at both of them showing to you a smile over their faces. And, you believe in them and believe in this smiling face they have put on for you and decide that they are right…that there is not going to be anything that will happen to you for hitting this school bully. As you are traveling on your way to the school, you continue to run through all of those events that will happen…those events that will take place based on the good advice that your parents have told you about. You see yourself hitting this bully in the school and then you see him falling down and crying out loud. This makes you very happy with yourself from this thing that you have seen, this vision of things that should happen, so you continue to gain in your courage all the way there.

"Finally, you reach the school ground. And, when you do, there he is. There is the bully and he is talking to another smaller kid. With all of the strength that has been building up in you, all of this courage that has come to you from seeing those events the way you would like for them to be you rush over to the place where the bully is standing. You yell out his name and tell him what you think of him. And, just after you have finished this announcement, you hit him. However, after you hit him, things do not work out the way you have seen them – not at all. Instead of falling down on the ground and crying, the bully looks at you and smiles. This is the kind of smile that tells you that you had your shot and that now it is time for his. With such a surprised look over your face you see his big hand meet with your face. And when you finally see it meet you that is the last thing you remember.

"Everything blacks out and you remember nothing more until you see one of the teachers standing over you and shaking you by the shoulder. Seeing that you are not in very good shape, the school decides to send you home. And when you reach home your parents look very surprised at the way you look. The teacher who has brought you home explains to them what had happened and your parents very quickly begin to yell at the teacher. To yell at this one who had been so kind in bringing you home… this one who was not even around to intervene in the first place. Looking at your parents, you begin to wonder why they are yelling at this teacher when it was their own advice that you were following. But, not wanting to interrupt them, you wait to say anything until the teacher leaves.

"Finally, when your parents ask you if you are all right and they see that you will not die, they assure you that this will not happen anymore and they say they are sending you to another school. To one that will not allow bullies to do such things. And this is agreeable to you because you had heard one of the kids at the school say this bully was really going to make you pay for what you had done to him.

"All of this is the kind of lesson we are speaking of when we speak about the emotions, little ones. The parents have not yet learned to see through their own emotions sufficiently to share with the child what has come to them. And, the child, only having his parents to follow, have not seen anything other than what they have shown to him. The parents feel the pain of this emotion that they are feeling when they see the hurt that has come to their son. And the son feels the best way to get out of any situation is to go away from it.

"In both cases, little ones, the parents are running away from a situation with the belief that if they will not deal with it, if they will not work with it, then it will go away on its own. And, the child learns that this is a very workable lesson to hold onto. And, when the time will come to him when even greater lessons will come to him then he will do the same thing. Then he will have the believing that if he will ignore or run away from those events that are coming to him, those same events that are being presented to him so he may learn from them, then he will avoid any more pain and suffering in his life path.

"However, as we have been willing to share with both of you, these are the eyes that see on the path of the others. This path that travels to the left. Now, let us look at this same event as it would be seen from the path that leads to the right…the path that leads to the spirit. As we will share with you those same things that happened before, we will begin with the place where the child comes home to his parents and shares with them what had taken place at the school. And, as he will share with them those events, they will sit down with him and begin to share those same kinds of events they too had gone through when they were his age.

"You see, little ones, when one will travel on the path of the spirit, there is no shame in being human and for making what appeared to be mistakes when one is trying to achieve a decision for himself…these parents who are traveling on the path of the spirit…this path that leads to the right. They will understand that this child they have been given to raise does not have an understanding for those things that have come to him. And, holding this understanding in the front of their thinking minds, they will share with him that they too have had this kind of experience…this kind of experience with a bully of their own.

"However, the difference in their sharing with this child of theirs, and the sharing that was done by the parents who were traveling on the path that leads to the left, these parents will show themselves in all the light of truth they can find. What this means is this. They will show themselves as the strong and weak portion of themselves. They will not be afraid of sharing with this child that they too were afraid and that they too did not know what to do. They will also share with this child that they do not always know the correct way to make a decision. And this is one of those times. But they will be willing to share with their own face of truth those things that they did with their bullies and what happened to them. They will be willing to share the frustration and the hurting they went through with him and they will share with him that there were a good many lessons they had gained from this experience as well.

"While they will share with this child they have been given the opportunity of raising that there is no answer that they will be able to give to him, they will also say that they will share, in detail, all of those things they had experienced. They will share this with him so they can come to their own conclusion. They will also share with him that this is a problem that only they can come to decide on…to reach a decision that will allow them to take on the responsibility of their own actions.

"However, with this knowing that will be shared from these parents. There will also come another knowing. And, it is a knowing that will assist them greatly. Not only in the times that are on them now but for all of those seasons that are yet to be borne to them. These parents will present this young one with a great gift. And this is a gift of explaining to him what the true definition is of a friend or one who will offer one assistance.

"They will share with him that for one who will have your own best interests in the front of their thinking minds – that there will be a mark to them. And this mark is in the knowing that they will stand next to you. That they will stand strong next to you but they will also give to you the freedom of working your own way through your problems. That this freedom is very necessary in order for there to be growth.

"To do anything else this would be to stop one's growth on their path. This would stop their growth because to do anything different would mean that they would be willing to do your work for you. And, this is not a good thing. So this small one will begin to see the value of knowing that a true friend to them will be one who will stand strong next to you while you are working your way through many events that will come into your life path…and, this knowing that will over time grow into understanding. It will then give to this young one the wisdom that is needed…this wisdom that will come to him only when the path of the spirit is followed. Then they too will be in the place of passing this on to another. And this knowl-edge that will be passed on to another will be by their actions as well as deeds and speaking words.

"It is only when one will have the understanding for those things of knowing that this will be seen, little ones. And this is the face of truth that is being carried on our speaking words. Only when you will have an understanding of those things that have been offered to you to learn from will you be allowed to live them. And as you will live them there will come to you the wisdom that will allow you to see how to share them with oth-ers.

"The difference from this situation that we have been willing to share with you and the one of the parents who are traveling on the path of the others, is that they are not willing to live their truths. They are not willing to do this because there is no truth in their believings to live. And without this living of those things that you will come to know and believe in, little ones, there will not ever be a wisdom that will come to you...a wisdom that will be seen and felt by those who are close to you.

"Until this wisdom will come to you, others will only have the sounds of the words you will tell to them. They will not have anything more because there is nothing more to them. It is only when one will be allowed to live those things they believe in will they be seen for what and who they are in truth. And those things they will have been willing to share with others – those things will be seen as truth...a truth that will not wash away with the passing of the seasons.

"Now, these parents who have been traveling on the path that leads to the right...this path of the spirit...they will also confront their child with the recognition that this problem of theirs will not go away. That if it is not handled in this day that is with them, that it will ultimately have to be confronted in some other time or in some other place.

"They will also explain to their child that there is no running away from this problem...that there is no running away or hiding from it. This is not possible because even if they were to move away from this school that when they would go into another one there would be another bully that would confront them. And there would be that same problem looking at them once again. They will explain to him that this takes place because this bully is not as he seems to them at this place in their seasons of the life path they are traveling.

"They will share with him that this bully is not to be looked at in a way that would give to them the face of another person. But this is an event that has been presented to them. And it is to be looked at as an event. An event that has been presented to them to look at with the face of receiving something to learn from…as having something for them that is needed by their spirit within them.

"They will further explain to their child that this bully has not come to them as a person. That they have come to him as an event to learn from. And the one thing they must come to the place of understanding for is what this lesson is trying to teach to them.

"As they will continue with their explanation to them, the parents will share with them that when one will continue to travel through this domain that is the Earth Mother's, that all of those things that they are…that those things will become like a magnet to others — *to those who are experiencing the same things as they are.* For those things that they will have learned from…those things they are working their way through to understand from…that those who will have a need of those qualities in their own life path…then they will be drawn to them.

"And this situation of the bully is not any different from all of this. The parents will share with their children that there is something within the child…something that has been calling to this bully that has allowed him to be attracted to the child. And it is this something that has come to the child that the bully needs to see. And this need to look at this part of the child, whatever this part of the child is, is what has caused this bully to single them out among all of the other children.

"That this bully has come to them because he has responded to a call *they have been making.* And, if they do not want to have other bullies come to them, then it is up to them to look within themselves to see what it was that was making this calling for such an event come to them in the first place. They will also share with this child of theirs that unless they will make the efforts of looking for whatever this is that is calling this kind of an event to them to learn from — if they are not willing to go within and perform the work that is needed…this work that is needed to come to the place of understanding for this — that there will always be another bully attracted to them. That there will always be another of these kinds of events that will come to them no matter where they will go and no matter what they will do.

"For those parents who are traveling on the path of the spirit, they will see the great need of sharing this kind of understanding with their child. They will see the great need for him coming to the place of understanding for this kind of learning because they will also have come to understand what it will mean if there is not learning gained from all events that will be presented to them. They will share with this child of theirs that this life path is much like a magnet for lessons that are needed...like an attraction to all things that we have a need to learn from. And until we will come to know ourselves better we will not see the value in learning from those events that will be presented to us. That until we will be willing to learn from them, and, to have an understanding from them, then we will continue to attract all things to us that are not desirable at all. We will continue to call on those things that are needed by us to learn from.

"They will share with this child of theirs all of those things that are coming to them. They are doing so not out of any kind of punishment. For this is not the truth to their being. They are coming to you out of love and the need for your growth. When one will travel on the path of the spirit, little ones, there will be great amounts of sharing and understanding...this understanding that will come from this willingness of sharing those things that have come to you from another.

"And, this is what has been taking place from this situation that we have been willing to expand on with you, little ones, this situation that has come from looking at one situation from two sides...from the side of the ones who will travel on the path of the others as well as from the ones who will travel on the path of the spirit.

"Now, there is another part of this sharing that we still see a need in the both of you. And this is the need that comes from understanding that from these emotions that are all around the event or lesson that has been presented to you there is a great lesson to be learned from them as well. A great lesson that is within these emotions if one will not become trapped inside of them, that is.

"You see, little ones, when one will first see this emotion that is shrouded over the offering, over this offering of an event that is coming to you, there will be a reaction that will come to them. *And this reaction holds the clue for you to use.* A clue in how you will be able to work your way through these emotions and come to learn from the event that is being offered to you.

"Now, the emotions are felt in the same way regardless of the path one will travel. And to this place nothing varies. However, what will change is this. The ones who are traveling on the path of the others, this path that is led by the body and fed by the emotions, they will continue to be caught up in these emotions. And, all of their efforts will be in a small circle of events that will come to them…a small circle of events that will take them nowhere. At least, nowhere they would wish to travel.

"And when these others will get caught up in those emotions that will come to them, they will do so at the expense of missing out on the lesson that is being presented to them…this lesson that is needed by their own spirit that will allow them to advance to the next higher place.

They will remain caught up in these emotions, because to them, this is what has been told to them what reality is. And so they will continue to hold onto those caught up feelings of themselves inside of those emotions that will come to them. They will remain caught up in them because they have not yet learned to look past them…to look past them and see the face of lesson that is being presented to them to learn from.

"You see, little ones, one of the great laws that has been set into motion by the Great Spirit is this. For all those things that will be needed by your spirit, those things that are needed to learn from, that until you will be willing to accept, learn, and understand from them, you will be destined to repeat them. And this repetition will be done even as new offerings and lessons will be presented to you.

"For this kind of learning that will be presented to your spirit, there is no looking away. For those things that you do not wish to learn from, they will continue to follow you all the way back across the great spirit waters and even into the waiting place. They have been designed for you to learn from. And for this, there is not any other choice that is given to you. No other choice except in the amount of time that you will be willing to carry this baggage with you.

"Keep in the front of your thinking minds, little ones, the teachings that have been shared with you from those speaking words of Grandfather and

Two Bears. They allowed you to see the many circles that are given to all who will enter this domain. And it is from these circles that we have come to see how the Great Spirit has designed all lessons that will come to us.

"As we begin in this domain of the Earth Mother's, little ones, we do so completely immersed in the sleep of illusion. And it is this sleep that keeps us in the place of wondering if life will ever move forward when we are of short seasons with the Earth Mother. When we will have reached this place of the short seasons, we will continually be asking why time takes so long to pass us by. And, why does it always seem to take so long for tomorrow to come to us.

"However, when one is a small child of these short seasons, well, they are expected to act in this way. And, there is none who would come to expect anything else. But the reason for this expectation has been forgotten by many, little ones. And this too is another of the parts of the face of lesson that the emotion will bring to us. When the small child is of short season, they are so immersed in the sleep of illusion that for them there really is no time. And it is from this frame of reference that we make this point for both of you to learn from.

"As the child will grow, they will be expected to complete this first circle of their life path. This will mean that they will be expected to gain in their levels of understanding for all of those things they have had presented to them…all of those things that have come to them in the form of events. And, it is the same with them as it is with all who have entered this domain of the Earth Mother's. For them, these events will be covered with the face of emotion as well.

"But many who will look on their face as they will encounter these emotions that will come to them, these same emotions that will shroud this lesson that is coming for them to learn from, they will not see the same kind of face over them as the one that will come to them. They will not see the face of fear or the face of hurt or the face of trying to run away from these events because of a fear from those things we call the forerunner of the lesson — this place called the emotion.

"And, it is from this face they will continue to see on the children that they will be in a place of wishing they too were still in this place…in this place where they would not feel the things from those emotions that they do. How like it is to see those who continue to travel the path of the others want to regain those seasons…those seasons of their own life path when they also reacted to those events and the emotions they brought to them just like the young ones do now.

"Many of them will even go so far as to want this so much that they will begin to wear this face…this same face that they once wore when they were young. However, from what we have been willing to share with both of you, these examples of what so many are willing to do, keep in the front of your thinking mind that this is just another effort of not having to work with those things that are being presented to so many. This is another means of hiding from themselves.

"And, because of this kind of hiding, little ones, those who will do this… those who will continue to hide behind many things. They will not ever complete one circle of their life path. One circle out of so many that all must successfully pass through before they will come to a successful conclusion. Remember, little ones, remember that all things that are within this domain that is the Earth Mother's, that all of them are based on the circle. And, it is this circle that will keep bringing you back to the place you were before if you will not make the effort of learning from those things that had been presented to you…those things that you have a great need to learn from.

"However, as we have been willing to share with the both of you, there are not ever any times or events that will come to you as a punishment. And, because all of these great laws that have been set into motion in this domain, because all of them are such a natural occurrence to the spirit who is within you, there is not ever a feeling of bad associated with them. This only comes to you from the body part…this part that has been willing to carry your spirit around for you.

"So it becomes a mark of those who are still sleeping, little ones, when they will wish to become as they were in those past seasons. It is this mark of the illusion that is continuing to lull them into seeing things not for what they are but for what they would wish for them to be. And it is this same falseness of the illusion that allows them to believe that all things are all right even when they are so busy trying to hide from themselves and all of those things that are being presented to them.

"Now, little ones, when one will travel on this path of the spirit, this path that leads to the right, they will also see those events that will come to them. Those same kinds of events that come to all who are here and they too will be covered with the great emotions that are all around them.

"However, the difference from the way this is seen by the ones who continue to travel on the path of the others and the ones who will travel on the path of the spirit is this. The ones who will travel on the path of the spirit will see this emotion, that is being carried in the front of the lesson being offered, as something of a test for them…as a kind of test that will be presented to them as a review of all those other events that had been offered…all of those other events that had come to them in those seasons that have since passed by them.

"For them, little ones, they will see them as a review of those things that they have not yet learned from. And to see this take place in the life path of any is truly a great blessing…to observe a wonderful path that is blessed greatly by their actions as they continue to advance their spirit in all they will come to do here.

"As you both have the knowing, little ones, that for those who will travel on the path of the spirit, the ones who are willing to make their own efforts for all things they will come to see and understand, that they will see the wonderful blessings that are continually being offered to them.

"However, for them to see this time in their life path, they will first have to go through many tests. And it is from those tests that they will see the benefit of working their way past the emotions of all events that will be presented to them…those same events that will be presented to them so they may advance their spirit to the next higher place.

"It is from this working their way through those emotions that are carried on the front of all events that they will have come to see the great advantage of making their own efforts in working their way through them… those emotions that may at first come to them as something that is causing them to hurt or feel the pain of loss.

"However, with the passing of more and more seasons on their life path, and with the reassurance of seeing the blessings that have been coming to them from doing these things – these things that we have been willing to share with you of working their way through those events and not running or hiding from them – they have come to know that this is the correct path for them to travel.

"From this path that they have willingly taken unto themselves, they will see that to run or hide from these events, they are in truth running or hiding from themselves and one of the great truths that has been taught from the silent brotherhood is that this is not possible...that you cannot run or hide from those things that are of yourself.

"And with this in the front of their thinking minds, they will stand strong with their spirit. They will stand strong with their spirit and look onto the face of each of these events that will be presented to them...each of these events that has come to them to share a learning with their spirit. And in the front of each of their thinking minds, little ones, is the face of truth for each of them. This face of truth that shares with them that all that will be presented to them in this life path – that for each event, each person and each situation that will come to them – that each of them has been designed specifically for them and no other will possess the ability of seeing this. Not in the way that it was meant to be seen.

"So, as they will stand and face these events, little ones, they will come to know that just behind each of these emotions that will come to them... these emotions that are always on the front of these lessons...that once behind them they will find something that will be of a great value to them and the spirit who is them from within. When they will have an emotion come to them, one that will cause them to feel something that is not liked, then they will hold onto the knowing that this feeling from the emotion that has come to them...that this is not anything that has come to them in a way of punishment for something wrong they have done. For any to think in this way is the furthest from any of the great truths that one can come to.

"They will hold the knowing and believing that the reason they have been feeling this badness from the emotion...the badness from the emotion that is on the front of the event that has come to them...that this reason lies within them. And, it has nothing at all to do with a payment of any kind for something they have done whether it be good, bad, or indifferent. They will be given the same understanding that was given to the ancient ones when they too were here in this domain of the Earth Mother's. They will be shown that for all of those things that they will ever come to feel from the emotions – and we say to each of you that this emotion comes to you from all things – that the reason they are feeling what they are feeling is because of a similar lesson that had been offered to you in those seasons of your past…a lesson that you did not take the time to work your way through the emotion of it and had turned away from it.

"It was when you had turned away from this lesson of offering, this event that had been presented to you, this is what had caused you to have a hole in your life path…a hole that will remain like an open sore until you have been willing to take the time to correct it. Keep in the front of your thinking minds, little ones, that for all things that will come to you in this life path, there will not ever be any that will be presented to you out of a punishment. And, when you will have this firmly embedded within you, then there will be no chance of ever slipping away from these things we are now willing to share with the both of you.

"So it is that when there is a hole within you, this hole does not become obvious to the one who is carrying it around with him. However, there is a danger in keeping it with you. And this danger comes to all of us because until we can come to the place of mending it or them, we will be trapped into this small circle that we are traveling around in. And, as it is with all circles, there is a lot of activity but there is no forward motion.

"To the ones who are still trapped in their sleep of illusion, the ones who are continuing to travel on the path of the others, this is all they will require. For them, any action at all gives to them the false feeling of forward movement. However, for the ones who will travel on the path of the spirit, they will know that they are not moving in a forward direction and they will ask for assistance…this assistance of the ones who have come to help them as well as the ancient ones, too. On the path of the others, this path that is led by the body and fed by the emotions, are only a very few circles there. So it becomes not as important to continue getting out of one and advancing to the next one.

"However, on the path of the spirit, there are many circles. And when those who are traveling on this good path will see others who are becoming successful in achieving their completion of one circle and going on to the next one, they will see the direction that they too will wish to travel and will attempt to do the same…but in their own way. This is one of the truths of any life path, little ones. Only you can travel the life path you and the Earth Mother have set for you to follow. If you will attempt at letting another travel it for you, or if you will attempt to travel another's for them, then you will be opening yourselves up to disaster. And, you will either be walked on or you will be walking on another. But, in any case there will be nothing gained and there will be nothing learned except the frustration that you will carry around with you.

"Now, the circles that are with us, they are with us in all things and must be completed before we are allowed to even attempt to come to the next one. And, little ones, for each circle one will successfully complete while they are traveling in this domain of the Earth Mother's, they will be one step closer to their return to become one once again with the Great Spirit. And, this is the desire to all who have a spirit to follow."

This one called Calling Thunder paused in his speaking words for a few moments. He was looking over to the places where Cheeway and I were sitting. And, I could tell, from those many times of my past seasons what it was he was doing. He was looking to our within places…our within places where our spirit resides to make sure we were able to keep up with these speaking words he was willing to share with us at this time. However, I was sure that while he found we were able to follow many of the speaking words of sharing, he would also find that there was a slight confusion over us on the concept of the circles within the path of the spirit…those circles that we would all need to complete before we would be able to go on to the next one.

"Think of it in this way, little ones," came the continuation of Calling Thunder's speaking words. "Think of yourself walking to a place you have a great desire to get to. And, during this process, there will be many holes in the path you are following. Holes that will be filled with mud and other such things that you do not desire to share the clean clothes you are wearing with.

"Now, as you will continue to travel on this path, this path that you know will take you to the place you desire to go to, you will have the knowing that you will have to do this one step at a time. That is, before you can take another step in this direction, you will have to first complete the one you are in the middle of.

"However, if you will not have the willingness nor the patience to do such a thing, then you will find that if you will attempt to take the next step before you have completed the one you are now in the middle of, then you will have a great fall. And this fall will not only dirty the clothes you are wearing but in this process of falling, you will most likely come to hurt yourself. And this will cause you another delay at arriving at the destination you are wanting to get to.

"So, one must first complete one step at a time before the next one is attempted. But, there are many processes to each step one will take. And those processes, if any are left out, will result in not keeping the correct balance and once again you will fall. You will fall because you will most likely lose your balance.

"How like the circles that we must complete before we attempt to enter the next one. Think of each of these circles on the path of the spirit as you would a step in the same way that we have been willing to describe to both of you these steps that will eventually bring you to the place you have a desire to get to.

"If you will not be willing to bring all of your forward motion to a completion before attempting your next step, then the next step will not take place in a very successful way. And this is the same for the circles that must be completed before attempting to gain entry into the next one. If the one circle is not completed and you will attempt entry into the next one, then you will end up falling on this path of the spirit and in this process, you will most likely hurt yourself. And, in the process of these falls, you will also end up becoming out of balance to all those things that will come to you. And, this imbalance will create a lack of understanding for those things that are of you.

"Now, as those who will continue to travel on this path of the spirit, as they will see many others who are completing their own circles and bringing to completion those things that had come to them while they were within it, they too will hold the desire to advance their own spirit in this direction as well. They too will see the direction they have a need by their spirit to travel in. But when they will attempt to follow in this direction, this direction they have seen others who are traveling this same path as they are, they will, in many cases, find that they cannot do those same things they will have seen in those others do.

"They will find that while they may be able to mirror those same things they have seen in another on this path of the spirit, they will find they are doing just that. That they are only mirroring them but they are not attaining any needed levels of understanding for doing them. Those needed levels of understanding that will allow them to continue doing those things they have seen the others do. Those others who are continuing to advance ahead of them on this path of the spirit.

"Now, little ones, we will wish for you to remember that while one will travel on the path of the spirit, that it is not ever important to do as another will do. For these things they will do are those things that are needed by their spirit. And this will not be the same thing that is needed by yours.

"However, what is important to remember is that while you must only be concerned with those things that are needed by your spirit, that the ones who are advancing on this path of the spirit, they will share with you the movement and direction that may be traveled. And it is from all of those fine examples that are being lived on this path that will allow you to feel many of them…to see many of them until your spirit from the within place will share with you which one of them is right for you to follow.

"But there is another danger that will be placed in your path to understanding, your path to understanding all things that are of you on this path of the spirit. And this danger that will come to you will be in the form of not listening to the calling voice of your own spirit for those things you are seeing. For if you will not listen to it, little ones, then there is a great risk of falling over to the path of the others…of falling onto the path of the others and away from the path of the spirit. Now, even while it is possible for you to gain entry onto this path of the spirit once again, you will have found that there has been a great deal of time that has been lost to you…time that cannot be made up for in this domain.

"This danger will come to you when you will see the ones who are advancing nicely on this path of the spirit. And you will see the direction they are traveling and you will attempt to follow them. But, because you have not closed up all of those holes within yourself, those holes that have come to you from those seasons of your past and the times that you have not worked with those events, those offerings that had been presented to you, you will find that each time you will attempt to follow one who is ahead of you on this path of the spirit that you will fall and lose your balance once again.

"Once again, little ones, we are willing to share with both of you that none of this is done in punishment for any of those things you have done in your life path. Rather, they are being done to you for those things that you have not done. And this is the reason you will fall down when you will try to follow this direction that you have seen come to you from those who are also on this same path of the spirit.

"What will become of those who will continue to do this thing, little ones? For those who will continue to try to follow another before it is their time, they will come to the place of believing that none of that which they will see is for them. And that the closest they will ever come to attaining such things for themselves is to only see it but not ever to attain it. You will see them as you will continue to travel on this path with the Earth Mother, little ones. You will recognize them as the ones who are always running and chasing after those things they need. But just as they are about to catch up with them they will give up. They will either give up on getting them, or when they will attain them, they will end up throwing them away.

"And all of this comes to those who have experienced the same things we have been willing to share with you about the path of the spirit or even on the path of the others. They will have become so used to not being able to attain what they will wish to follow after, they will bring this over to the body part of themselves. And they will become very confused with all those things they will desire in their life path. They will become very confused with them because they will not have the understanding of why they desire something or someone so much to begin with. But once they have it or them they no longer desire it.

"And, little ones, all of this takes place within another great law that was set into motion by the Great Spirit. It is a law that shares that all things that take place above will in time follow in those places that are below. And for the path of the spirit or the path of the others, this means that what is experienced by your spirit on its path, will also become followed by the body as well. All of the actions that your spirit will take will also be taken by the body part of yourself. Unless there is an understanding for what is taking place on their life path, those who would follow in the path we have just described to you will be caught in this same circle of their path. For them, there will not ever be a leaving of it. There will be no escaping of it because they will not be willing to do the work that is required to come to understand what it is they are doing in truth.

"However, there is a way out for them, little ones. And this is one of the many things you will be required to work with for those quests that are still ahead of both of you. The way out for all who would wish to take the time and effort for themselves is to complete this circle they are currently trapped inside of. And, to complete it, they must be willing to look on the face of the emotions that will come to them…those emotions that will come to them in front of all events that will be offered.

"For within the emotion that will precede the lesson, little ones, there will be a great lesson that will be learned from it. That is if they are willing to stand strong before it with their spirit. Stand strong before it and learn what it is they must do. As you have both been prepared with from the teachings of Grandfather and Two Bears. You hold the understanding that there is nothing to be learned from the emotions of any situation. That to remain in them for any time would not be the wise thing to do.

"And, for this, we share with you that it is correct. For emotion in itself does not hold any learning for any of the spirit walkers in this domain of the Earth Mother. That is if they will remain in them for long periods of time. But, this is not what we are referring to, little ones. This is not the place of the emotion that we are now willing to share with you that holds a great lesson. The place we are sharing with you from this place of seeing is this. That when an emotion will come to us, this same emotion that is always carried on the front of each of the events to the ones who are traveling on the path of the others, this comes to them as a warning…a warning to them that if they will look through this emotion to see the face of the lesson that they will be greatly hurt. And for them, this causes a great fear – a fear of the unknown. And since they do not have an understanding for this process of the unfamiliar, they will continue to see this process through the eyes of fear and will continue to run and hide from it.

"Now, for the ones who are willing to travel on the path of the spirit, they will not see it in this way. That is, if they have experienced at least a little of the progress that is here on this path for them. You see, little ones, when one will travel on this path of the spirit, they will come to taste the freedom that is within it and themselves. When they will come to advance themselves on this path, there will be such a wonderful blessing that will come to them that it will strengthen their spirit part greatly. And as we have shared with each of you before that when something will take place on the spirit part that it is only a matter of time before it will also take place on the body part.

"It is from these achievements that are to be made on the path of the spirit that this knowing comes to them. This knowing that will in time lead them to the place of understanding for those things we are speaking of. And, little ones, the more understanding we will have of ourselves and all things that are around us, then the stronger we will become in the ways of the spirit that are continually with us.

"But for now, little ones, we will go back to the place where we were discussing the way out of the circles…those same circles that are with us all to teach us from. And those same circles that we so often get caught up in and feel trapped. The key to getting out of these small circles, little ones, lies in what there is to learn from those emotions that will come to us…those emotions that are on the front of the lesson we are being offered from the events that will cross our life paths. You see, these events do not begin from the time that we will see them as something to learn from. They have been with us from the very first breath one will draw upon entry into this domain of the Earth Mother's. And, they will not stop until we have left this place, little ones. This will give to each of you an idea of what we are here for.

"We are not placed into this domain to rest or to have a place where we will not have anything to do. We all come into this domain that is the Earth Mother's so we will be able to learn. And from this learning comes understanding and wisdom. And, from them both comes the ability of our spirit to gain entry to the next higher level. Gaining entry to the next higher level brings us closer to the place of being joined once again with the Great Spirit. And, this is what it is all about.

"Now, all those events that have been presented to you from the very first season of your life path have come to you at the right time and in the right path. As we have been willing to share with you, there is nothing that is ever presented to you by accident. All of these events and people who will cross your life path have been designed by you and the Earth Mother when you were sitting in council with her.

"Also, there is no thing that has ever been done by yourself that was not done to perfection. And all of those things that you are currently doing now, well, they are just the same way. They too are all being done perfectly. Now the proof of all of this is you and what you have become in this day. Think of all those things that you can see now. Think of all those things that you can give value to and think of how well you can now recognize what it is that you have to do while you are in this domain. You are now a sum of all those experiences that have been offered to you from the past. Those same experiences that have come to you have done so in order to make you into the person you are today. And the person you are today is the one that is needed by your spirit to learn from.

"So many will try to always be aware of all things they are doing. They will do this in an attempt of not doing anything that is not correct. However, when they will look back on all of those things they have tried to do, all of those things that they have tried to exercise their own control over, they will see that there was not really any control of their own over those situations. If they will look on these events of their past, they will see that all they were doing was what was needed by them or another. And those things were planned long before they had entered this domain.

"Remember, little ones. Remember that all things you will do in each day that you are here, that all of them are done to perfection. So it is not of any value to try to predict any kind of control over them not only for yourself but for others as well. The thing to keep in the front of your thinking mind is not this thing called control. Because this word is residing deep within the spirit of illusion. And this is all that this word will bring to you. It will only bring to you those things that are not real and will show to you those things that do not exist. When you think that you are in control of those things that are taking place around you, then take a good and deep look into your within place…this within place where your spirit resides.

"Because when you will hold onto this believing that you are actually controlling anything, then you will find that you have in truth lost sight of the spirit who is you. You have wondered off from the path of the spirit and fell onto the path of the others…this path where only the body is satisfied and the emotions are the only food. When you will catch yourself and see that those things that you are doing are done to perfection anyway, and to think on the controlling aspect of anything is to waste your time, then you will be in a place of seeing clearly these things that we are about to share with both of you. This path that will allow one to get out of the trap of the circles they are in.

"And, as you will begin to see this, little ones, then you will also see why it is so important to listen and understand what it is that may be learned from these emotions…these emotions that are always in front of the lesson that is being offered to you from every event. Circles of a life path have been with all who enter this domain from the time of all our beginnings. And, those same principles and truths that were once with them those many seasons ago they are still there. And, they hold the same weight of importance to them.

"Before we will come to the place of our sharing with you, little ones, this place of sharing with you what the emotions carry with them, let us first look at the path these circles are in. Then when you will hold an understanding for this, it will become clearer to both of you what we are willing to share. This sharing of what it is the emotions in the front of lesson carry with them. As we have been willing to share with each of you, there are many circles of a life path on this path of the spirit. And within each of these circles are many lessons that are located within them. Now, as no two spirit walkers will carry the exact same life path with them, then you must hold the knowing that no two people will have the same needs during this time they are with the Earth Mother. And, this will mean that some will begin in one circle of learning and another may begin in another.

"But this is because of the lessons that are needed by the spirit who is within you. And those needed lessons are to only be found in the circle that has been allowed to carry them. So when you will see someone who is of the same number of seasons as you and they are not traveling in the same circle of learning, then do not question this. This is something that is not important for you to have a knowing for. What they are doing…this has been designed by their spirit and the Earth Mother. And, what you are doing…this too has been designed by you and the Earth Mother.

"There is no way of ever changing another, little ones. And both of you have been prepared that to do so is to waste your time while you are in this domain. If you will wish to attain the freedom of the life path you travel, you will have to find it from within yourselves. And, once you will find this freedom for yourself, then you will be more willing to allow this same freedom in another.

"This is only natural, little ones. For when one will travel without the needed levels of understanding for themselves and all things that are around them, then they will not be willing to allow another to find something that they themselves have not yet learned to find. It is only when one will have experienced the understanding and the clarity of vision, these things that will allow them to see what has been with them all the time, only then will they hold the understanding that all of their needs have been with them. And they only have to walk to them to receive their blessing.

"When this has taken place, little ones, then they will be ready to accept the freedom of another. And by accepting this freedom of another they will be willing to allow them the direction of travel they need. For they will hold the understanding that it is their spirit who is leading them and not the guidance of another who is in this domain of the Earth Mother's.

"Now, when all of this has taken place, they will look at those things they will have entered this domain to do...those quests they have offered to the Earth Mother and all of her children...these same quests that will assist them and their needs for the coming of this new age we must all enter. And, when they will see what it is they have entered to do, there will be a knowing that will fill them...a knowing that will share with them a great secret...a great secret that many will spend an entire life path searching for, but so few will ever find.

"Now, in this beginning of the seeing part for them, this seeing part that will share at least a partial knowing of what it is they have entered this domain to perform, what they have brought with them in the way of talents of their spirit from within, they will only be shown a part of this great discovery. Only a part of it, because for them their test is not yet over...this test that has been given over to the ancient ones who are always seeing us and these things we will do.

"There is another test for them to go through if they are to continue on this path of discovering those things that are of themselves. And this test is, as all things are, not only in this domain that is the Earth Mother's to guide in but in all domains that are of the Great Spirit. And this is from the truth that there will not ever be anything that will simply be given to another. This is just not possible because of the terrible results that come from it.

"Think of it in this way, little ones. Remember all of those things that you have come to receive and have been willing to perform the necessary work for. And, when you will review them you will find that because you have been willing to make payment for them, a payment of some kind, then you have come to hold them with much more respect and given to them a higher value than you would have if you had not been required to work for them.

"Now, as all will have in this domain, think over all of those things that have been given to you. Those things that have come to you that did not require you to perform any work or give any payment for them at all. Think of them and try to remember how long or how high you valued them. When you will look on them with the eyes that can see, we are sure that you will not see any of those things that had been given to you remain for long. Nor will any of them have held a high meaning for you. And, this is the way of all things that are in this domain, little ones. When you will give something away, then you are not only giving it away but you are also giving your permission for it to be thrown away and not valued at all by the one who has been in receiving of it.

"And this is the face of lesson that is applicable to what we are now willing to share with both of you. This is the same reason for there being another payment for the ones who are beginning to see what it is they have entered this domain to perform...and those talents that their spirit has brought with it to do these things.

"You see, little ones, when one will begin to wake from their sleep of illusion, this sleep that comes to all who will enter this domain that is the Earth Mother's, they will wake from this sleep in a complete state of confusion. But this confusion is one that comes to them not out of vengeance, even though many of them will come to see it in this way in the beginning. It comes to them in a way that will allow them to see all things that are around them through the eyes of truth...these eyes that are of their own spirit within them.

"In the beginning, they will believe that they have lost all things that have been close to them...all of those things they once had come to believe in and lean on for their support of those things they had been doing in their life path. They will believe this because this is in truth what is taking place for them. It is when one will begin this wakening from their sleep of illusion that they will begin to see through all those things that had been around them...to see through those things that do not carry the weight of truth to them...to see through them as if they do not exist because in truth, little ones, they do not.

"And during this time of their beginning of awakening, they will only be seeing those things that would have come to them eventually. But now... now that they are awakening from this sleep, they are able to see this while they are still able to do something about it. It is sad to say this, little ones, but most of the ones who will enter this domain of the Earth Mother's, most of them will not awaken from their own sleep of illusion until they have crossed the great spirit waters and are standing in the waiting place… this place where their spirit family resides.

"And it will be then that their spirit family will ask them what they have done with all of the time they had been given here in this domain. Why they did not try to awaken themselves from this sleep of illusion and see those things that were being offered to them. But the for the one who did not make the efforts of wakening themselves from this sleep, they will not have an answer they will be able to share with them.

"For them, they will only be able to stand before them and shake their heads from left to right. A motion that will share that they do not know why. And, for all those things their spirit held a great need for, those things that their spirit entered this domain to learn from, they will have to go through all of this once again. But when they will do this there will be another payment they must be willing to make for this opportunity with the Earth Mother. And, it is a payment that is not an easy one to make, little ones.

"So it is that when one will begin to awaken from their sleep of illusion that they will have this feeling that all things have been taken away from them. That all they once held to as a security of their knowing and believing has left them. This will be the beginning of their awakening, little ones. And, if they are able to see this as a beginning, they will be well on their way to learning…to learning those things they had entered this domain to gain from.

"However, it will be from this beginning of the wakening period, little ones. It is from this point forward that they will come to know the ones we call the Spirits Of The Flame. For it will be from this place forward on their path they will come to know what it is like to be without anything, anything at all. It is from this place they will see what it feels like to know all things they have ever held close to them be taken away from them. But in the truth of the matter, they have not been taken away at all — they have been dropped away. And this process of dropping them away has been done by themselves."

"But for this time that we are willing to share with you, we will continue with the lessons that will come from the emotions…those same emotions that will come in the front of all lessons that will be offered to you. We will come back to this time when one will experience the Spirits Of The Flame. We will do this when first you have come to see the importance of the lesson of the emotion and what it is they are offering to you to learn from.

"Now, little ones, as it is with all who enter this domain, there are many lessons that are needed by each spirit. And the difference of these needed lessons is so great that no one spirit will have exactly the same ones that another will have a need for. And, it is from this difference that we will begin. We have been willing to share with you both what takes place by one who is traveling on the path of the others. And what they will do when they first encounter this emotion that we are speaking of. We have shared with you how they will continue to look away from them and see them as something that has come to punish them. But, this is not at all the face of truth to what has taken place. This is not their reason for being brought to them.

"For those who travel on the path of the spirit, they will have encountered these same kinds of events…these same lessons that are being presented to them and they too have this same coating of emotion that is around them. However, they will not react in the same way as the ones we have shared with you about did…the ones who traveled the path of the others…the ones who have found the path of the spirit. They have held onto the same kind of events that have been presented to all. You will see them and you will know what we are speaking of. They too will have gone through similar events that had come to them. You will find, as they will share parts of their life path with you, that all you had experienced will be very similar to those things that had come to them. Remember, similar is not the same as being identical.

"However, what will become the mark of one who will travel the path of the spirit from the ones who will travel the path of the others…the difference is that for those who have found the path of the spirit, they have come to understand what it means to them to look away from those events that are being offered to them. They will have come to know that when they will look away from an event that will be presented to them, that they are, in truth, not looking away from the event but they are looking away from themselves. They come to understand that all things that will be presented to them in this life path they are traveling are coming to them in the right time and in the right way for their learning. And, if they are to look away from them, then they are setting themselves back…back into a place of not learning…a place of not learning those things they have entered here to learn. There is another difference that will distinguish those who travel the path of the spirit from the ones who do not. This difference comes to them because at one time in their seasons of the past, they had been presented an event…an event that had come to them with a great learning lesson for their spirit.

"And, when this event had come to them, it was not resisted, it was accepted and they learned then this was a good thing for them to do. That it was a good thing for them to do because there was a great benefit that had come to them. And this benefit was that they had, perhaps for the first time, learned to look through this face of emotion and see all the way into the lesson they were being offered…this lesson that blessed them in a wonderful way. And from this first experience they held within themselves, this is what had allowed the growing of their spirit from their within place…this spirit who is them and allows them to gain daily in the strength they need so that they may continue to look straight onto the face of emotion. To look straight onto this face of reminding and see into the lesson that is being presented to them.

"You see, little ones, this emotion that we have called the reminding, it is of great value to those who will have the willingness of spirit to learn from it. And, it comes to them in the same way that a child will cry to the parents when it is hungry but has not yet learned their way of speaking its needs yet. From those things both of you have seen in this case, this case of hearing the small child cry, the parents will have to do many things until they can come to the place of understanding what these cries of this child mean. And for those who will travel on the path of the spirit, they too will have to make many attempts at understanding this thing called the emotion of reminding…this same emotion that is on the front of all events that will come to you.

"However, for the ones who have found this path of the spirit, they will have an experience or two to draw from. And the strength that they will find in these experiences will be of sufficient levels to allow them to gain in their strength of spirit…this strength of spirit that must be present before one can come to believe in themselves. When one will look into this face of the emotion, they will see many things come to them. Many of them will be of the caliber that are not pleasant. And it is because of this face of the emotion of reminding is not often pleasant that we will need this strength of the spirit to stand strong before it.

"Now all of this will require a great deal of effort on your part or on the part of the one who will stand and confront their own emotions that will come to them. But, as they have come to understand from those experiences they have already gone through, the blessings and gifts that await you will be more than worth the work you are now being required to expend on this event…on the working your way through the emotion that has come to you first. For you will hold onto the understanding that once this emotional part of the lesson is over, there is only the seeing of the face of lesson…this lesson that you and the Earth Mother had designed especially for you.

"And, for the ones who have found their way to the path of the spirit, they know and understand this. It comes to them…this looking at this emotion. It is like them looking at one of their own children. And, the truth of this is that this is exactly what has come to them, little ones. It is in truth one of their own children. This is a child of theirs because it has been the result of their own planning for those things they needed to learn from and the willingness of the Earth Mother to allow them to come into life. So it is that from this way of looking at all of these events that have brought you into them and all of those who have crossed your path with an event they have brought to you. All of these things have been designed and prepared by the spirit who is you and the Earth Mother. And all of them have come to you in exactly the correct time.

"Now, as it is with all who have found this path of the spirit, this one path that will lead to the spirit's advancement, they will have found a great value from these emotions that are on the front of all these events that have come to them. They have found that they are not only necessary to look at them, but they will have found that there is a great reminding to them for those things that still need to be worked on as they will travel on this path of advancement for the spirit.

"When an event will come to them, it will do so with the same weight as it will come to all…with this same weight of emotion that all others feel from it. But since they are willing to listen to the reminding of this emotion, for them it will not last as long…this feeling that is being given to them from these emotions they will find they do not reside with them. Not in the same way they will do so for those who travel on the path of the others.

"You see, little ones, when one will be willing to perform the work that is required of them while they are in this domain, they will see that there is an immediate reward for all of those actions they will be willing to do. And one of these rewards is the ability of seeing all things for what they are and not; as one who is still in the sleep of illusion would see them only as they would wish for them to be. This emotion that is carried on the front of each event is not any different. And, when it can be seen for what it is, then there is a great messenger that is seen from it. A messenger that is willing to share with you what it sees. A messenger that is willing to share with you all of those places that you cannot see and which ones are still weak and need to be worked on.

"Remember what has been shared with you both from the teachings of Grandfather and Two Bears. That it is only when we are within this domain of the Earth Mother's that we will see things for what we would wish for them to be. And this truth to the great illusion is only valid here. But it is because of this truth that we have come to look at this way of speaking as we have. And because the illusion has allowed us to see that our two-legged way of expressing themselves as the only valid path to speaking, well, we have missed out on many others…those many others who are willing to share with us.

"We have missed out on this because we have not been willing to listen with the ears of the spirit nor have we been willing to see with the eyes of our spirit. When another will speak to you or share their speaking words with you, you have been taught that there is an accepted form of communicating these thoughts and ideas. And this acceptable way of expressing oneself is through the mouth and the utterances that will come out of if. Because so many have been willing to accept this as their truth, they have forgotten the many other ways of communicating. They have closed themselves off to all others who are willing to share with them and assist them in coming to a higher place of understanding themselves and all things that are around them.

"On the one hand they will tell many that there are more than words that will be able to describe something. But on the other hand they will tell those same ones that unless they can express it in words, in those same words that all of them have agreed to as being the only ones they will accept, then this is not a real form of knowledge. Then they will look around themselves and wonder why they often feel so trapped by those things they have taken unto themselves. They will wonder why there are not other forms of life they can relate to. They will continue to wonder on this because they are only willing to look at themselves and this very small part of life they are in.

"Now, when one will find this path of the spirit and they will come to the place of understanding that there is only their way of being but there are also others who will have their way as well, then they will have begun to see that the place they occupy is actually very small. But all that is in it is very necessary for them to learn from. And they will spend great amounts of time in coming to understand that there are more living things around them than they are themselves. They will see all of the children of the Earth Mother first. And they will recognize all of them as their brothers and sisters, little ones.

"They will look at all of the green ones and see that they have a spirit path they are following...they will look at all of the standing children, the rock children, the earth children, the crawling children, the water children, the sky children, the winged children and so on. And, when they will see them, they will know that they too are alive and deserve the same kinds of consideration as they request by others. It is when they will come to see that there is life in all things that are within the Earth Mother that they will begin to understand that they too have a path to travel. And that it is the same kind of path they too are following.

"And, when they will have come to this place of understanding, little ones, then they will be willing to listen to the possibility that they too might have things on the path of wisdom to share with them...to share with them from their own learning and willingness to understand. This will be the beginning, little ones, the beginning of those who travel on the path of the spirit to see once again. And to remember that all that is around them is also filled with a life of its own. And that each life has their own path to follow and does not need you to interfere with it.

"So they will come to see these other children of the Earth Mother as being alive. And in doing so, they will come to consider them sacred...as sacred as they consider themselves. Once this place is attained by a spirit walker, they will come to feel their ways of speaking to you...their own ways of sharing those things with you that your spirit holds a great need for. And it is from this understanding that you will come to know their ways of sharing with you are much more refined than the ways you were once using...those ways of speaking with the mouth that you once found to be so efficient but now find so lacking...so lacking in the ways of expressing those things you are now finding within yourself.

"When one will first feel the speaking from any of the children of the Earth Mother, they are very surprised. Very surprised at this because this is something that they had been told did not exist. That this is something that was just not possible. But in order for them to advance any further on this path they have just discovered they must be willing to allow this kind of thinking fall away from themselves. And, the only way for this to fall away from this is to come to the place of understanding it and how it relates to those things they have a need to do here.

"Now, little ones, this new way of communicating is only a way that is much more efficient and not as limiting as the way of using only the mouth to speak with. And, as you will find, all children possess this ability of speaking and sharing with us. It is only the ones who are still trapped within the sleep of illusion that have forgotten how to do this. And for them perhaps it is better that they remain asleep because of what is coming to this domain very soon.

"However, for the ones who have awakened from this sleep of illusion, when they will feel this emotion that is being carried on the front of these events of offering these events of learning, they will see this emotion as another of these children of the Earth Mother. And they will see it as one who is trying to communicate with them. And, from the understanding that all things that are within this domain that is the Earth Mother's, that all of them hold life within them. They will come to know what this message of the emotion carried on the front of each offering is to them.

"For them, they will not see it as something that has come to hurt or punish them at all. For them who have woken from their sleep of illusion, they will see this thing called the emotion for what it is and not be fooled into thinking it is something that it is not. And what this emotion is on the front of each event that will be presented to all in this domain. It carries the lesson of reminding. This lesson of reminding that shares with all of us how far we have come to travel on this path that is ours to travel when one who is firm on this path of the spirit…when they have done all of the preparing for those things they have come into this domain to perform. They have been initiated through the many tests that the ancient ones have lain before all who would wish to undertake them. And having passed successfully through all of them, they are now ready to face themselves and all of those things that are of them…these things they have been successful with, as well as those things they have not been as successful with.

"And this is the face they will have a great need for as they will make their attempts at standing strong before these emotions that have come to them. They are able to stand strong before them to learn from them because they have found the path to their within place…this within place that is where their spirit resides. They will also feel the same fears that are held by all others who will come to see these emotions, little ones. They too will feel the fear from them as they too do not hold a complete understanding of themselves and all things that are around them.

"However, this face of fear that will come to them on this event will not be as debilitating to them as it would be for those who have not found their way to the path of the spirit…this path that has been designed by themselves to learn from. This fear that will come to the ones who have found this path of the spirit…it will come to them as something of a calling voice…a calling voice that they will recognize as the one they have often heard before. And this calling voice to them will be the same one as they have heard from their own spirit as it would call to them to learn. For them this is their time of testing. The time of seeing for themselves those teachings and understanding that have come to them. To see which of them will assist them in this time of their need. And it is also a time for them to reach decisions. These decisions that will be presented to them from seeing which of the teachings will assist them. And which of them will not.

"During this time of standing strong before these emotions of reminding, little ones, without the assisting of those things you have come to know and understand from the many lessons of your life path, well, one simply could not stand in the face of these great and wonderful offerings to them. They would not have the strength of their spirit to guide them through those places they are being asked to look at…those places where they have not ever gone through before. And it is because of this newness that will be presented to them that they must follow those things they have learned on this path of the spirit in order to find their way.

"They will see those things that have been shared with them in those many seasons of the past then. They will see them and remember them well as they will begin to employ their wisdom. And when they will find any of those things that have been shared with them…those things that had been told to them would assist them greatly in their time of need… when they will find that they do not hold the weight of truth to them, then they will cast them aside and later allow them to drop away from themselves. To drop away as something that did not hold their own weight of truth for them.

"As they will stand strong before this emotion, they will feel many things from it. They will feel the pain of loss, the hurting of being lost, or many other things will fill them up…fill them up to the place of them believing they cannot hold any more. For if they were to attempt to fill themselves with one more thing that they would surely go crazy and not find their way back to the one they had known of before…this place they were standing on when this event had first come to them.

"However, as it is with all things that will be presented to any in this domain, these emotions are not coming to punish or to frighten you away. They are affecting you as they are doing so that you can see what it was that you had turned away from in the seasons of your past. So you will be able to now look at this offering that had been presented to you so long ago – this same lesson that you had turned away from – this same lesson that you had continued to turn away from until now. You see, little ones, when you will be filled with a feeling of being uncomfortable or being scared and frightened from this emotion that has come to you, this emotion that has been carried in the front of the lesson you need to learn from, it is only giving to you these feelings because these are the lessons that you have not yet learned from over the many seasons of your life path.

"From the first time when this same lesson was offered to you, you turned away from it and tried to either ignore it or put it away someplace where you would no longer have to work or think about it. However, each time you would do this, it would leave you with an open hole...an open hole in yourself that would allow many things to come into you...many things that would come into you that you would have no control over. No control over what it was that was coming into you because you could not see them...because you would not even be aware of their presence in you. And those things that have come to us that we are not aware of, we cannot learn from them. We cannot understand from them. And this is why we are affected so greatly by this emotion that has come to us. This is why without the strength of our spirit from within us we are not able to stand in the front of them to listen to what they are trying to share...to recognize this remembering they are trying to tell us about this hole that is within ourselves.

"This lesson that is being carried to us on the back of these emotions, these lessons of reminding to us, they are always showing each of us who and what we are really like in this day we share with the Earth Mother. They are sharing with us how we have done those things we have done. And, they are letting us know that there are still many more things on our life path that continue to need work on. As it is with all living two-legs, little ones, none of them will ever want to be criticized for those things that are a part of themselves. To them, there is only their perfection and to suggest anything less, well, this is a great blow to their ego...this same ego that will continue to keep them asleep.

"But with the presentation of these emotions, they will come to each of us in such a personalized way that they cannot be ignored for long periods of time. They are so personalized that we may choose to ignore them for short periods of time but as the seasons pass us by, they will win. They will win because they know each of us very well...because they are in truth a part of ourselves. And the way they will come to us is one that will make us feel very bad and worried about things that we cannot see. When this will take place, we will tend to give these unfounded feelings such weight that we will eventually give them life. We will give them life so they may come to us in the same way we are worried about them.

"However, when one who is traveling on the path of the spirit has gone through this kind of event several times, then they will have come to see what things these emotions are presenting to them. They will see this because of the continual repeating of them. It is from the repeating of those things we are to learn from that they are learned from. And this is due to the kind of life path that is made available to all who will enter this domain of the Earth Mother. It has nothing at all to do with the level of intelligence of another.

"This repeating is done through many events so that all sides of them may be seen. So one will be able to see that there is more than one reason for all that is around them. And these reasons will lie within the levels of understanding they will attain. Now, for the emotion that comes to the ones who continue to travel on the path of the spirit, when they will feel them come to them, there will not be any less of a lesson for them than there is for the ones who still travel on the path of the others. And the reason for this is that all is within this domain that is the Earth Mother's. Freedom of choice is always kept by all.

"However, it is very sad to see so many of them willing to let go of this freedom that could be theirs. To let go of it so they might be more accepted by another. This kind of action does not help them nor does it assist anyone else. It only clouds the ability to see themselves for who and what they are. Now, with these things in the front of your thinking minds, you will be more able to see what it is we are willing to share with each of you now. When an emotion of any event will come to you, it only has one thing to teach, and this one thing is a reminding to you that there is a weak place within you. Then it would do you very well to listen to what is being shown to you. For if you will listen, then you will receive a strong clue on how and where you need to go in order to fix this weak place. And, when you will fix it then you will most likely be allowed to leave this current circle you are in and be allowed entry into the next one.

"Keep in the front of your thinking minds, little ones, that it is only when we will have finished one circle, when we will have learned from the circle we are currently in, then we will be allowed to enter the next one… this next circle where we will find even more lessons to learn and advance from. And, when one will remain in the circle they are currently in, then they will come to know many things. They will come to know them very well because they are always being repeated to them. All of those events and lessons that they had seen before they will see them again. And for one who is stuck in any of these circles, well, this is only as far as they will go for any of the efforts they will make while they are here. And this is a very limiting factor because until they have prepared themselves sufficiently, prepared from coming to understand those things that have been offered to them from this current circle, they will not learn more of themselves nor those things that are around them.

"And this is the reason there will only be two or three circles ever found on the path of the others…this path that is traveled by those who have not yet learned their way to the path of the spirit. Now that you can see why it is so important to see ourselves for what we have become, why it is so important to hold an understanding of the need for fixing all of these holes that have been left in us, these holes that have been made and expanded for each time we have turned away from those events and lessons that had been presented to us, then you will also come to see why it is important to fix them. Because without fixing them there will not be any chance of any-one leaving the circle they are currently in and advancing to the next one.

"Without this progression on any life path, little ones, there will not be the full realization of those things that any who have entered this domain to learn from learn. These offerings that will come to you, these offerings that have been designed by you and the Earth Mother from the time you were sitting in council with her, they will not be revealed to you until you have been prepared for them. You see, little ones, this is also a great truth that each spirit part has agreed to before entering. They have agreed to this part of their life path so they would not be able to receive or understand those lessons that had been designed for their spirit to learn from until they were sufficiently prepared for them.

"And this reminding of the preparing is the emotion that has come in the front of them to you…this emotion that is being carried before the les-son that you are in search of. Unless one can come to understand the value of the emotion that is before them, they will know that they are not ready to see the lesson that has been offered to them. They will not be ready because there are still holes within them that have still not healed. And because these holes are from their current circle and the event or lesson is from the next one, it is just not possible for them to see nor to understand those things they are not yet ready to encounter or embrace.

"So it is for the ones who will travel on the path of the spirit, when they will see one of these events come to them, they will encounter the feeling of the emotion that has been presented to them first. And, they will feel this reminding of the emotion and know that if what they will feel from it will be something that is not good then they will know that they do not understand a part of themselves…a part of themselves that is very important to what they have entered this domain to learn. They will have this knowing that until they will come to the place of understanding these things about themselves, they will not be allowed to advance one more step on this path of the spirit…this same path where there are so many more lessons for them to learn from…so many teachings they may come to see the light from understanding for.

"So, when they will feel this emotion that is filling them, this emotion that is always present on the front of all events that are ever presented, they will feel this badness of feeling from it and know. They will know what this lesson from the emotion is for them. They will know that this part of the event is sharing with them that there is a place on them that has a hole…a hole that has not yet been repaired by them. For those who have come to understand what it is they have next to do they will continue to advance on this spirit walk they are doing with the Earth Mother. And for them, there will not ever be an event presented to them that they will not be willing to work and learn with.

"However, for those who are still new to this path of the spirit, the ones who have not yet come to the place of seeing completely and clearly with the eyes of the spirit, they will have to learn these next steps well. For it is only through them that they will come to succeed in doing those things they are seeking to do."

Chapter 15

▼

LOOKING THROUGH THE EMOTION

"When one will feel this emotion come to them, it will bring to them a feeling of something bad. Something that is bad to them or even a feeling of apprehension. Then they will have to stand strong in their spirit and face this. They will have to look closely at this emotion because it is here they will find the next step to travel…this next step that is very necessary for their continual advancement on this path of the spirit.

"It is only by looking closely at this emotion that they will be allowed to see things that have not yet been known to them. And it is from this emotion that they will have to learn to see it well enough to see the face they will need to place over it.

"When one will look at this emotion that has come to them, this emotion that has also made them feel very bad, they will have to see it in its entirety. And, when they will do this, they can then put a face and a body over it.

"By placing a face and a body over it, little ones, they are allowing themselves to see it well enough to recognize it. To recognize it at least well enough so they will be able to see it when they will encounter it again… when they will encounter it on their review of all their seasons past.

"You see, little ones, as we have been willing to share with you before, the reason this emotion has such a feeling over anyone – a feeling that is not a pleasant one to look at – it is only because this same lesson has been offered to them before. This same lesson that is still residing on the back of this emotion they are experiencing on this day we are speaking of.

"However, from those many seasons that have passed them by when this lesson first came to them, they had turned away from it. They did not choose to look at it and see what it was that was being offered to them to learn from.

"And ever since that time, that first time this lesson had been presented to them, they have been turning away from it. And it has been through their turning away from this offering that has caused a hole to form in them…this hole that we are sharing with each of you that has given to them a bad feeling from this emotion they are now feeling.

"Now, the lesson will not ever go away from anyone, little ones. It is not something that you can put out of your thinking mind and believe that it will just go away. For lessons are not like that. They will continue to follow you to all places and thoughts that you will have.

"And, even though they may not be accepted nor understood by you, they will have already become a part of yourself. They will already have found a place within you. When they will find a place within you, and you will not have an understanding for those things you are needing in this life path, they will have to continually remind you to look at them. And it is by this reminding to you that they will have to present themselves to you from the outside…from this outside place that you are at this point accepting all things from.

"So, as they will continue to remind you, as they will continue to come to you from the outside, then they will have to find a place to exit and then re-enter you from. And this is what has caused this hole to form within you…this same hole that will also allow other things and events to enter and leave.

"When there will be enough of these holes within you form, there will be many things that will enter and then leave at their own convenience. And this will also give to you another feeling…a feeling of not being in control of anything that is in your life path…that you have become the victim instead of the student.

"Now, each time that this lesson or event will come to you, come to you as you yourself have requested it to do, then it will have to share with you its direction of travel, and its location of the time and the place that it has been allowed to be born into. This will be carried to them on the face of the emotion…on the same face of the emotion that has come to them with these bad feelings.

"Now, for the ones who will continue to turn away from this emotion, they will not ever come to the place of understanding what it is that they must do. And for them, they will continue to remain caught up in this emotion and will not find any of those answers they are seeking. All they will find is that for each time this offering of the lesson will come to them the emotion that is on the front of it will only grow stronger…stronger to them but it is to remind them that it will not go away and to look and work with it is much better to do than to look away.

"Next, for those who will have found the strength of their spirit to look straight onto this emotion and to give it a face and body, this face and body that will allow them to recognize it for what it is, they will be on their way to seeing those things that are being presented to them. And, they are well on their way to fixing up the hole that has been put into them from their past seasons. And in a way that will allow them to understand what they need in this circle of the path before being allowed to advance to the next.

"Now, as they have placed a face and body to this emotion, they have still not learned anything from it. Not yet anyway. Before they will gain anything from this event that has come to them, they will have to take this new face and body of the emotion and its feeling that has been given to them…they will have to take this picture of this feeling they have been receiving and review all of their seasons of their past.

"They will have to review all of those other times when something had happened to them and had caused them to feel in this same way. And when they will have come to this time and this place, for each time they will encounter a similar feeling of what they are now going through, they will have to look through these things that had happened to them and make a determination of what they had done. They will have to look at all of these things they had done to see where they had turned away from this offering…where they had turned away from it and how. Once this has taken place, they will then have to make the determination of why they had chosen to do such a thing. Why they had turned their own back on themselves and the learning that had been presented to them.

"It is through this reviewing of these events that had taken place in their past that they will see what things they have done because of themselves and what thing they have done to themselves either because of others or through the direction of someone other than themselves. Now all of this will become uncomfortable to those who will be willing to look through all of these events of their past, little ones. However, it will not make them feel as bad as this emotion that has come to them in this day. And this will give to them a wondering if they are now not being affected so greatly by those feelings of their past as they once thought of them as affecting them.

"But, we will tell you the truth, little ones. It is not that those feelings from the emotions have become any less in those seasons of the past. It is not that they have been lessened at all. It is only that now they are looking at them through a comparison of the emotions and feelings they are having in this day they are in now. And when they will compare those things of the past with those things of today the feelings and emotions will not have been built up as much then as it is now. And this is why they do not feel as strong then as they do now.

"However, for each time they will find this same kind of feeling that had come to them, they must make the determination of why they had done what they have done. And it will be through this learning that they will come one more step closer to answering the questions they have. These questions of how to learn to work through the emotions that have come to them in order to see the lesson that is being offered.

"When they will come to the first time in their past seasons that they have a memory of such a feeling that had come to them, they will have found the first time they had turned away from this lesson. They will have found the first time they have turned away from the learning that had been offered to them. Which had not only caused them to have a hole within themselves but it also marked the first stop on their being held within this circle they travel in now...this same circle that they are trying to get out of.

"It will only be when they will have come to accept this event that had been offered to them from those past seasons that they will find what they have held a great need to understand in this life path of theirs. They will also find those things that they once turned away from were because of their listening to others tell them how and what they should be and not from those things they had come to know of themselves.

"It is at this time when they will discover that all of those seasons they had been listening to the many others tell them how to live their life and what they should and should not do. Only at this time will they be able to see how much of their time was not used for themselves and their growth of the spirit within them.

"However, they will also come to the understanding that all of those things they had done were very necessary for them...that they were necessary for them to learn and later understand from them. They will hold the knowing that without all of these events that had come to them for all of their seasons, that they would not have come to be in the place where they are now. And, from the way they will now feel about themselves, there will be a great acceptance for themselves and all things they will do. There will also be a good feeling for themselves and where they are now…now that they have come to understand what it is these emotions will bring to them to remember. They are not trying to punish them or to make them fell bad. They are only trying to share with them those things they still need to work on.

"And, when they will come back to the place they first were, this place where they were standing before this emotion had come to them, they will find that those things they once felt from them are no longer standing in their way. That these emotions that had once made them feel so bad that they could have caused them to remain stuck in them and learn nothing have been dissipated and are no longer standing in the way of the face of the lesson…the face of this lesson that is still being presented to them. When they will have come to dispel these emotions through understanding themselves, they will see what was needed to be learned by them in the first place. And as it is with all things of truth, this lesson is very simple and does not require much work on their part at all.

"This then is the lesson that is contained within the emotions that will always come to us, little ones. If we will choose to learn to remember from them, then there will only be growth for our spirit and we will increase our levels of understanding in this life path we are traveling. However, if we choose to turn away from them and keep this process up, then we will not ever escape from this place we will have boxed ourselves into…this place that will make us feel lost, unhappy, trapped, and without any progress at all. Whichever choice we will make, little ones, this will determine where we will come to on this life path. The choice will allow us to see the great doorway that is being presented to us…or it will only show to us the wall…the wall that we will continue to run into time after time."

Part 3

To Travel Next To
The Spirits Of The Flame

Chapter 16

▼

WHEN THEY SPEAK

This one called Calling Thunder had paused in the speaking words that he had been willing to share with Cheeway and myself. We could feel his eyes looking deep within each of us and it was in a way that was not bad. It was in a way that we had both become used to from spending so many of our younger seasons with Grandfather and Two Bears. As this seeing was being done, I was thinking over those speaking words that had been shared with both of us, especially the ones earlier that had shared with Cheeway and myself about the nature of the spirits of the flame. Not wanting to be left behind in my thinking thoughts, those same ones that I did not have a firm hold on understanding for, I asked, sitting in a very straight position, "Calling Thunder?"

"Yes, little one," came his response. "What is it that I may be of assistance to you on?"

When I heard these speaking words, I was shocked. And looking over to the place where Cheeway was lying, I could see that his mouth had dropped open...open and even larger than I had ever remembered it going. It was hearing these speaking words come to us from this one called Calling Thunder that had caused such a strong reaction from both Cheeway and me. His speaking words that had been shared with us were the same ones that had been used by Grandfather and Two Bears so many times before...and when we would both be at a place that was similar to the one we were in now. It would always be when the both of them had offered each of us so much information on the topics of the path of the spirit. When they had given us so much that they would see from the face we were both wearing that we were about to ask them a concerned question. But a question that they each knew we had formed within us long before we did. And when they would hear us finally come to the place of placing our speaking words to it correctly, they would always respond in the same way...always respond in the way that Calling Thunder had done just now. It was almost like a confirmation that Grandfather and Two Bears were still with us. And, they were using this shell of the one called Calling Thunder to allow us to hear them more clearly. However, with all of this in the front of my thinking mind, I was not willing to ask such a question of him in such a direct manner. And, from the look that had now covered Cheeway's face I could see that he was feeling the same way. But, with so much in the front of our thinking minds, I held the knowing that Cheeway would not mind if I were to pursue this matter in a more indirect way. In a way that would not only reflect respect for this one who had come to us and in a way that would allow each of us to see those things that had been offered to us more clearly. Those things that had been offered would also include this small clue that had been given to each of us. This clue that I was now going to pursue from this one called Calling Thunder.

Come Back To The Beginning Of Seeing The Spirits Of The Flame And How It Seems As If All Things Are Being Taken Away From You But In Truth They Are Being Allowed To Fall Away By Yourself.

About the Author

Patrick "Speaking Wind" Quirk, a Native American author, lecturer, and publisher, was raised by Grandfather, Two Bears, and White Eagle of the Pueblo People. He knew them as Spirit Callers, but in today's terms we would call them "SHAMAN". He, and his brothers, Cheeway and Nahe, were raised in the mountains of northern New Mexico by Grandfather and Two Bears for almost twenty years of their early life. This is where they were introduced to the ways of the spirit.

However, these teachings were to be put asleep for a time, and were not to be remembered until the time was right. But before the time was right, Grandfather, Two Bears, and White Eagle left, with their bodies; and several years later, Cheeway and Nahe ended their journey with the Earth Mother as well. That left Speaking Wind, alone, to sort and process what he had been given to share.

When Speaking Wind, Cheeway, and Nahe were very young, they were placed in a boarding school for several years. And this became the first of their experiences from having the control of others attempt to bury their spiritual beliefs. During their boarding school experience, they were not allowed to speak their people's language, or practice their spirituality. And there were placed on them many scars of abuse for breaking these rules.

During the boarding school years, they, as well as others who were either mixed, or full blooded Native Americans, were not taught to read or write. Instead, they were marched to the back of the school and picked up by residents, then taken to their private homes and farms, where they would work, for no pay. They would be returned to the boarding school only when it was time for them to learn of its religion.

However, they had asked too many questions from the teachings of Grandfather, Two Bears and White Eagle. Questions the teachers could not answer. So, they were labeled as "Spawns of Satan" and forced to leave so they would not influence the children who were not following the "devil's evil ways."

When Speaking Wind, Nahe, and Cheeway entered the public school system, they could not read or write. They had not been taught. So not only the teachers, but the students, called them dumb Indians. That left a mark on them, and gave them the determination to pursue their academic goals. Cheeway completed his doctorate and worked as one of the leading archeologists in the Yucatan Peninsula, uncovering many of the ancient writings of civilizations that related to the sacred writings of the Pueblo People.

Nahe pursued a career in law enforcement, then went on to become the Sheriff in a small town in New Mexico. Speaking Wind attained two undergraduate degrees, two graduate degrees, and completed one-half of his doctorate. He taught in the school of business at the University of Phoenix, then worked as a consultant in Asia, and for almost sixteen years, as a consultant in Europe.

However, for Speaking Wind, all of this was to end in 1993 when he died and was taken to the lands of The Ancient Ones. This is where he was not only reunited with Grandfather, Two Bears, White Eagle, Cheeway and Nahe, but also the "GREAT MESSENGER." This was when the "GREAT MESSENGER" gave Speaking Wind a message to bring back…a message that was to be shared with all who had the eyes to see, the ears to hear, the heart to feel, and the willingness of spirit to understand. It is a message of love, a message of hope, but most of all, it is a message that can replace fear with understanding for everyone.

It was at this time when Speaking Wind was told it was time to begin his work and return to Turtle Island (The Continental United States) with his son, White Raven. Speaking Wind and his son traveled together from the time White Raven was six.

For the next five years, Speaking Wind and White Raven toured the United States holding seminars and lectures. In these, Speaking Wind presented Native American spiritual practices and performed healing ceremonies to all those who were ready to receive them. One of the most compelling of the ceremonies he performed were the spirit drummings. During some of these, a dimensional "portal" would open and people looking into the eye of a stranger would be able to see an aspect of their own spirit as they truly were. Many times this image would be something that needed to be worked on.

But it was the drumming at Kinlock, one of the sacred areas in the land now known as Bankhead National Forest, which always resulted in different manifestations. Many times, people heard native flute music playing. And on more than one occasion, several people admitted to actually seeing images of the Old Ones.

Times were very fast paced for Patrick during the 1990's. Years of a grueling seminar schedule and many overnight hours of working on his latest manuscripts finally took their toll. On December 22, 1998, Speaking Wind crossed over. Or, as Patrick would say, he allowed his robes to fall away and leave the Earth Mother.

Since his departure, his physical presence has been greatly missed. But his spirit has visited many of us. And while his teachings are carried forward in the form of his books, manuscripts, and recordings, it is his personal impact on a small circle of friends and seminar acquaintances that will remain with us for the rest of our lives.

Washte Speaking Wind.

www.ingramcontent.com/pod-product-compliance
Lightning Source LLC
Chambersburg PA
CBHW030518020726
47494CB00004B/1144